GILL PRATES

(with John F McDonald)

The Girl Who Made Me Dance

A woman's journey to find meaning,
purpose, truth and freedom

Published by Gatecrasher Books
London – England

www.gatecrasherbooks.co.uk
www.thegirlbook.com

Copyright © 2019 Gilmara Prates and John F McDonald

Gilmara Prates and John F McDonald assert the right to be identified as authors of this work, in accordance with the Copyright, Designs & Patents Act 1988

All rights reserved, including the right to reproduce this book, or portions thereof in any form. No part of this text may be reproduced, transmitted, downloaded, decompiled, reverse engineered or stored, in any form, or introduced into any information storage and retrieval system, in any form or by any means, whether electronic or mechanical without the express written permission of the publisher.

This is a work of fiction.
The characters in it are fictional.
Liberties have been taken with some locations.

Hardback ISBN: 978-0-9957515-6-9
Paperback ISBN: 978-0-9957515-3-8
eBook ISBN: 978-0-9957515-5-2

Cover image: eugenepartyzan (stock.adobe.com)
Design and typesetting: www.shakspeareeditorial.org

To–

my parents and heroes, Helena and Juarez

my fiancée and the love of my life, Keeley

the memory of John, my dog and best friend

Contents

1. DNA 3

2. Harassment 10

3. Valéria 18

4. Travel or Treatment 28

5. Africa 38

6. History 47

7. Breakdown 54

8. Treatment 62

9. Mia 69

10. Lovers 76

11. Italy 85

12. Dancing 97

13. The Hungarians 104

14. A Happy Ending 113

15. The Vineyard 122

16. Brazil 130

17. Maria and José 137

18. Alone In a Crowd 144

19. Coming Out 152

20. Omens 161

21. The Breakup 174

22. Hedonism 184

23. The Ghost 195

24. Close to Why 204

25. The Convent 213

26. A New Life? 224

27. The Quantum 232

CHAPTER 1

DNA

The undercarriage of the Qatar Airways Boeing 787 Dreamliner was coming down as the jet approached Hamad International Airport. She'd already drank half the hip flask of absinthe, Devil's Springs vodka and Zevia ginger ale that she called her headkick cocktail. She hated flying, which was really unfortunate, because her job took her all over the world. But she needed a few hits of strong liquor to keep her up in the air.

The jet banked suddenly and ascended steeply back into the infinite azure of the sky. She drained the rest of her customised cocktail in one gulp to steady her nerves. The pilot's voice crackled.

'Sorry about that folks, another plane jumped the queue. We'll circle and land shortly.'

Her heart stopped trying to leap out of her mouth as the Dreamliner came back around and this time landed safely.

She was relieved to get back on solid ground, even though she hated going through customs at Doha. They had a way of making you feel you were doing something wrong, even though you knew you weren't. And now they'd installed the new iris scanners and DNA chips, rather than regular passport and visa requirements. It was called Universal ID and would eventually be rolled out around the world, but for now it was only the rich Arabs who could afford it.

It was the first time she'd been to Doha since the new technology came into use and she'd had to go along to the embassy in Mayfair to be scanned and to give a DNA sample for customs. She hoped their damn computers didn't malfunction. Alright, it was faster than thumbing through paper documents, but she had an aversion to machines – they seemed to be taking over the world.

It was the beginning of the holy month of Ramadan and sharia law was being observed more strictly than normal, people were being stopped for one triviality or another. She passed through the automatic iris and DNA checkers without a problem, but some sharp-nosed security guard detected a whiff of alcohol as she walked past him.

'Madam …'

She kept walking. He followed – tapped her on the shoulder.

'Madam, yjb 'an tati maei.'

'I'm sorry, I don't speak Arabic.'

'You must come with me.'

'Why?'

'Just come.'

The security guard was armed, so she decided not to argue with him.

He took her to a private office, where she waited alone until he came back with an immigration official carrying a file. The official was wearing the traditional white thawb and chequered ghutra. She was dressed modestly enough, in a business suit and medium heels, so that couldn't be the problem. The immigration man looked her up and down, then checked his file before speaking.

'Ms Gabriela Pereira?'

'Mrs.'

'You are here to attend a trade show?'

'That's right.'

'Do you realise it is an offence to be drunk in public in Qatar?'

'I'm not drunk.'

The immigration man and the guard spoke urgently to each other in Arabic. Then the guard produced a breathalyser and the immigration man smiled. It was a sly smile, a smirk rather than a smile, as if he'd won an argument.

'Would you care to …'

'No!'

'We can take a blood sample if you refuse.'

She knew it was pointless to protest, so she blew into the machine. It read .15% – .02% was the official drunk limit in Qatar. She was still defiant.

'Alright, so I had a drink on the plane to steady my nerves, especially after that aborted landing. I suffer from aviophobia.'

They both gave her a puzzled look.

'Fear of flying.'

They still didn't understand. How could anyone be afraid of flying? Wasn't it the safest way to travel?

'Wait here.'

The immigration man left the room, followed by the security guard, who locked the door from the outside. She desperately wanted a cigarette, but she promised Valéria that she'd quit and hadn't brought any with her. She was worried now, there was a remote chance she could end up being detained in a Qatari prison – not very nice at all!

Then something in the corner of her eye broke into her disquiet. She focused on the file the immigration man had carried into the room – it was still on the small wooden desk. She looked around for cameras, but couldn't see any. Of course, that didn't mean they weren't there. It was a risk, she was in enough trouble, but she couldn't resist taking a look. Slowly, cautiously, she turned the file toward her and flipped it open. Up to that point, she'd never known much about her genome and what it meant. She'd never really given it much thought.

The first thing she read was her ancestry: 60% white European, 30% black African, 5% Aboriginal and 5% Middle Eastern. It stunned her. How could that be? Alright, she realised there was indigenous blood in her make-up and maybe even some Semite, considering she came from European settlers in Brazil, but the 30% black African shocked her. She'd always considered herself to be white, now this file was implying she was mixed-race.

Her eyes moved down to where an even bigger shock was

waiting. The genetic report also contained a health analysis and this alleged that a defective tissue existed on gene TMEM56 of her DNA signature – hypermethylation of that gene was linked to systolic heart failure. She could see she had two years to live – the technology was even able to predict it to the day – Fourth July.

She fell back onto one of the plastic chairs in a state of inert disbelief. There wasn't a clock in the room and her phone had been taken away, so there was no indication of time. Time, in fact, stood still. The earth no longer spun on its axis. Everything outside the sterile white room may have been moving, but she had become inanimate, waiting for her own particular Godot.

She remained like that until the door opened again and the immigration man re-entered.

'Mrs Pereira …'

She didn't respond, just looked straight ahead, as if in a trance.

'Mrs Pereira, after consulting with my superiors, we have decided to deport you back to Great Britain.'

She heard the words vaguely, distantly, coming toward her in slow motion down a long echo chamber. The immigration man moved closer.

'Mrs Pereira, did you hear what I said? You may consider yourself lucky.'

His face appeared above her, materialising out of the haze of disbelief. She stirred – shook her head – tried to bring reality back from where it had fled to.

'I need to make a phone call … please.'

The immigration man left the room. A few minutes later, the security guard came back with her bag, including her mobile. She tried to call Valéria, but couldn't get through, and she was still in a state of something like shock when she called work. She checked her watch – 4:30 pm, Arabian standard time. They took her to a restricted area to await a plane to take her back.

'Could I have some coffee?'

The security guard who stayed with her obliged and she sipped it in the surreal silence. He stood close by, keeping an eye on her. She turned to him.

'When will I leave?'

'Soon.'

Her voice sounded strange, as if it belonged to someone else, not her – someone she didn't know, had never met. A complete stranger. Suddenly she was hungry and realised she'd had nothing to eat since a very light breakfast of scrambled egg and sunflower toast at 5:30 am that morning. She considered, in a hazy, dreamlike way, asking the guard if he could get her something to eat, but she didn't. It would have been inappropriate. And, anyway, she wasn't really that hungry.

She drifted in and out of a semi-conscious state, while she waited. Thoughts invaded her mind from time to time – considerations of things. Like life. And love. Her job – because she didn't quite consider work to be a part of life, not a defining part in any case. Unless, of course, you were one of those people who lived for their work, which she did not and never had. Or unless you were a dedicated doctor or explorer or philosopher or priest, whose work was their life. But there wasn't much to get existential about in marketing, was there? Not in a life way. Maybe in a comfortable, elegant, heady, stimulating, narcotic way, but not in a real-life way. Not in a "this-is-your-life" sense. Perhaps she was wrong, but she didn't think so. And what if you could really choose? If you had a real choice work wouldn't be your life, life would be your work. Wouldn't it?

The security guard coughed and the sound brought her back to reality, but only for a short while. She thought about love – or what people liked to term as love. And there were different kinds of love. She loved Valéria, she was sure of that, in a sensual, lovers way. She'd loved her father when he was alive, in a warm, safe, maroon way. She didn't love her mother – at least, she wasn't sure if she loved her or not. She definitely felt something for the woman, but she didn't know if it was love or some counterfeit emotion that might easily be mistaken for love. She'd also had a few fleeting relationships with females before Valéria, but they'd been brief and of a purely sexual nature, so they hardly counted as love. They'd all been frenetic, clothes-strewn-on-the-bedroom-floor, and bodily fluids, and marks in various places that weren't there beforehand. Come to think of it, she could remember very little about the relationships she'd had with women before Valéria. But none of them were what anyone could seriously call love. She'd never been close to her half-brothers and half-sisters back in Brazil and she had no firm friends – no dog or cat or religious deity to speak of. So, that was the extent of her experience of love – Valéria.

It was 6:00 pm and she'd been sitting there forever, with still no sign of the plane that would take her back to Britain. In a way, she didn't want to go back, she didn't want to move, she just wanted to sit in that airport seat forever. Do nothing, just stay still and let the long seconds tick by slowly in what was left of her life. The restricted area was assuming a familiar, comfortable ambience – a place where she didn't have to face the future, face what was ahead of her. She wanted to stay there forever, because she felt safe – the nightmare scenario she'd just become aware of couldn't get to her there. But she knew she couldn't stay. She'd have to go, sooner or later.

Life was such a complicated thing, at least at the human level. Maybe not at the universal or the infinite or the quantum or sub-quantum. But here at the human level, things were certainly extremely complicated. Were they not? She tried to imagine how it might all be made simpler – how to simplify it all but, no matter how long or how hard she thought, it all came back down to one common denominator. One way to do it – make it simpler. There was only one way – in the end.

But there was no time for that now.

The immigration official returned and he and the security guard escorted her out of the terminal and across the tarmac toward a Boeing 777. They took her up the stairway, on to the plane and installed her in a first-class seat. There was no one else on board, just her.

A stewardess approached. She had red hair and black eyebrows and smelt of Eau Sauvage pour Femme.

'Can I get you something?'

'Double whisky, please.'

The stewardess gave her a look that said, 'you can't possibly be serious'.

'No alcohol until we are in the air, I am afraid. Something to eat?'

She just nodded her head, even though she was and wasn't hungry, just to get rid of the stewardess and her irritating voice. The immigration official left, but the security guard remained in place, in case she made a break for it, back to the safety of the restricted area.

The stewardess came back with chump of lamb with chermoula spices, along with a glass of sparkling mineral water.

'Enjoy.'

She said it with a smile, as if she was serving it in a five-star hotel and not a deportation plane. The meal was half-eaten when she came back to take the plate away. Other passengers were beginning to board by then and soon the aircraft was almost full. It took off at 9:00 pm. The security guard had already disappeared, like a mirage – a visual fallacy that had never been there and only gave the impression of presence.

CHAPTER 2

HARASSMENT

Gabriela Pereira, known to her friends as Gabby, checked into the Swissôtel in Bremen, northern Germany. After depositing her luggage in her room, she made her way to the foyer to rejoin her colleagues from Palexion Limited, where she worked as Communications and Marketing Manager. They were in Bremen for a conference and she was the only female in the delegation of ten – six from the Mannheim head office and four from the London office. They had lunch and attended the conference opener in the afternoon. Later, Gabby took a shower and went down to dinner, during which she drank a few Doornkoat-Tini's, a cocktail made with schnapps. The drink wasn't really to her taste, but she liked to try out new mixtures when the opportunity arose.

She wore a conservative business suit and shirt, with medium heels, so that she'd fit in with the testosterone-heavy ambience. Working in a male-orientated environment had taken its toll on Gabby. Being the only female manager out of a total of twenty-five meant that, in her mind at least, her personality had to change. She had to be less like herself and more like them to fit in. So, she became less passive and more aggressive in order to be taken seriously. She changed her dress code to Savile Row trouser suits and Crockett & Jones business shoes, keeping her designer handbags as the only relics of her previous fundamental femininity.

Despite intense disinterest, she learned the basics of football, enough to be able to offer semi-informed comments during major tournaments. She took up golf so as not to be excluded from decisions that were made over G&Ts at the nineteenth hole. She studied all she could about the masculine world, without a boyfriend or husband to observe at close quarters. She never bored her male colleagues with trivial feminine gossip and she knew from experience that complaining would be considered as whining.

Once, earlier in her career, she was asked to serve tea and coffee at a meeting of her peers and she complied, even though she felt like pouring the beverages into their crotches, scalding their egocentric genitals. No, she didn't cry or show emotion and that stoicism brought fast-track promotion. Her faux positive attitude to the "survival of the fittest" work ethic earned Gabby praise, but little did they know it was all a self-constructed façade, one that damaged her sense of self-worth on a daily basis. Deep down, she knew she was betraying her true nature – professional success had come at a cost and she increasingly wondered if that cost was too high.

After dinner, in the bar, the men talked loudly about work and tried to impress the boss, Günther Engels, a Bavarian-Swiss entrepreneur who believed he was the new commercial messiah. Gabby soon got bored of the vying for position and retired to her room. About a half-hour later, there was a soft knocking on the door.

'Who is it?'

'Me … Günther.'

'What do you want?'

'To come in.'

'I'm in bed.'

'I need to talk to you.'

Gabby was reluctant to open the door. She'd had encounters with Engels before, on his frequent visits to London. He was in his late fifties, dark-haired, slimly built and over six feet tall. He was always immaculately groomed and Gabby was sure he was probably the epitome of the older, sophisticated man for a lot of women – but not for her. He always made sly comments about how daring she looked – he never used the word sexy, but it was implied – and at times came closer to her than he needed to be. This made Gabby very uncomfortable, but she didn't complain about it. She couldn't risk losing her job, which she'd worked so hard for. It was a man's world in the selling business and she'd had to prove herself twice as much as her male colleagues. But, despite her intellect and resilience, she was often unsure of her own coping mechanisms – sometimes becoming anxious and irritated with herself for not asserting her total opposition to Engels' unwanted attention.

Despite advances in equality in the workplace, it was still a world where women sometimes cried alone in corporate bathrooms, unable to cope with the verbal, and often subtly physical, abuse. Nothing that could be construed as a sackable offence – just innuendo, sexist joke, sly wink or gesture, picture or video on a phone, leading question, unwanted offer, insinuation. But it all added up to harassment and women had to keep quiet about it or become a victim of even more ridicule and retaliation.

'Run to daddy.'

'Oh, are you gonna cry now?'

'Boo hoo.'

'She's just a little girl at heart.'

And so on.

Many women took voluntary sabbaticals, or even maternity leave, to get away from the constant violation of their right to be female. Some never came back. So, Gabby kept quiet, not wanting to face the job market in search of that one perfect position where she'd finally feel truly appreciated and respected for her abilities, for being a woman, for bringing a different kind of thinking to the hairy-armpit, chauvinistic approach of winning at all costs. But that job didn't really exist, and she knew it.

'Gabby … let me in. I just want to talk.'

She got out of bed and threw a dressing gown over her naked body. She was still reluctant to open the door.

When she reached it she listened, hoping he'd go away, but he was still outside, still knocking softly. She was afraid he'd attract the attention of some of the others and then there'd be a scandal – she'd be talked about, joked about, they'd superimpose her face on pornographic pictures and circulate them.

'It's late …'

'I know, but this is important.'

She opened the door and Engels entered her room. She could see he was inebriated, possibly even very drunk.

He pushed past her into the hotel room and sat on the double bed. She immediately regretted letting him in.

'What do you want to talk about?'

'Come here. Sit next to me.'

'No.'

He stood up, smiling in that way some men do – men who are used to getting their own way. He moved closer to her. She moved away.

'What is wrong with you, Gabby?'

'Nothing.'

'Then, why …?'

'I want you to leave.'

'No, you do not.'

He grabbed her and turned her toward the bed, pushing her backward until she fell onto it and he fell on top of her.

'I'm married, Mr Engels.'

'So what? So am I.'

'You don't understand.'

'What do I not understand?'

'I'm married to a woman.'

Engels' mouth fell open and he was stunned for a moment.

'You are a lesbian?'

'Yes.'

A cynical grin broke across his face.

'I can cure you of that.'

Gabby was really angry now and she managed to get out from under him, telling him to leave her room immediately. He was so full of alcohol he thought it was a game and he wouldn't go.

'You want to play? I like games. I too can play.'

Engels started to circle around her.

He was saying weird things that made no sense – random comments in German she couldn't understand. It was as if he was ranting or raving and she wondered if he'd taken something other than alcohol.

Then he grabbed her and held her close to him. She could smell his breath, feel his heart beating very fast. She tried to pull away, but he was strong and held her tighter. He was trying to kiss her and she was turning her face away. He kissed the top of her chest that was visible under the dressing gown, all the time saying weird things.

'I can make you rich, Gabby.'

She was scared.

He was laughing hysterically and nodding his head, saying he wanted to see her naked and trying to pull off her dressing gown. When he didn't succeed, he started to take off his own clothes

Gabby froze, knowing she had to get past him – get to the door. But it was if she was paralysed and couldn't move. He was half-naked and grabbed her again and pushed her back toward the bed. She began to fight against him, but this just excited him all the more, as if it was a new part of the game he believed they were playing. Gabby fell backward onto the bed again and he was on top of her again, pulling her dressing gown to one side.

'No, Günther! No!'

He stuck his penis into her, pushing back and forth. She hit out at him and tried to get free, but he was too strong and too heavy. So she just went completely limp and lay there like a rag doll. He kept thrusting for about five minutes, but he was too drunk to ejaculate, so he gave up in the end.

When he finished he stood up and faced her, still lying on the bed with her hand over her mouth. She felt sick.

'I am sorry.'

She couldn't tell if he was sorry for raping her or for not being able to ejaculate. It didn't matter. He gathered up his clothing and stumbled out of the room. As soon as he left, Gabby rushed to the bathroom and threw up, then she turned

on the shower and sat under it until the water turned cold –
even then she stayed there, trying to decide what to do.

She knew she should call the police and report the rape,
but she was in Bremen and who would believe her. He hadn't
ejaculated and, anyway, without thinking she'd washed away
any DNA evidence there might be. He'd say it was consensual
and everyone would believe him. By the time she got back to
London it would be too late.

Gabby turned the shower off and lay on the bathroom
floor. This was just too surreal. Nothing made sense. Why had
he done this to her? He had plenty of women who would have
willingly had sex with him, so why her? Was it because she
was out of bounds? Was that the challenge for him? To have
something he knew he could never have. She was sobbing for
a while before she even realised it.

By then she was barely able to breathe, gasping and saying
the same word over and over, speaking out loud to the empty
room.

'No! No! No!'

It was as if she'd ended up on the other side of a mirror
and could see herself through the glass, calling to herself to
come back. She felt like she was an imposter and the image on
the other side of the mirror was the real Gabby Pereira.

She got up off the bathroom floor and wrapped the
dressing gown around herself. Then she went back into the
bedroom and opened a window to get some fresh air. She cried
again, feeling like she didn't want to live this way anymore.
Perhaps it would have been better if Engels had killed her, he
was a coward for leaving her alive – that was the worst thing
he'd done to her.

The hotel room was four stories up. She climbed onto
the window ledge and looked down at the street below. She
was barely able to breathe. It was a long drop and it would
definitely kill her. She imagined her body lying broken at the
bottom and the evil thing he'd put inside her coming out –
rising out of her dead body like black smoke. And she'd be
clean again. Herself again. The police would come and Engels

would get into trouble – get arrested – maybe go to jail. Maybe not. Maybe he'd say he didn't know her, that she was just some crazy woman. Drunk. On drugs.

She began to lean forward. Further. Further. She closed her eyes.

'What are you doing?'

Gabby turned to see her father standing in the room. He was holding out his hand and she slowly stepped back down from the window and came across to him. He put her into the bed and sang one of his songs to her until she fell asleep. Then he closed the window.

Next morning Gabby decided to cut her hair off. She chopped at it with the small manicure scissors from her bag. She cut it because she hated it. What was the point of it? It just got dirty and she had to wash it to make herself look attractive. She didn't want to look attractive. She didn't care what she looked like when looking attractive got her abused like that – degraded and dehumanised. Cutting her hair had a kind of symbolism to it – like in the film *Dark Angel,* where all the clones were shaved to look identical, even the girls and boys looked the same and they had no names, just barcodes.

If you stripped someone of their external individuality what were they left with? Their internal individuality? Their humanness? Their thoughts and feelings and morals? Human in the most basic form, not obsessed with their external selves to the point of not knowing who or what they really were anymore? The reality of being human, the reality of freeing what was underneath, what mattered most?

Gabby felt plastic, as if she was fake, walking around pretending to be human, pretending to be a person, and she was sick of it. Sick of feeling like she was a cypher of her real self. Her hair was a pretence, a trivial thing, skin deep, a physical representation of her mental state. She felt out of control and didn't know what was important anymore. She didn't feel in touch with herself or know what the point of anything was. She had the scissors in her hand, they were close to her throat –

The turbulence of the descent through the clouds into Heathrow Airport woke Gabby from her fretful sleep. That same dream – nightmare. Maybe it was brought on by her phone call to Günther Engels from Doha? She hadn't told him the truth about the headkick cocktail, or the immigration man, or about being deported. She'd just said she felt unwell on the plane and her Medical Diagnosis App, or MDA, had advised rest and a visit to her GP. Engels wasn't happy, he'd have to find a last-minute replacement, but he agreed that she should take some sick leave and let him know when she was fit to come back to work.

He never mentioned the incident in that hotel in Bremen two years earlier, and neither did Gabby. Maybe because he didn't remember, or maybe because he was ashamed – either of what he'd done or of being unable to ejaculate. Gabby never mentioned it because she wanted to forget it. Yet still the bad dream came back.

CHAPTER 3
VALÉRIA

Gabriela Pereira fell in love with Valéria Torres on a trip to Brazil twelve years previously, when she went to São Paulo for a month to see her family. She stayed with her mother, who had retired by then.

The city hadn't changed much and was in full Christmas swing. All the shop windows were decorated and sandwich-board Papai Noels were ringing bells in the sweltering sun. There were street traders peddling food and plastic toys and cheap cigarettes and counterfeit branded goods from stalls and boxes. Hundreds of people going in different directions. All in a hurry, trying to outpace each other and ignore each other at the same time.

Sounds filled Gabby's senses. The shrill, screaming noise of police and ambulance sirens. Impatient drivers hooting their horns in an impossible gridlock and shouting and swearing at each other. Local buses with people hanging off the doors and windows and crowding on top of the roofs. Emaciated stray dogs with mange and ticks and fleas. Flies everywhere. People sleeping on the pavement, with the scurrying throng tripping over them. Food smells mingled with the stench of sewage from a distant canal or peripheral river and the faint, smokey odour of urine drifted on the midsummer air. It was a world full of energy and garish colours and bits of sky and shop windows and nervousness.

Gabby wondered why she'd come back. It wasn't as if she was close to her family. Her mother had always been on the road when she was young and she'd been passed around from one house to another. Maria only retired shortly before Gabby left for Europe, so they'd never had a chance to get close and really know each other. But she was here now, so she might as well make the most of it.

The sun was unable to break through the cloud cover and the light was as translucent as in a Monet – with objects in the foreground moderately in focus and the distant vista hazy, with soft outlines blending into each other. She walked through the teeming streets with her friend from way back, Jorge, not really caring where they were going or what they were going to do. Just shooting the breeze, ambling through the city centre and watching the illegal street mascates run away when the police came.

Most people were migrants from the north of Brazil or from Colombia, come to São Paulo for a better life. Without skills or education, they couldn't get a job and ended up in poverty. Living from glimmer to glimmer, in the hope of finding some luck.

They stopped at a small café when they got hungry and bought cassava chips and bacalhau and drank sugarcane juice. Gradually, the enthusiastic streets emptied of daytime workers, to be replaced by the night people – drinkers and clubgoers and drug-peddlers and pimps and pushers. Sirens constantly squalled past like excitable harridans, and the doormen hulked about hump-backed in the shadows, looking for sex from homeless street girls. It was an unpredictable place during the day, but at night it was gaudy and greedy and always on the verge of anger – constantly disturbed by the sounds of the city night and hooded spectres leering past in the neon lecher-light.

'Let's go somewhere nicer, Jorge.'

'I thought you liked the seedy side, Gabby?'

'That's you, not me.'

He laughed.

'Let's go to Cracolândia.'

Cracolândia was to the south-west of the city centre, in the Luz region of São Paulo. It was very affluent in the 1960s, with plush hotels and theatres and shops and restaurants and only the very rich lived there. It stretched from Republican Square and spread to São João Avenue through to Luz Station, which was built by the British, who taught the Brazilians how to play football. Now it was populated by the destitute homeless and the once five-star hotels, the theatres and cinemas had long since degenerated into porno palaces, frequented by perverts and prostitutes.

The people in this place were all crack addicts – hence the name. Crack had a short-lasting high, so everybody was always on the edge, constantly waiting for their next fix. It was a graphic place, with people wrapped in dirty blankets or slumped on damp, stained sofas and old mattresses or just lying on the pavements. Whole families floated like flotsam on a rat-infested sea of sadness. Most of them looked dazed, shuffling along in a psychotropic world, with glazed eyes and dirty faces repeatedly illuminated by flashes of fire as they smoked a mixture of crack cocaine residue and anything else they could find, like crude hemp or tobacco.

Jorge told Gabby there were about 2,000 homeless people here, but nobody could tell for sure because they came and went, or died, or got killed or taken away to be tortured by the police.

'Why did you want to come here, Jorge?'

'To get some gear, of course.'

People were fighting and screaming at each other. Mothers of young children were weeping and wailing. It was the dirtiest place Gabby had ever seen, streets and streets of filth and faeces with piles of stinking rubbish everywhere. People vomited and defecated and urinated openly all over the place. The smell almost choked her. And it wasn't just the place that stank, so did the people. Most looked like they hadn't had a bath in years and had been wearing the same old stained clothes for just as long.

Some were searching through big municipal garbage containers for scraps of food, or gathering up fruit and vegetables discarded from the street markets. Others begged from the late-evening passers-by, who tried to ignore them as they hurried along – almost running in their eagerness to get past. The place was infested by insects of all kinds – mosquitoes and beetles and flies and maggots crawling all over the ground. Gabby could see rats and dogs scavenging for food and the drinking water came from fountains that people washed in. It was difficult to tell the age of any individual, because the intensive use of crack residue made them all look a lot older than they actually were.

Whole families were addicted – generations waiting for their next fix. A legacy of despair, passed down from father to son, mother to daughter. The pungent stink of crack cocaine was everywhere, like burning plastic, and its acidic haze stung Gabby's eyes.

Cracolândia was an epidemic that spread to everyone who became associated with it. People came there looking for friends or relatives who had disappeared and ended up addicted themselves and stayed. There was a constant, fluctuating population who were prey to the drug dealers. Children as young as four or five could be seen smoking the pipes – and they would never live to adulthood. But nobody cared – not the police nor the politicians nor the church nor the general public. The newspapers constantly called for the place to be burnt to the ground or bombed or blitzed – along with the people in it. And the government would have gone along with it if they could have got away with genocide.

The police made a few token excursions into Cracolândia every now and then, just to prove to the newspapers that they were doing something about the place. But they just beat people up for fun, kicked them and sometimes killed them. Who was going to complain if a crackhead got crippled? Nobody. Rich boys drove past in their flash cars and threw petrol bombs out the windows, setting fire to people who ran around screaming as they burnt. Children as young as two or three were sexually assaulted, with their parents' consent, in exchange for money to buy crack.

But Cracolândia was a convenient place for many, safe from police attention. Most high-level dealers who plied their trade there lived outside it. Police took bribes from the dealers, politicians took bribes from the police and news magnates sold papers full of lurid stories that the safe people liked to read and thank their lucky stars they did not have to live in such an awful place. So, Cracolândia was convenient for everyone, not just the unfortunate addicts who lived there.

The tragic thing about it was, they believed this was the only way of life for people like them. They didn't know any better and considered it their lot for being born poor or disadvantaged. They lived for the day. They had no dreams and no future and no fixed place in space and time. The only thing that motivated them was their next hit – their window in the wall. They longed to look through it again, if only for a brief moment. They were hopelessly addicted to their addiction and that longing of the soul was their only raison d'être.

There were two kinds of poverty in Brazil: rural poverty with hunger and backwardness and no amenities like shops or showers or television; and urban poverty with squalor and filth and disease.

Urban poverty was worse.

Gabby was sorry she'd come, but she had to stay with Jorge.

Jorge approached a group of kids whose average age was about thirteen, with the oldest being no more than eighteen. They were random arrangements of small muscles and bone, held together by leathery skin. Mostly boys, but maybe a couple of girls – it was difficult to tell. Androgynous in their mutual squalor and emaciation, they gathered in a square with some trees and concrete benches and with tall buildings all around. They eyed Gabby up and down suspiciously. Jorge spoke to them.

'You have some candy?'

'You have some dinheiro?'

Jorge produced a wad of reais and the street kids' eyes lit up. It was a dangerous place to be flashing money, boys as young as ten carried heavy handguns. But Jorge had obviously done business with them before and they knew him. Gabby was nervous and didn't like the idea of Jorge buying crack.

'What's candy Jorge?'

'It's nothing, just a new legal high. It's not against the law.'

Jorge made his purchase and they left Cracolândia, much to Gabby's relief. They went to a club where they drank caipirinhas and were joined by some of Jorge's friends. Later that night, they all went back to someone's apartment in Itaim Bibi, where they began smoking the stuff Jorge had bought in Cracolândia. They puffed at it from a miniature brandy bottle with a hole knocked in the bottom. There was some kind of gauze in the neck, with the little "candy" rock on top of it and they heated it with a lighter.

'What is that stuff, Jorge?'

'I told you, Gabby, it's nothing … it's called a legal high. It just lifts you up.'

'Are you sure?'

'Sure I'm sure. Take a hit, you'll see.'

Gabby was hesitant, but the others encouraged her, so she took a long puff of the white smoke from the hole in the bottle and sucked it into her lungs.

Gabby felt her heart beat harder, like it was going beat right out of her chest. She breathed out and it hit her, took her breath away. The feeling was so strong it blew her off her feet – almost blew her head off. She fell back onto a sofa and gasped and gasped and gasped, lying there with her eyes closed and mumbling to herself.

'Oh my god, this is crack!'

She looked over at Jorge, but he was busy doing his own blast. Gabby crept toward the kitchen to drink some water, hoping that would dilute the high she was feeling. Now she knew why people were willing to kill for this stuff; why crack addicts became thieves and muggers and ruined their lives over it.

The high lasted about half an hour and, when she was finally able to speak, she got really angry with Jorge.

'This is crack.'

'It's not crack, Gabby.'

'It is, Jorge!'

'Stop calling it crack!'

'That's what it is.'

'It's blasting coke!'

That's what he called it. He wouldn't admit it was crack, even though Gabby knew it was.

When the hit wore off she was scared, more than scared, she was terrified – horrified in case that one hit had made her an addict.

'I hate you, Jorge. I hate you. We can never do this again.'

Gabby kept away from Jorge for the rest of the holiday but, by New Year's Eve, he'd persuaded her he was sorry and wanted to make it up to her. She'd been drinking in the afternoon at Fran's Café, with some of her cousins. He turned up later with another young man called Flávio, who suggested they go on to Autorama at Ibirapuera Park for some fun.

'No drugs!'

'I promise you, Gabby, no drugs.'

Autorama was a car park during the day, but it metamorphosed into a forbidden hangout for the LGBT community from late evening into the early hours. Gabby had never been there before and, when they arrived, she thought she'd made a big mistake, just as she had with Cracolândia.

As they drove around, she realised it was mostly inhabited by young, half-naked men and she felt a sense of unease. The men posed and flexed their muscles to attract "clients", while others openly engaged in masturbation and oral sex. It was alright while she was still under the influence of the cachaça she'd drunk at the café, but the effects soon wore off in the fresh air, so she asked Jorge to take her home.

There were on their way out, driving slowly, when Gabby noticed a small group of three standing by themselves. Two of them were young men, but the third was the most beautiful girl she'd ever seen.

'Stop the car!'

Jorge brought the convertible to a halt.

'Go ask her if she's entendida, Jorge.'

'Are you sure?'

She wasn't sure, but she still said yes.

'Only for you, Gabby.'

'You owe me!'

Gabby held her breath as Jorge approached the group. She could see him speaking to the girl, who looked across toward the car and smiled. Jorge waved to Gabby to come over, but she hesitated – she'd always been a bit conservative when it came to connecting with other women, a legacy from her traditional upbringing.

Once they were out of the car, Jorge and Flávio became distracted by the two young men in the group of three and soon disappeared with them, leaving the two females alone.

'Hi, I'm Valéria.'

'I'm Gabriela … my friends call me Gabby.'

'Can I be your friend?'

'Sure.'

Valéria was eighteen at the time, five years younger than Gabriela. She was slim, tall for her age, with brown eyes, olive skin and long straight hair that cascaded down her back like an ebony waterfall.

Without warning, Valéria took Gabby's head in her hands and gave her a long, lingering kiss. Gabby gasped for breath when their lips finally parted. Valéria smiled coquettishly.

'Well, you said we could be friends.'

It was hot and temperatures were reaching the low thirties, even at night, so they climbed into the back of Jorge's car, which had air con. Valéria immediately took off her top, to reveal her small, well-proportioned breasts. Gabby was amazed by the girl's forwardness – she'd never met a woman who behaved in such a provocative way so soon after connecting. Gabby wasn't sure what to do in the face of this impertinence, but some instinct lifted her hand and placed her finger on the corner of Valéria's mouth. There was a tiny pulse – a faint rhythm just under the skin. Then she allowed her hand to slip down, to caress the nipple that pouted at her.

'We need to go!'

Suddenly, Jorge and Flávio were at the window. Things hadn't gone well with the two young men, either because other people considered them to be their property, or some drug purchase had gone wrong. Now a dangerous situation had developed. Valéria kissed Gabby again and jumped out of the car. Jorge and Flávio jumped in and they sped away before the women had a chance to exchange phone numbers.

The days and nights slipped by like clouds gliding across a satin sky and Gabby was making the most of her time with family, especially with her estranged mother, Maria. On the last day of the visit, Luana, one of her cousins, took her for lunch at the Mercado Municipal, a food market in the centre of the city. Gabby loved the sights and smells in the hall – it was truly an assault on the senses. They had prawn pastel and caipirinhas and it was almost a perfect ending to her trip. Only one thing would have made it better. As if by some magical mind transference, Gabby's phone rang.

'Hello.'

'Hi, Gabby, it's me … Valéria.'

'How …?'

'My friends know Jorge. They got me your number.'

'Where are you?'

'Ilhabela beach.'

Gabby asked Luana to take her to the beach where she met up with Valéria. The two girls spent the rest of the day and late into the evening together. A group of young people lit a bonfire and drank beer and played music, but Gabby couldn't stay the night, as Valéria wanted her to, because she had to be at the airport early the next morning. Valéria gave her a book about fate and destiny called *Maktub* – on the inside of the cover, she'd written "o que será". Gabby left without saying goodbye.

Next morning at Guarulhos International Airport, Gabby was sorry she hadn't arranged to meet Valéria again sometime, or at least said goodbye – or au revoir – tchau – anything. Then her phone rang again. It was Valéria.

'You didn't say goodbye.'

'I don't like goodbyes.'

'I might come to London …'

'When?'

'When I finish my studies. Maybe next year.'

And that's the way they left it. They didn't arrange to meet, it was an unspoken thing. They both knew Valéria would come to London and they'd be lovers.

CHAPTER 4
TRAVEL OR TREATMENT

On the way to her apartment in Kensington, west London, Gabby tried to decide what she was going to tell Valéria. She didn't want to lie, but she didn't want to alarm her lover either. In the end, she decided just to play it by ear and see what happened. It was 3:00 am when she got in and Valéria was still in bed. Gabby didn't want to disturb her, so she slept on the couch, or tried to sleep – fitfully, restlessly.

Valéria was an administrator at Charing Cross Hospital, a job she liked, but she wanted to move up to a senior managerial role. She was ambitious, even more so than Gabby. It had been a problem between them for some time, as Gabby wanted children but Valéria didn't. Gabby considered it a crime if everything she'd done up to now, moving to the UK and working so hard to secure a good living, was for nothing. It would all be futile if she couldn't have children. It was what she wanted most. What use were all the material things in an empty space?

She'd questioned the role of her femininity and not having children left Gabby with a sense of worthlessness which sometimes pervaded her entire being. Alright, she conceded it was a role society still imposed on women, even well-educated women, and she completely accepted that having children wasn't the ambition of every female. She respected that. Her mother was, of course, a little frustrated that she was still not a grandmother and Gabby didn't like disappointing her – again. The first time was when she came out openly as gay. But it was mostly an identity issue with Gabby – it involved what she considered to be her true identity as a woman, not the false identity she'd manufactured for herself. Having a child would bring back an essential part of her that had been missing for so long.

They'd started living together a couple of years after they first met at Autorama in São Paulo. They'd corresponded via email at first, then Valéria moved to the UK to be with Gabby. Gradually, they fell deeper in love – a love that was precious and all-consuming for Gabby, but a little less so for Valéria, who was the more practical of the two and less transcendent in her ideals of what the quintessence of romantic idealism should be. In other words, Gabby wanted perfect love, whereas Valéria was happy to settle for what most relationships are – compromise.

Both women were vaguely aware of having known each other from the beginning of time. Gabby was vaguely aware of Valéria's connection to her, in the way that all things were connected, interacted with each other, died and became each other, existed together in the quantum of all things and all times and all places. Valéria was also vaguely aware of Gabby, but in a more recent context – if recent could be used in the context of all things and all times and all places.

Gabby couldn't remember when the connection began – sometimes she experienced mysterious flashbacks, or flashforwards, she wasn't sure which – but the visions scared and excited her, so she left them alone. Most of what Gabby knew from previous existences had been lost. She forgot about the god of everything that was inside her, part of her, just as it was in and part of everything. She forgot what her role was in the great geomancy, the universal understanding. She forgot what had come before, or what came before what was before. But she was aware of the animal in her, the powerful basic instincts inside her that needed to be acted upon.

What had come before wasn't relevant to Gabby, at least not until she saw the DNA prophesy in Doha. Now she was focused on the ring, the cycle, the circle of her life that was in danger. Valéria, on the other hand, was more in the moment, the basic necessities, and that came from her life in Brazil, before London, when everything had to be fought for. She didn't see that the great intuitive understanding of the first consciousness had been lost over the millennia, that the increasing self-obsession and immersion in the "I" culture had gradually replaced the all-embracing oneness of her ancient ancestors. Valéria was a professional woman and, as such, she had a very narrow vision of both past and future – whereas the indigo child in Gabby was more developed.

The new perspective that caused her flashbacks scared Gabby, until the DNA test. She hadn't known what it was or where it came from. She hadn't realised that she was the connection, the conduit between distant past and unimagined future. Valéria didn't understand the forces that were at play within Gabby, absorbed as she was in her work and surrounded by her colleagues. She couldn't see that Gabby's loneliness came from an ache inside her – to rejoin her past and her future, so that all three became one. All along the timeline, there were fragments of them both – essences in the ethereal light wave between past and present and future. Essences that manifested themselves in an incompleteness – at the separate points in eternity.

Gabby woke in a sweat.

Cold perspiration covered her body. She tried to remember what had happened in Doha, the nightmare that was so real it caused her to wake up in this state, but so obscure she couldn't make any sense of it. She climbed off the sweat-soaked sofa and headed for the shower. It was 5.00 am and she knew she'd never be able to get back to sleep now. Under the piercing shower-rain, she experienced a feeling of extreme loneliness again. It was fleeting, momentary, a sense of nostalgia that sometimes came and pierced her heart. She didn't know where it came from. It had arrived for the first time about a year ago and came upon her unexpectedly, intermittently, since then.

After showering, she made some decaf and spread a thin layer of cottage cheese on a couple of crispbreads, but she had no appetite. Gabby always tried to eat a healthy diet and she exercised regularly. Her job in marketing was unspectacular, but it, and living in a big city, required that she be fit and healthy and she tried her best to accommodate that requirement. In fact, unspectacular was a word that could be used to describe Gabby Pereira and her recent life – up till now. Now it all seemed irrelevant.

She'd been feeling disorientated for some time. The sensation started to manifest itself on her psyche about the same time as the nostalgic feeling of loneliness arrived. It was as if someone, or something, was trying to communicate with her through an emotional sense of loss. However, the message was opaque, distorted, ambiguous and she couldn't be sure if it was a message at all, or just her subconscious playing tricks on her.

Gabby got dressed and looked out the window at the approaching dawn. A new day, unlike any she'd experienced up to now. Now she knew her fate – the very day of it. She watched the brightening sky and thought that life was really such a strange thing – so important and self-centred at ground level, yet so minute and fragile on the universal scale. This was no great profundity, it was a normal, everyday thought and, thinking it, she began to feel a bit better.

As she walked from the window she had a flashback – or flashforward – like something from a movie. It only lasted a second or two, but it momentarily disorientated her. It was a face – a face from a dream. Not a human face, or at least not human as she knew a human face to be – rather a morphing visage, half image and half numeric code, appearing and dissolving somewhere on the mesolimbic pathway of her brain, dancing between the synapses and neurotransmitters and receptors and tracts. It wasn't the first time she'd had one of these evocations, but she was a marketing executive and, as such, she dealt with trends and facts and numerical predictions – stuff that could be rationalised and proven with graphs and test results. Alright, her intuition told her that not everything could be explained, that there was much to be discovered. But she believed that, eventually, everything would be logical, in human terms. However, for now, she was seeing these things, these visions, and she couldn't explain them. Even if she could, she wasn't sure she would have wanted to. They unnerved her.

Gabby sat down heavily on a chair and took a couple of deep breaths. The vision, or whatever it was, had disconcerted her, taken her by surprise. She wasn't expecting it so soon after the trauma of yesterday – it had ambushed her when she wasn't prepared.

She took a sip of water from a plastic bottle she'd taken out of the fridge, then turned on the television, which she immediately turned off again, because it was all about the negativity that manifested itself on a global scale as greed, with the richest in society wanting to be even richer at the expense of the poorest in society. People who weren't the everyday, shabby, gutter rich, but the obscene super-rich, who were out of touch with every reality except their own, out of touch with what they really were and where they came from. So out of touch they believed themselves to be the nouveau gods. They were brainwashing the population with television and trivia and personalised religions, so that everyone was forgetting they were part of a oneness that was whole, not fragmented, nor splintered into millions of little egos, all competing with each other for shallow, worthless prizes.

And she was part of it.

The negativity was manifesting itself everywhere. In the media, where nobody addressed the real issues of the day, but increasingly obsessed over celebrity and the shiny little trinkets of illusory reality, the fool's gold of stardom and wanting to be special, at the expense of everyone else. It manifested itself in selfishness and suspicion and cynicism and a hardening of hearts. It was spreading across the planet and was affecting all aspects of human life. It manifested itself on a personal level inside Gabby, with an increasing sense of frustration and disappointment. It was as if negativity was growing inside her, spreading like a virus through her nervous system and her genes and her brain functions. She was feeling levels of negative emotion that were alien to her – fear and doubt and a kind of paranoia. It was as if some natural equilibrium inside her very soul had been disturbed.

The colours in the room blended into a chromatic soup and time travelled at a pace that was unique to Gabby's concentrating mind. Gradually, the interior of the apartment grew brighter and shapes and colours faded into nothingness. Gabby saw the half-image/half-code face in front of her again. Only this time the features were more distinct. The emotional sense of loss wasn't so acute – as if it was dissolving in the allness of the moment. It was a beautiful, intrinsically female, face. Not beautiful in a humanistic way, but in an eternal, wave-like way – coming and going, appearing and disappearing, like an apparition coming out of a mist, then fading back into the opacity, before becoming visible again. It was smiling, not in a way that would be recognisable as a smile, but in a way that was all-encompassing, as if the whole face was a smile – as if it was not made up of parts – of eyes and nose and mouth and chin and ears, but was just a face, the component parts inseparable and indistinguishable from the whole.

The smile reassured Gabby and she lost her apprehension. There was something eternally glorious about the vision, something familiar and welcoming, like a glimpse of a long-lost friend in a crowd, or a piece of music heard in the distance that rekindled an overwhelming déjà vu. The eyes were starlight and the mouth was the moon and the skin was the sun and the hair was strands of shining double-helix. The face spoke to her, not with a string of words – she didn't hear it, she just knew. The complete meaning came in the one instant, not in the clumsy focus of separate sound symbols, but as a complete understanding.

A hand appeared in the vision. It reached out to Gabby in the lightroom that was once the apartment where she lived. There was nothing in the lightroom but herself and the vision and the words that weren't really words but an entire concept. No walls, no floor, no ceiling – just light and face and voice and Gabby, floating in dimensionless suspended animation.

'I've come to warn you.'

The sound was not a sentence, the complete meaning of the words was conveyed instantaneously – warm and friendly, a blanket enveloping a cold body.

'Warn me?'

Gabby heard her own words in the same way as she heard the words from the vision, an unambiguous question with a complete meaning.

'About the girl.'

Something cold touched her foot – the bottle of water she'd taken from the fridge had spilt across the floor. It brought Gabby back. The colours re-emerged and Gabby felt the unbearable loneliness come back and pierce her through the heart.

It was about 7:00 am when Valéria finally woke up, surprised to find Gabby returned from a trip that was expected to last a couple of days. She was concerned.

'Why are you home so soon?'

'Wasn't feeling too well.'

'What is it? What's the matter?'

'Nothing, just an upset stomach.'

'Are you sure?'

Gabby pretended not to hear, as she made her way to the kitchen. But, by not answering, Valéria knew something more serious was wrong.

'What about work?'

'I called Günther Engels, he gave me some sick leave.'

'You look very pale, Gabby. Maybe you should come to the hospital, get checked over.'

Again, Gabby didn't answer. She'd been awake most of the night, which had given her time to consider her options.

'Valéria …'

'Yes, Gabby?'

'I want to go to Africa.'

'Africa? Why Africa?'

Gabby had her convincing reason ready.

'We've been everywhere else … Europe, the US, South America, China, Australia …'

Valéria looked sceptical, she was less impulsive than Gabby, preferring simple things like conversations with close friends, or playing her guitar in the evenings, or crunching the dry leaves under her feet in autumn. Whereas Gabby liked the new world that had been created by marketing moguls and sold to the public, the illusion of a new reality, the artificial feeling of belonging that manifested itself on television screens and billboards.

'I have to go to work, let's talk about it tonight.'

'Can we go somewhere later … to eat, I mean?'

'Of course. You book.'

They sat by the fireplace in the Goat Tavern, a seventeenth-century pub on the High Street. Gabby had a pint of traditional ale, which she loved, while Valéria sipped an orange juice because she didn't like alcohol. Gabby's voice was cordial, even though she wasn't feeling it inside.

'Did you miss me, Valéria?'

'Didn't have time to miss you, did I.'

Gabby hadn't quite figured out how to tell Valéria what had really happened in Qatar. She looked at her lover with a deep sense of loss, even though Valéria was sitting opposite her.

'Do you know how much I love you, Valéria?'

'I think so.'

Valéria's eyes narrowed, she didn't know where this was coming from or what it was leading to. She stood up.

'Have you been cheating on me, Gabby?'

'Of course not! I'd never do that.'

'Then why are you acting like there's something really terrible on your mind?'

Gabby fell silent. Her reluctance to speak only made Valéria more suspicious.

'I'm going, if you don't tell me what it is … right now!'

Just then, their food arrived. Valéria looked as if she was going to punch the waiter for interrupting her – then she sat back down. As it was, she was attracting attention from the tables close by.

Gabby had ordered Hunter's chicken with dressed salad garnish, even though she hadn't much of an appetite. Valéria wanted rump steak with grilled tomatoes, onion rings, garden peas and fries, because she was really hungry after a long day. But now her appetite was similar to Gabby's.

Gone.

They pushed food around their plates until the waiter finished fussing. Gabby was the first to speak.

'I didn't have a stomach upset.'

'What?'

'In Qatar … I was held by immigration in Doha.'

'Why?'

'I drank some headkick on the plane.'

Valéria rolled her eyes.

'I told you that stuff's too strong. What were you thinking, Gabby?'

Gabby raised her hand to curtail Valéria's chiding.

'They checked my DNA … found a defective tissue on the TMEM56 gene.'

'What? What does that mean?'

'I have two years to live … or to die, depending on how you look at it.'

She lifted the pint of ale to her lips and took a long drink from the glass.

Valéria said nothing, she just sat there as if dumbstruck, her mouth half open, displaying the food she'd been chewing. Finally, she shook her head.

'No! I don't believe it. How accurate can a DNA test in Qatar be?'

'They have the latest equipment at the airport, Valéria.'

'I don't care. We need another test, here in London.'

Dinner was over prematurely. Gabby called the waiter and paid him, as Valéria put on her jacket.

'Is there something wrong with the food, madam?'

'No, it's fine.'

She had to hurry after Valéria, who was already going through the door.

They drove home in silence.

Through her job at Charing Cross Hospital, Valéria knew a lot of DNA clinics in London and she insisted on a second opinion. Gabby, on the other hand, was reluctant to have the diagnosis confirmed beyond a shadow of a doubt. Valéria countered with, even if that proved to be the case, the survival rate for even the most malignant types of heart disease was excellent nowadays and new treatments were being discovered all the time.

They lay in their king-sized bed, bodies entwined in the comfortable clinch of familiarity – the yin and yang of life and love. Gabby was thoughtful.

'I can't waste any time, Valéria. If I only have two years left, I need to do things … tests take too long.'

'They don't.'

'Yes they do. They'll send me from one test to another … it could take months. I have stuff I need to do.'

'Let me make some calls, Gabby. Talk to a few colleagues.'

'No. I want to go to Africa. Come with me, Valéria.'

Valéria sat upright in the bed, a look of disbelief on her face.

'Are you out of your mind? You need to get well, you need treatment, Gabby. What's in Africa?'

'My past.'

CHAPTER 5
AFRICA

Gabby was intrigued about the 30% black African genes the DNA test had revealed and did some research. Her origins pointed toward West Africa, along the coastline from Senegal to Nigeria. She discovered that slaves were transported from there to Brazil and she wanted to travel to Dakar to find out more. She'd always been interested in the subject of slavery and the African diaspora, not from the generic perspective of public condemnation, but from a more personal point of view.

Her own ancestors, of Portuguese extraction, were slave owners on their plantation in the state of Bahia, back in the eighteenth-century. Her personal life had now been turned upside down by the discovery that one of those ancestors had probably had a pe na cozinha – in other words, mated with one of the slaves and she was the linear product of that union, despite the fact that she'd been brought up as white – notated on her Brazilian birth certificate. Now Gabby wanted to understand what it meant to be black – the challenges, the disadvantages and advantages, the seriousness and solace of it. Perhaps that way she could come to terms with who she really was – a melting pot of multiple races.

And a terminal heart condition made her journey of discovery all the more urgent.

It was the first time Gabby had set foot on the African continent and the first time she'd travelled neither for work nor pleasure, but for self-discovery. She was an admirer of Nelson Mandela and his resilience, altruism and determination in achieving what he had during his lifetime, against all the odds. She felt small and insignificant when she thought about her own legacy to the world – whatever that might turn out to be. And she hadn't much time left to make her mark. She deeply regretted having wasted so much of her life in what she now saw as irrelevant and selfish pursuits, that had no positive impact on humanity.

Once settled into the Hotel du Phare Les Mamelles to the south of the airport, she unpacked her Sony HXR-MC2500 to record her experiences. She didn't know what she was looking for or where she was going to find it. All she knew was that Senegal was where she was meant to be at that moment in time – it was a starting point.

She decided to walk the mile and a half along the Route de la Corniche Ouest to the magnificent *African Renaissance Monument*, 150 metres tall, nearly four times the height of *Christ the Redeemer* in Rio. She lit a cigarette and observed the statue from a distance, before taking the steps up to its base. As she climbed, Gabby wondered if Africa would ever be able to emerge from the desolation of its past – the ravishing of its resources, both human and natural, which scarred its present with poverty and inequality. In a way, it was like her own South America – *Christ the Redeemer* overlooked millions of poverty-stricken people in favelas just as, in Senegal, millions still felt the effects of hundreds of years of the slave trade and its attendant corruption and cruelty. Both statues represented hope and freedom from oppression, but the irony lay in the fact that freedom was still as inaccessible as the summits of the statues themselves.

In the middle of the afternoon, Gabby took a taxi north-east, past the Golf Club and Lake Malika and the Lac de Mbeubeusse to Lake Retba. It was a forty-kilometre journey and she wanted to take a swim in the pink water and cool off from the hot, semi-arid June climate.

The lake was separated from the Atlantic Ocean by a narrow corridor of terracotta coloured dunes, with magenta samphire bushes flourishing on white sandbanks. She floated on the pink water, coloured by *dunaliella salina* algae, looking up at the deep blue of the infinite sky, regretting that Valéria had refused to come with her – saying she wouldn't be complicit in Gabby's reckless disregard for her own well-being. Gabby had been angry at her lover to begin with, but had already forgiven her and was looking forward to renewing their relationship when she got back to London.

As she floated close to the shore her thoughts were interrupted by a young voice, coming from a group of salt harvesters.

'Who are you?'

She turned to see a boy of about ten, smiling broadly as he filled up a bucket with salt rocks from a shallow wooden boat.

'My name's Gabby. And you?'

'Ibou. Is not the water too salty for swimming?'

'Isn't that the main attraction? Apart from the beautiful colour.'

In some areas, the lake was over 40% salt and the harvesters stood chest high in the water for seven hours a day, loading their wooden piroques, because metal boats would just rust away. The men coated their bodies with shea butter, or beurre de karité, to help prevent wounds and infections. Lake Retba was a tough place to earn a living, where the men were paid 60 cents for filling a bucket and the women 5 cents for carrying it.

Gabby was intrigued by the serious look in Ibou's eyes – a look of early responsibility she recognised. She'd seen it in the eyes of street children, begging for money in São Paulo. Coming out of the water, she called after the boy and his mother.

'Hey, Ibou!'

He stopped walking and placed the heavy bucket on the ground.

'Yes, lady?'

'I'm a tourist and I need a guide.'

'How much you pay?'

'A hundred dollars American … for one day.'

Ibou ran after his mother and Gabby waited as he spoke to her in an animated fashion. Then he came back.

'Mother say yes.'

'Good. We should meet here at 9:00 am.'

Next morning, Ibou was waiting for Gabby when she arrived at the pink lake. He jumped into her taxi and they headed for Gorée Island. It was an hour's drive and she tried to get to know the young boy on the way. They spoke to each other in a mixture of French and English – French being Ibou's first language and he was trying to learn English.

She discovered that Ibou, like herself, had lost his father when he was quite young. The man was killed in a bar argument with a Casamance rebel. Ibou pulled a small amount of Lake Retba sand from his pocket and blew it at Gabby's eyes – she was immediately able to see what happened to his father as if she was standing in the bar when he was shot. When reality returned a few seconds later, she saw the boy smiling at her, as if he knew what she'd just seen and he knew that she'd seen similar visions before.

'You are psychique, Gabee.'

They arrived at the Avenue de la Liberation and took a boat to Gorée Island, two miles offshore, to see where African slaves were held before being shipped around the world. They joined the guided tour of the House of Slaves, first built by the Portuguese in 1536. Entire families were separated and herded into small stifling cells. Gabby touched the thick stone walls and stood inside the claustrophobic holding areas. She read the surviving signs over some of the doors: "Hommes", "Jeunes Filles", "Enfants", "Cellule des Recalcitrants". Then the infamous "Door Of No Return", where the slaves would be forced at gunpoint on to the rocky shore, carrying eleven-pound metal balls that were permanently chained to their ankles or necks to prevent them trying to escape into the water. The sick and injured would be weighed down with chains and thrown to the sharks from the walls above.

Gabby could feel the tears welling up in her eyes as she held on to Ibou's hand. Her story belonged to both sides, the masters' as well as the slaves', and she was overwhelmed by feelings of both shame and courage. It was Ibou's first visit.

He didn't cry, just held her hand in silence as he listened to the guide describe the horrors. The value of a male slave was based on weight and strength – the ability to perform heavy work, like a beast of burden. The women were valued on the appearance of their breasts and their virginity – virgins were more valuable. Children were valued according to the quality of their teeth.

At the end of the tour, Gabby sat in the shade, exhausted by the terrible distress she felt. Here was the real essence of who she was – who she truly was. Ibou sat next to her. After a moment or two, he finally broke his silence.

'Humans are cruel.'

She placed an arm around his shoulder.

'Very cruel, Ibou.'

The boy didn't know how cruel, and maybe that was something he'd have to learn as he grew. He didn't know about ancient civilisations built with the blood and sweat of slaves. He didn't know about medieval torture chambers and burning witches alive. He didn't know about Auschwitz-Birkenau, or Wounded Knee, or Mỹ Lai or Srebrenica. He didn't know about rendition and the secret black-site torture centres set up around the world by so-called civilised countries, like the USA and the UK.

Yes, there was no limit to human cruelty.

Afterwards, Ibou showed her around Dakar – the zoological gardens, the Immeuble La Rotonde, the Rond Point Jet d'eau amusement centre, the shopping malls, the restaurants and bars, until it began to get late.

'Now I should take you home, Ibou.'

'I can find me way, lady.'

'No, I'm responsible for you.'

They took another taxi, this time to a poor neighbourhood in Niaga, north-east of Dakar and south of Lake Retba. Ibou lived with his mother and five siblings in two rooms in an area bustling with an end-of-day market selling fruit, vegetables and grain. The boy guided Gabby through a burgundy curtain that served as a door to the humble dwelling.

'Fatima … is mother.'

Gabby offered her hand, but Fatima hugged her instead and kissed her three times in the traditional fashion – left cheek, right cheek, then left again.

'So good to meet you, Fatima … and who are these beautiful children?'

Ibou introduced his two sisters and three brothers: Omar, who was nine; Awa, who was seven; Bineta, who was six; Elhadji, who was four; and baby Momo, who was eighteen months. Gabby touched each child on the head in greeting.

The room was chaotic, filled with pots and pans and hanging clothes and the paraphernalia of family life. Fatima offered Gabby a cushion to sit on cross-legged.

'You will stay for reer.'

Gabby knew that was the Wolof word for dinner. She accepted, so as not to offend.

'We do not have much to offer, but we share with open hearts.'

Gabby was touched by the generosity of this woman who had nothing but was still prepared to share. She knew many people with plenty, who were greedy for more and begrudged giving a penny to a hungry beggar on the street.

'Thank you Fatima.'

Fatima spread a white cloth on the floor and placed a large serving platter on top. They sat in a circle round the food. Fatima passed around a bowl of water for everyone to wash their hands. Dinner was a single-dish affair of thiéboudienne, a fish-and-rice staple which they ate with their hands. Fatima offered Gabby a hibiscus drink called bissap, which she found very sweet, but refreshing.

When it was time to leave, Gabby wanted to pay Fatima for the food, but the Senegalese woman refused her money.

'Then I'll pay Ibou what we agreed for the day.'

Gabby gave the boy a hundred dollars as promised, which he immediately handed to his mother.

'And a bonus of fifty dollars for being such a good guide.'

Everyone was happy.

The next day, Gabby headed to the Archives Nationales du Sénégal on Avenue Malick Sy to see what she could discover about her ancestry, if anything. After four tedious hours of dusty files, all she found were listings of European ships that arrived in Dakar between the fifteenth and eighteenth centuries. It was a wild goose chase. Why would the slave traders identify the black people they kidnapped? It was futile – Valéria was right, she should have stayed at home. Sweat ran down her forehead in the dingy room, where only one middle-aged man sat some distance away, concentrating on an archived newspaper.

'Excuse me, sir … '

He looked up slowly, seemingly irritated by the interruption.

'Yes?'

'Where can I find information about the people who were kidnapped by the Portuguese?'

'Do you have a name?'

'No.'

'Age? Gender?'

'No, nothing … apart from my DNA.'

The man shook his head and returned his attention to the newspaper. Gabby stood up to leave.

'You could try the Catholic Church records.'

This surprised Gabby. She knew the Catholic Church was supposedly against slavery and that some priests had tried to protect slaves and aboriginals in Brazil. But why would they keep records? The man read the look of puzzlement on her face.

'Let me explain … although the Church did not trade in slaves, it persuaded slaves that it was their destiny to be oppressed, just like Jesus, and that, by enduring that oppression, they would receive their reward in heaven. It stopped them from killing themselves because suicide would block their entry into paradise.'

'And where can I find these Catholic Church records?'

'Lisbon.'

Gabby stayed in Africa for two weeks, not really wanting to travel to Portugal, but she couldn't find what she was looking for. In the end, she had no other option. At least she'd found something in Africa – her time with Ibou and his family. That experience was worth the journey.

The Arquivo Nacional da Torre do Tombo in Lisbon was guarded by gargoyles representing death, good, evil, tragedy, comedy, war and peace. Gabby wondered how many secrets had been stored inside for centuries, as she entered the fortress-styled building. She'd considered letting Valeria know that she'd be extending her absence, but decided against it. She didn't need another argument. Life was too short – at least hers was.

She was given a pair of thin white gloves to examine the rare collections of books and archived documents. She found the Catholic Church section, which contained thousands of letters from the missionary priests of the Portuguese Crown. After searching for a while, she came across an archive dedicated to family genealogy. She found the Fidalgo family, who were the antecedents of her mother's Bento family and one of the most prominent during the colonisation of Brazil, but nothing associated with the Pereira family. Gabby was convinced the 30% black African in her DNA came from her father's side and not her mother's. Nevertheless, she filled a trolley with journals, epistles and registry documents and went to one of the private rooms to read.

The Fidalgos who went to Brazil wrote back to their relatives in Portugal from their sugar plantation near the town of Ilhéus, in the southern coastal area of Bahia. The patriarch, Antonio Fidalgo, had sixty slaves.

It was all very interesting, but there was nothing in the records about anyone called Pereira. After hours of searching, she was about to call it a day when she came across a rolled-up painting of the Fidalgo family, with an obscure signature and the date of 1871. In the foreground was a man who could only be Antonio Fidalgo, standing beside a seated woman who was presumably his wife, Delores Fidalgo, and they were surrounded by six children of varying ages. Was it Gabby's imagination, or did Antonio look very like the middle-aged man she'd met in the archives in Senegal?

Unravelling the picture further, Gabby could see a black slave woman standing in the background, holding a small child with light skin. A letter fell out – it was dated the same year, from Delores Fidalgo to her sister Rufina, saying that a slave called Dandara had given birth to a child with light skin and she suspected her husband to be the father. This wasn't what Gabby was looking for – it was her father who had the dark skin.

Dandara walks through the plantation at Ilhéus, a bucket of water on her head and a baby on her back. Gabby follows. With each step she takes, the child grows older, until Gabby can see it's a young girl, walking beside her mother; then a teenager being set free when slavery is abolished in 1888; now a woman riding a horse with a handsome cavaleiro; then marrying the cavaleiro. Gabby listens to the priest reciting the marriage vows and stating the names of the bride and groom.

The groom's name is Pereira.

'Wake up … wake up, Senhora!'

A security guard was shaking Gabby's shoulder. She'd fallen asleep on top of the pile of papers.

'OK … está bem Senhor.'

She replaced the documents and left. Had she discovered that her maternal great-great-grandfather had sired a child with her paternal great-great-grandmother? Could that have caused the defect on the TMEM56 gene of her DNA?

Or was it just a dream?

Gabby no longer knew the difference.

CHAPTER 6
HISTORY

Gabby was born in Vitória da Conquista, one of the many cities founded by the Portuguese, and fought for in bloody battles with the, now almost extinct, indigenous tribes. Her father, José, was an uneducated, semi-illiterate man with a good heart – but a good heart alone wasn't always enough to put food on the table for Gabby and her four step-siblings. His odd jobs as a horse trainer and labourer only took the family so far and they relied on the garment business Gabby's mother, Maria, ran. But Maria's local clients began to desert her after her divorce from her first husband, who was a brute who beat her.

Something else bothered Gabby's parents even more than their poverty. Gabby cried a lot when she was a baby and nothing seemed to make her happy. She was in pain when she passed urine, which was always very yellow. The local hospital diagnosed that her kidneys were not functioning properly and would get worse as time went by. She'd probably need a transplant, but that couldn't be done until she was older, and then only in São Paulo. So they did what they could and her father loved her and looked after her more than his older step-children, because her mother was often on the road, looking for new clients for the clothes she made.

Apart from the kidney complications, Gabby had a fairly normal, if traditional, upbringing. She was baptised and christened in the Catholic faith and was told to ask for the blessing of her parents in the morning and before going to bed. She was instructed to pray to God and Jesus twice a day to help her endure her affliction and to always remember the ten commandments, which she had to learn off by heart. She became fascinated and, at the same time, afraid of churches. When she eventually realised she was gay she became deeply conflicted by the opposing constructive and destructive forces Catholicism exerted upon her – the unquestioning certainty of her faith and the guilt of being gay.

There were rare times spent with her maternal grandmother, Ester, in Paraná, when her mother was on the road and her father was working. They'd watch the Rio Carnival on TV and cheer the Portela samba school because they liked the white and blue flag. Ester was blonde, with the most beautiful blue eyes, which contrasted greatly with Gabby's father, who had dark skin and brown eyes. Ester didn't like dark-skinned people, she called them darkies and frequently commented that they should be whipped.

Being black in Brazilian society was synonymous with shame. Gabby's step-brothers and step-sisters would ask her why her lips were so thick, like those of a negroid person and unlike theirs. It had to be because they had different fathers. This hurt her as a child, but became a source of amusement when she came to the UK and saw women having Juvéderm pumped into their lips to make them fuller. Esther said Gabby's father was mulatto and the young girl came to fear the word as something ugly, even though she didn't really understand the contradiction – how could a man as beautiful as her father also be ugly?

Her father became the single most important person in her early childhood. She had a passion for horses, just like him, and he'd take her riding on the farms where he worked and taught her to be an accomplished horsewoman almost before she could walk. When her illness was in abeyance she loved spending time with him and his horses in the fields and on the beaches of Ilhéus and Porto Seguro in Bahia. They'd make a fire and he'd cook curau and they'd drink cocoa milk and he'd play his guitar and sing to her and they'd watch the stars travel across the night sky until it was time to go home to bed. Gabby was sad when they had to move away from that beautiful life.

By the time Gabby was five, her illness had deteriorated and it was feared that if she didn't get a transplant soon, she'd die. So the Pereira family sold what they could, packed their bags, and took a bus south to São Paulo. The journey lasted over thirty hours, along the BR-381 motorway, stopping for food and toilet breaks and being harassed by road guards looking for bribes to allow them to continue. After enduring the longest and most uncomfortable journey of their lives, they finally joined the influx of nordestinos swarming into Brazil's biggest city. It was a massive megalopolis, covered by a mushroom of polluted grey clouds and surrounded by the dead Tietê river, that stank of faeces.

Their final destination was the menacing Jardim Brasília neighbourhood in the eastern zone. It was a shanty town, a place of thousands of unregulated constructions that housed the nordestinos who arrived daily in paus de arara. The Pereiras had two rooms in a house, with one bedroom for the whole family to sleep in and a small kitchen for cooking. Toilets were shared with the other residents and were always filthy. The accommodation had been arranged by Gabby's godmother, Carmen, who'd moved to São Paulo from Vitória da Conquista a couple of years earlier and who lived in the northern zone. José said it was just a beginning and things would get better, but they had to save Gabby's life first.

They woke early the next morning, after sharing a couple of mattresses on the floor. Maria wanted to ask her affluent family for help, but José said no. They'd shunned her when she'd divorced her abusive first husband and she didn't need to go crawling to them now. They'd say, 'we told you so' and laugh in her face. But Maria was a woman who made her own decisions, so she wrote a letter to Esther in Paraná.

In the meantime, Gabby was turning purple and time was running out for her – it was even painful for her to stand up. Maria stayed with her older children while José took Gabby to the Santa Casa Hospital, the largest health complex in South America, where an appointment had been made by Carmen. He had to carry his five-year-old daughter in his arms into that busy place, with hundreds of people moving here and there, all going somewhere, all with somewhere to go. He reported to reception and they were directed to the paediatric waiting room – where they waited.

Other patients were being called: a baby who was so small it was in a shoebox; a girl who'd eaten undercooked pork with maggots that had travelled to her eye and were eating it from the inside.

'Gabriela Pereira!'

The voice came from a tall, bearded doctor in a white coat. José picked Gabby up and took her into a consultation room.

'I am doctor Matos. Please sit down.'

A female doctor joined them, scanning a file in her hand.

'This is my colleague, doctor Sinclair. She is a specialist in kidney disease.'

Doctor Sinclair looked up from the file.

'I have Gabriela's case notes from the hospital in Vitória da Conquista. Let us see what we can do.'

The doctors examined Gabby and took urine and blood samples. José could see from the frowns on their faces that things were serious.

'Results will be back in two days, mister Pereira. We will call you.'

'I do not have a telephone.'

'Oh … very well. Can you come back here then?'

'And bring Gabriela with you.'

By then, Maria had received a reply from Esther. All that needed to be done for Gabby would be done – remotely. Maria was given the address of a lawyer in the Pinheiros district. He would arrange everything.

When José took Gabby back to the Santa Casa Hospital, the same two doctors saw them again. The news wasn't good. Normal function in one of Gabby's kidneys was badly compromised and the other needed treatment with a medicine that was only available from the United States or Japan.

'What does it mean, doctor?'

'It means, mister Pereira, that your daughter needs an urgent kidney transplant … and I mean urgent.'

'Can you give her one?'

'Unfortunately, there aren't any available that match her tissue type and blood group.'

'We can put her on dialysis until one becomes available.'

'How long will that be?'

'It could be a day, a month, a year … perhaps never.'

José put his head in his hands. It was all his fault. The headless chicken malumba from his ex-girlfriend in Bahia had caused this. Now his daughter was suffering and might die because of what he'd done, leaving that crazy woman to marry Maria.

'You could give her one of yours, mister Pereira.'

'Could I?'

'If it is healthy enough … we would have to do some tests.'

'What are we waiting for?'

José's kidney was acceptable and the operation was a success. Gabby received the best aftercare at a number of private clinics and was given the medication needed to stabilise her other kidney.

After recovering from the operation, José was none the worse for losing a kidney and he was fully back to normal after a few weeks. Gabby needed ongoing supervision, as any kind of infection could have disastrous consequences. But she, too, pulled through and, after about six months, she was healthy enough to go to school.

It still left the Pereiras with the problem of making a living in a strange city where competition for every job was immense. José helped Maria out as a feirante, selling the clothes she made at local markets. Her older children were sent to boarding school through the combined intervention of her own family and the family of her ex-husband. On school holidays, José and Maria took Gabby around the country to festivals and pageants where they sold their goods. It wasn't long before they could afford slightly better accommodation.

Gabby's ongoing treatment prevented her from having a "normal" life, like other children. She required extra care and could no longer ride a horse or eat certain staple foods like pork, tomatoes or oranges. But the close relationship with her father continued, even as the relationship with her mother deteriorated because Maria was back on the road, seeking out buyers from further and further afield. Gabby and José were always together, jumping in puddles and dancing under the water which poured down from the guttering of people's houses in the summer heat, imagining the stars they could no longer see through the city smog, eating curau and drinking cocoa milk like they used to.

Then her father died in a fire when Gabby was eight.

She was alone after that.

Losing her father so early in life made her look for elusive answers all around her. Life itself – the meaning of it. Sometimes she thought she had the answers, that she understood the what, the where, the how and the when – but didn't know the why. The why answer eluded her. As she grew older, she had flashbacks of the farms and the horses she'd loved so much when she was younger, of being chased by an angry cow, of never asking members of her family for anything, of doing her homework alone. She used her student's reduced price ticket to go see ballet and jazz and theatre productions alone. She was always alone after her father died, even though a part of him was inside her.

She always enjoyed reading and she kept a diary from the age of thirteen until she was twenty-three. Despite her poor origins, she developed a taste for the finer things in life, like the opera and art-house cinema; she visited museums and photographed architecture. It was always inside her, that wanting to experience everything, and she knew she'd have to leave Brazil to do that.

Being bright was Gabby's greatest weapon during her teenage years. While her peers went to the cinema or the shopping mall or hung out in bars, she read books or went to the opera or practised the ballet steps she learnt during her free lessons at the Theatro Municipal. She hated São Paulo and, in particular, the Jardim Brasília neighbourhood. There were too many bad memories there that she'd rather forget: being mugged in the streets and robbed of her watch, her phone, her bicycle; being bullied at school because of her standoffishness; seeing the effects of drug dealing and youth delinquency – the shootings and the knifings; her mother never being around for her while she was growing up.

As an adult, significant parts of Gabby's childhood came to her in the flashbacks and she didn't know if they were real – if they'd actually happened. She even had visions of things that might have occurred before her childhood, things she couldn't possibly have known about. These flashbacks were triggered by strong emotions and she was never sure if they were true or illusional.

Poverty was a disease, just like ignorance. Gabby knew this because her father had told her so when she was just a child. It was a curse, and she meant to escape from it at all costs. Many of the people around her had little or no education and survived on the bare minimum, but they endured their lot and were thankful for the blessing of healthy children. Gabby wanted that blessing too, but only after she'd made a better life for herself.

To do that, she would leave – as soon as the time was right.

CHAPTER 7

BREAKDOWN

Gabby kept an old briefcase in the shared garage of her apartment in Kensington. It was made of dark brown leather, with a single handle.

She dusted it off and opened it carefully. There they were, the shadows of her personality, her most feared memories that she'd imprisoned there. Pictures from her childhood – small black-and-white photos of her father in his cavaleiro outfit, holding his guitar. A relic of the Easter festival at Ouro Preto. A burnt dog collar. An old song sheet. A melted plastic guitar plectrum. They began to float up, rotating around her like miniature planets.

It had been an occasional ritual of hers to open that Pandora's box, to see if the ghosts lurking inside were still under control. Now the fragments of her inner self surrounded her, spinning faster and faster. There was no light. The floor felt like starched fur and the sky outside the garage was blood-red. A far-off door opened and let in just a little illumination. Everything was wraithlike. Shifting. Insubstantial. There but not there. A voice – whispering. A face hovering above – in the semi-light. Concentration bringing it into being and lapse of attention allowing it to fade back to foam. Unseen. Skin moving. Being moved by unseen fingers. Numbness creeping inch by inch along. All feeling floating away.

Then blackness.

A tall nurse with a long, pointed nose gave Gabby a small dose of adrenaline to bring her round. It was 2:35 pm and she'd been out for seven hours, with no sign that she'd come to of her own volition. The nurse wasn't taking any chances. Gabby woke suddenly, as if she'd jumped out of a really bad nightmare. She was agitated and didn't recognise her surroundings.

'Where am I?'

'You're at Charing Cross Hospital, my dear.'

A doctor in a white coat appeared from nowhere and sat on the bed beside Gabby. He started to take her pulse. She pulled her hand away.

'Please take it easy, Gabriela. I am Dr Boulger.'

He spoke with a thick French accent and gestured to the nurse, who propped Gabby up in a sitting position and handed her a glass of water.

'Drink slowly.'

Gabby grabbed the glass in both hands and gulped the water down in one.

Still confused, Gabby tried to get off the bed and noticed, for the first time, that she was wearing nothing but a hospital gown, tied at the back. The nurse prevented her from getting to her feet.

'Is Valéria here? I want to see Valéria?'

The doctor tried to calm her.

'You were brought here alone, Gabriela. You were found unconscious in your garage with an empty morphine bottle beside you.'

'What? Found by who?'

Dr Boulger looked enquiringly at the pointy-nosed nurse.

'A neighbour … I think. She called an ambulance, and the police.'

Gabby was still confused, trying to remember what happened.

'What about Valéria … she works here …'

The nurse shook her head. Dr Boulger intervened.

'You took an overdose, Gabriela. Do you have any recollection of what occurred before you took those pills?'

A very long silence followed, then Gabby began to cry. Huge tears rolled down her face and dripped off her chin on to the bed.

She remembered.

Valéria was gone when Gabby returned from Africa. There was a note:

> *My Darling Gabby,*
>
> *By the time you read this I will have returned to Brazil. I cannot stay here and wait for you to die, unable to help you. I wanted you to seek treatment but, instead, you went off to Africa for almost a month. That is a month you could have used to help your condition. I contemplated staying and trying to convince you when you came back, but I know you well enough to understand that you will only do what you want to do. We would have argued and I would have felt like a monster. You have a right to live the rest of your life as you see fit – it is your life, not mine. And I love you too much to make that life unhappy for you, which I would do if I stayed. I have found a good position at a hospital in Rio and perhaps without me you will find someone to have children with – if it is not too late. Everything I own is yours. I leave with nothing but my memories.*
>
> *Forever,*
>
> *Valéria xx*
>
> *PS: Do not try to contact me. This is for the best.*

Gabby did try to contact her – she tried and tried and tried, to no avail. She thought of flying to Rio, but she didn't have an address, didn't know which hospital, it would have been impossible. And what if she did find Valéria and her lover refused to come back to the UK with her? What would she do then? Remain in Rio? Drink herself into the gutter? End up on drugs in a favela?

Mornings became a struggle, wandering around the flat in a state of something like despair. They'd been together so long – she didn't know what to do with herself. She was so used to Valéria being there, planning for the two of them, now her lover was gone.

At the end of a relationship a part of you begins to drown, and Gabby was drowning alone. Part of her was dying, in more ways than one. She found herself gasping for air and, when she finally reached the surface, she realised that love negotiates its own terms and always collects its dues from those who break its rules.

Even though Valéria was gone, she still lurked in small things – in wardrobe smells and bathroom brush-hair and freezer food and paint colours and the quiet desperation that Gabby felt inside her soul when she contemplated a new future alone. Her desire to live out the next two years as fully as possible were conditional upon Valéria being a part of it all. Her first instinct was to decline into pathetic self-pity, then, after a week of listless dejection, she got back up.

The next stage of breaking up was to exorcise the apartment, to get rid of what was redolent of Valéria. It all had to go – photographs, clothes, souvenirs, love letters, even the couch and the mattress. After that, Gabby disinfected the apartment from top to bottom, as well as scrubbing herself as hard as she could, in an effort to wash away every recollection, every ghost, every manifestation that permeated the space around her. Except for a snow-globe with a picture of them ice skating in Hyde Park one particularly cold January. The part of her that wanted to keep it had to fight hard with the part of her that wanted to throw it away. But there needed to be something – some reminder that the years hadn't been in vain, that they'd been happy once, many times, but that it hadn't been enough. Or maybe she kept it as a relic of the fragility of human relationships.

After the exorcism, she drank a bottle of wine and smoked a full pack of cigarettes, but it only made her melancholia return. What was the point of fighting her fate? It was useless to pretend she had two glorious years yet to live – maybe with Valéria, but not on her own. That's when she went to the garage and took the strong morphine pills that had been prescribed to numb the extreme kidney pain she was prone to from time to time.

Initially she just wanted to sleep, then she decided to prolong that sleep for eternity.

'Can I go home now?'

Her voice was hoarse from crying.

The doctor pursed his lips.

'We would like for you to stay overnight, for observation.'

'You're afraid I'll do it again, aren't you?'

'Well …'

'I won't, I promise.'

Dr Boulger considered the situation for a moment. He took the nurse to one side and they spoke quietly and earnestly to each other. Gabby couldn't hear them and she wanted to tell them it didn't matter, that she'd be dead in two years anyway – but she kept quiet. The doctor came back to her bed.

'I will allow you home … on one condition.'

'What's that?'

'You should attend the Priory in north London for a psychiatric evaluation.'

'And if I refuse?'

'We can section you, Gabriela.'

That night she had a panic attack. She tried to breathe, but couldn't, tried to force the breath into herself but couldn't control it. She sat down and drank some water, trying to calm down and centre on her breathing. It took ages. It was really difficult to regain a steady rhythm of inhalation and exhalation and she had to concentrate and keep focused until the panic subsided. She just wanted the mental torture to end. The worst part was that she couldn't change it – she couldn't undo the fact that she was going to die and the fact that Valéria had left her when she needed her most. She should be dead – the nosey neighbour shouldn't have found her in the shared garage.

No one was supposed to feel the way she felt.

The following few days passed in a series of panic attacks, which were replaced by inertia. Gabby wanted to scream – at everyone – at herself. She worried about the urge to kill herself coming back. She didn't want there to be a next time, but there almost certainly would be if things continued like this. She felt she had no control over her life or what was happening to her. She was emotionally damaged, but fighting against it was too traumatic – it was easier to give in. The psychological violence was so very exhausting that sometimes she just couldn't handle it – so she just let it happen. But when she felt like she was at the end of the road and couldn't go any further, she took one of the pills Dr Boulger gave her and went to sleep for a while, to get her strength back.

And hoped she'd wake up.

Gabby believed she was complicit in her own destruction – it seemed as if it had been destined to happen and there was nothing she could have done to stop it. She became completely isolated in her mind – cut off from normality. After the overdose, she wondered to herself if she really wanted to die. If the DNA test was right, death would come soon enough. If it wasn't, then she'd know when the time came. Maybe she should have done what Valeria suggested and sought a second opinion – and a third, fourth, fifth opinions. But what if they all came back positive? What if they all confirmed Doha?

It was the first time she started to consider that maybe she had a mental illness, as well as a defective tissue on her TMEM56 gene. Were the visions and flashbacks and flashforwards symptoms of madness? She began to ask herself questions. If she was fighting a mental disorder, was she winning the battle or losing it? Did she need help, or was she coping with it on her own? She couldn't really tell because, when she was happy and content, she felt she was OK and always had been. But when she felt low and depressed, it seemed as if she was depressed all the time and had never really been happy – as if she just pushed the bad feelings to the back of her mind for a while, but they always escaped and came back.

While she was waiting for the appointment that Dr Boulger had made for her at the Priory Hospital, Gabby felt as if the depression would never go away, no matter what she did or who she talked to – the negativity about everything – herself – the future she didn't have any more, that had been taken away so suddenly. It didn't matter where she went or what she did, the problem would never go away. She considered praying to a god she didn't believe in – and would that god respond? Speaking to god was acceptable to society at large, but god speaking back was schizophrenia. Everybody had an inner voice – so why were people who had a dialogue with that inner voice considered to be insane? And who could say what was madness and what was sanity anyway? It was all relative to who you were and what you'd experienced.

There, she was doing it again – crazy. Crazy. Crazy.

Gabby tried to "snap out of it", but "it" had such a strong compulsion that it was too difficult for her to fight against and she kept relapsing, just like alcoholics and addicts kept relapsing, even though they hated themselves for doing it. Then there was the fear – when she heard a knock on the door she felt scared, even though there was nothing to be afraid of. It was how phobias started – almost as if she needed to give herself a reason for feeling the way she did. It was a form of self-harm because she just didn't care about herself or what happened to her. Gabby began to realise that something was very wrong inside her head – but was that surprising, considering what she'd been through?

What she knew?

She was spiralling out of control, sinking into something horrible, being swallowed up by a sea of despair. Her soul had been taken over by some evil entity and the more she struggled against it, the stronger it became. She could never get away from it now – it would kill her on the fourth of July, less than two years from now. In the meantime, it would eat her from the inside out and she could hear it laughing in her head. She felt like an open wound – like her whole body was bleeding, like she was just a rag doll that was being dragged along a floor covered with vomit and urine and excrement. She'd be physically sick in the toilet, then lie in a bath of cold water for hours and hours, hoping she could soak off the sin that had infected her.

She'd sit on the floor, as if she was in a trance. She found comfort in the floor. The floor was her friend, it helped her hide from the windows, so nobody could see her. She started crawling everywhere, to the cupboards for food and to the bedroom and to the kitchen to make a cup of tea. She lay on the floor with the lights off, listened to music with headphones on and, if anyone came to the door, she'd turn the music up. If she couldn't hear them, they weren't there. Her mind was in turmoil and she felt a strange, compulsive urge to give in to the latent desire to try suicide again, only this time to make it more permanent – jump off a bridge, hang herself, leap in front of a train. If she'd had a gun, she'd have put the barrel in her mouth and pulled the trigger. She considered slicing her neck open with a knife, but she didn't have the courage.

It was as if she'd been shattered like glass.

Every morning was a struggle, tormented by the urgency of letting go of an exhausted love, enduring the mental and emotional anguish with a fake resignation. That was the most agonising type of pain, the pain she had to pretend wasn't there. She was drowning alone, every single day – a prisoner, under house arrest for something she hadn't done, feeling guilty for a crime she hadn't committed. The panic attacks continued – they came on like a black cloud in her head that she couldn't think through. It was a sense of impending doom that wasn't just impending, but real.

She'd cry and find it hard to breathe and get dizzy and couldn't calm herself down. After the panic attacks she'd feel as if she was going to explode, as if she was going to completely disintegrate. She blamed herself for everything – everything was her own fault. She was hugely distressed and needed help.

Then, the day before her appointment at the Priory, she grew cold inside. Her life was what it was and it would end soon, either by her own doing or by the flawed heart that would eventually kill her. But the biggest threat to that life was all this craziness – the prospect of going crazy worrying about it. So she stopped being afraid. She stopped caring. Life didn't scare her – death didn't scare her.

Not any more.

CHAPTER 8

TREATMENT

Gabby drove voluntarily to the Priory Hospital in north London, to which she'd been referred by the Charing Cross psychiatric team. The hospital's general mental health service treated residential and day-patients for a range of conditions, such as stress, depression and anxiety. The therapeutic interventions included trauma reduction, cognitive behavioural therapy, dialectical behaviour therapy, emotion focused therapy, along with movement-orientated psychology.

She'd been entertaining thoughts of self-harming and suicide since Dr Boulger had discharged her. Her mind punished her with dreadful questions to which there were no answers. Was her pursuit of success worth all the sacrifices she'd had to make? The sexual harassment and innuendo had turned her into a different person, one she didn't particularly like. Would she have been happier staying poor and having children, like some of her relatives back in Brazil? Was she being punished for something she'd done in the past and had forgotten? Was it bad karma? Or maybe life was just a constant stream of painful experiences – a vale of tears, as the Catholics said?

And now Valéria had turned against her as well as her atavistic heart.

Gabby passed the brick walls surrounding the hospital, through the rustic stone piers and wrought-iron entrance gates, along the long driveway through an avenue of trees, abandoned tennis courts to the left with rough grass and enclosing hedges. The main building was an imposing two-storey structure, with a three-bay central loggia supported by four giant Ionic stone columns. It was surrounded by an open lawn and pleasure gardens with picnic tables facing a narrow path to Grovelands Park in Southgate.

She was directed to a treatment room that looked like a hospital ward with no patients. There was nothing in the room except her and her nightmare. Her distressed soul floated around Gabby in the space that was neither large nor small, a space that just held her in its sanctimonious grasp. Pieces of lost time came and went in this cavity of uncertainty. She felt uneasy on her own, with everything distorted and compromised. She felt abandoned – betrayed – denied – dismayed. She began to pace about, looking for an alternative, but couldn't find one. She kicked at the door – no one came to tell her to stop. The nightmare was laughing at her frustration – lightly – somewhere far off, in the corner of an abyss that had no corners – a room that was part of the unbearableness of illusory reality. The sound of the laughter was yellow, reminding her of other sounds she'd heard. Transparent sounds. Silent sounds. Creeping up on her from behind sounds.

She kicked the door harder and this time they came, three female nurses, their faces set and grim. They glared at Gabby. She glared back – and suddenly they weren't nurses any more – they were ninjas. She knew they wanted to fight her, and she was no pushover. She'd had fight training when she was younger – Mauy Thai martial arts. So she danced about, shadow-boxing and launching kicks at their heads which never connected.

'You want me?'

'Mrs Pereira …'

'You want me you bitches?'

'Mrs Pereira …'

'Come and get me, then!'

They circled round Gabby, cautiously, not wanting to come too close and connect with her flying foot. The panic inside her grew and it made her see beyond herself, beyond the Priory Hospital, beyond north London. She found a walking stick and used it as a sword, swinging it round her head to keep them at bay, until she accidentally connected with one of them – maybe a flick to the ear, maybe to the ego. That was it! They all rushed her at once and she felt a sharp prick in her arm.

In the darkness she saw the Fenrir, whose jaws touched heaven and earth and swallowed Odin. And the flesh-eating horses of Diomedes, who ate the carcass of their master. And Francesca da Rimini, who was put to death for adultery. And the Fair Rosamund, who lived in a labyrinth and was poisoned by Queen Eleanor – hic jacet in tumba Rosa mundi, non Rosa munda. Falling. Falling. Gabby fell deeper and deeper down the well. Waiting for the water to break her bloody neck.

On the way down, Gabby saw herself as a child again, in Brazil. She could hear the songs and see the sights of her youth and smell her grandmother's cooking – pão de queijo and feijão tropeiro.

She fell past the years when she was bullied in school for being a clever A-Grade student; past the depression she'd suffered because no one spoke to her for a whole year. She saw her father's blackened body as she went down and down, until she hit the bottom and bounced hard.

During that period of tranq-teichopsia she sang and sang – songs she'd learned as a child in São Paulo, like repente and sertanejo. An angel sang with her and held her hand and she cried a river of salt tears.

The light finally came on again. Gabby's room was overlooking a delicate lake where children played in the pleasant weather of early autumn. A consultant was sitting close to her, a woman in her mid-forties, wearing a white coat over a colourful sari. The name tag pinned to the coat read Dr Sunita Rajwana.

'Let me introduce myself … I'm Dr Rajwana …'

'I can see that.'

Sunita smiled in the face of Gabby's hostility, and the smile blended rather surprisingly with the doctor's reassuring air of authority. Then Gabby began to cry, something she rarely did in front of strangers. Sunita held her hand in an attempt to comfort her.

'I'm here to help you, Gabriela.'

Gabby didn't know why she'd taken the overdose – yes she did, Valéria had left her. But it was more than that, people split up all the time and the relationship had been shaky for a while. She just felt so weak, unable to cope by herself – probably since Qatar. It was a kind of PTSD – post traumatic stress disorder.

She tried to explain how she felt to Dr Rajwana, without disclosing what she'd seen in that genome report in Doha. Would the doctor even believe her? Would Sunita Rajwana think she was completely crazy and maybe section her. As it was, she'd come here of her own accord, on the advice of Charing Cross Hospital. She didn't want her attendance to be compulsory.

'What's the problem, Gabriela?'

'Don't you know?'

'I know what you did. I want to know why?'

That unanswerable question again. Why?

'The thing is, I don't even know why I feel this way. Other women have gone through worse. I just feel so weak, not able to cope.'

'I know, Gabriela, human relationships can be disturbing at times.'

Gabby continued to talk and Dr Rajwana continued to listen. She talked for hours, days, a week. The doctor listened. Gabby took long pauses to breathe or cry.

During that time, she went on a journey inside her own subconscious. Sometimes she could understand what the doctor was telling her, and other times she couldn't. In the beginning, her mind wasn't focusing properly and everything was a bumble, a mumble. All a stumbling, crumbling, fumbling bumble – in her brain. Dr Rajwana's voice came and went, with its interpretation of her current psychological diathesis and its hypothesis on her course of treatment. The doctor talked of primary delusion and ego disintegration and cognitive epistemology and other things. Sometimes she sounded a little crazy herself – from spending too much time with crazy people.

They discussed her attempted suicide and Sunita's face frowned and her hands made little expressions of understanding. She said there might be too much dopamine in Gabby's brain – or serotonin – or histamine – she wasn't sure. She said Gabby's neurotransmitters were probably out of sync, causing surges of adrenaline. Or maybe it was something to do with her sleep patterns – or her mood inducers – or even her appetite. Either her histamine was low or her hormones were high or there were imbalances of zinc or zymogen or niacin or nicotimi-acid.

Or maybe it was her homocysteine levels. Or it could be something to do with her nerve cells. They kept talking – talking, talking, talking, talking and it seemed sometimes that the doctor was talking to herself and not to Gabby. About things – she talked about things like wheat gluten and opioids and exorphins and prostaglandin and prolactin and melatonin. And drugs. She talked a lot about drugs and she gave Gabby drugs and sympathy, to keep her safe – from herself.

Dr Rajwana didn't ask her about the thing she wanted to talk about – Valéria. Why she felt so hopeless without the woman who had shared her life for so long. So Gabby tried to answer that question for herself. Why? But she just couldn't focus on it for long.

Other questions came during that week of rehabilitation. Why her life was going to be cut short before she could do the things she really wanted to do, and the implications? Obscure thoughts of space and life and time and tiny little atoms and huge philosophies and death and madness and the meaning of everything and sometimes she could see it and sometimes she couldn't.

And when she could, a light shone at the back of her brain and she could smell the essence of the universe.

And when she couldn't, she felt something sad, like a loss. Like the death of a child.

She knew it meant something – even if the doctor didn't. There was something to the feeling of loss and hopelessness inside her. Something sublime and essential. The doctor couldn't see it, but she could. It was then that she caught little glimpses of god and she understood the state of mortality and the concept of infinity and saw beyond herself. Beyond the Priory. Beyond London. Beyond the world, the solar system, the galaxy, the universe.

And she flew away over the wall.

After six or seven days of treatment Gabby began to feel a kind of normality again – whatever normality was. The sense of loss diminished but didn't go away completely. It became bearable.

The medication modified the earlier lucid craziness that was too much to bear for any human being, the keenness of the equilibrium and the piercing purity and the colours and sounds and smells, and the knowing of all things.

She had no more thoughts of ending her life. Oh, she had challenging moments – intermittent bouts of depression that varied in severity – feeling lonely, withdrawn, vulnerable. But the doctor controlled it with self-management therapies and Gabby wondered if the condition had really gone away, or if it was still hiding at the back of her mind, biding its time, waiting until she'd been lulled into a false sense of sanity, when it would emerge again – laugh at her again – that yellow laugh. Sometimes she cried but, outwardly, she was managing, not letting anyone see her vulnerability.

She was coping and went home.

On the weekend, Gabby went to the supermarket, feeling a little woozy from the medication. She miscalculated how much she'd spent and was ten pounds short when she got to the till. She searched for her card, but couldn't find it. The cashier asked her if she wanted to put something back, but she threw everything on the floor and ran to the door, crying. She cried all the way home and didn't sleep that night.

The thing had taken over her body again and was speaking in a strange accent. The words were coming from somewhere outside her, even though the thing was inside her. The words were murky, they smelled of blood. She still needed someone to help her, so she called Dr Rajwana on Monday.

Back at the Priory for a second week, Gabby was worried they might keep her in against her will and never let her back out. She was confused and believed it was the drug regimen they'd put her on that was causing the problem.

'Can I stop taking the tranquillisers, doctor?'

'I wouldn't recommend it, Gabriela.'

But she stopped anyway, against the doctor's advice. She became jumpy – nerve-jangly. She lit up a cigarette inside the building, which was strictly prohibited, and set off the fire alarms, which really annoyed the nurses. More days passed, then something came over Gabby – weirder than anything she'd experienced before. Little shafts of light – quick flashes of lightening. Bright for an instant, then black again. Trying to get through what was left of the psychotropic straitjacket. She knew she'd passed into another world and wasn't in her human body any more. The orthomolecular entity she'd become tried to understand this parallel reality.

Shadows came and lay beside her. It was difficult to make them out – Jeanne of dreams, of le menu peuple? Dido maybe, with her hair and clothes on fire – Xanthippe – and Oenone, who may have told her the story of the rest of her life. "Soient bons, soient mauvais esperils, ilz me sont apparus." And she felt no guilt – no blame – no responsibility for the thing she couldn't control. And neither did god.

Dr Rajwana said, 'Same time tomorrow, Gabriela.'

She was back in her body.

Human again.

CHAPTER 9

MIA

On the third week of her outpatient's treatment, Gabby was wandering through the corridors of the Priory when she heard some enigmatic music coming from somewhere close by. It was both familiar and unfamiliar – music she knew, but being played in a different way – a different modality. She followed the sound to a large room, a dancehall or a theatre. About a dozen people were moving to the music, led by an elegant, petite girl, with a delicate, freckled face. She had long straight hair, part ginger, part auburn, tied back in a ponytail. Gabby watched as she instructed the dancers, smiling beautifully and guiding them patiently. Gabby's heart began to beat slightly faster as she watched, fascinated.

'Do you like dancing?'

Seconds passed before Gabby realised the girl was speaking to her. She blushed.

'Emmm … not really.'

'Why not?'

Gabby tried to think why not, but her mind was jumping about like a jackrabbit.

'I don't like close physical contact with people I don't know.'

The girl had come across to where Gabby stood in the doorway. The others continued to move to the music that was coming from a laptop on the floor.

'What about people you do know?'

The girl's eyes were laughing at her.

'Those too.'

'How sad.'

Gabby tried to change the subject.

'What kind of music is it?'

'Brazilian zouk.'

She was surprised.

'I'm Brazilian and I've never heard of Brazilian zouk.'

'It's actually an evolution of the lambada from the 1980s, but it incorporates more upper body movements. Come, let me show you.'

Before Gabby could object, the girl had pulled her gently on to the dance floor and was explaining the movements with exaggerated hand gestures and head motions. Gabby tried to resist, but only half-heartedly, and her natural sense of tempo and ballet training soon picked up the slow-quick-quick rhythm.

Her phobia of close physical contact with strangers dissipated through the sensuality of the girl's undulating body and flowing hair. It was a close connection embrace of long graceful steps, strong hip movements, body isolations and torsions, wild spins and whip-like head movements. The melody and pauses utilised different timing dynamics and Gabby could see how it was influenced by jazz, ballet and contemporary dance. Her body was in constant flux with the girl's, alternating close chests and cheeks resting on each other – the other dancers stopped to watch. Gabby had her hands on the girl's neck and allowed herself to be led in graceful, imagination-provoking movements. When the music stopped, everybody applauded.

'You're a natural, … ?'

'Gabriela … Gabby.'

'I'm Mia.'

Mia dismissed the class and invited Gabby to a nearby café, where they sat and drank mineral water. The girl wasn't Brazilian – she was a Londoner with an Italian background. It surprised Gabby that Mia knew something about Brazilian dance that a native like herself didn't.

'So, what did you think of Brazilian zouk?'

'It's left me a bit out of breath, as you can tell. Are you a dance teacher, Mia?'

'No, I'm a psychologist.'

It turned out that Mia held a therapeutic Brazilian zouk class once a week at the Priory. She was a consultant psychologist working for the National Health Service and wasn't specifically attached to the rehab centre. She already had a master's and was completing her PhD thesis.

'Dance can be very beneficial to cognitive function and mood, Gabby. It also relieves tension and mental stress. It's one of my three main interests.'

'What are the other two?'

'Women and winemaking. But that's me. What are you doing here?'

'I tried to kill myself.'

'Oh dear. Why?'

'My wife left me.'

'Your wife?'

'Yes.'

Mia was more than a little intrigued by Gabby's use of the term. Gabby explained that she and Valéria were legally married and referred to each other as wife as a joke and a way to surprise people at social gatherings. It transpired that Mia herself was bisexual and enjoyed the company of both men and women – a fact that Gabby absorbed with great interest. Then it was time to part company. Gabby didn't want her new friend to go.

'Can I see you again, Mia?'

'Sure, here's my card. Give me a call.'

An imperceptible breeze blew along the streets of Soho, which were filled with young crowds holding onto pints of Peroni or glasses of Pimm's Royale or flutes of champagne, making it difficult to drive past, especially in a BMW 4x4. A week had gone by before Gabby mustered enough courage to call Mia. When she did, the girl was happy to hear from her and they arranged to meet. Now Gabby's breathing was heavy and her patience was short, her fingers fidgeted on the steering wheel, waiting for people to cross the street in front of her. She couldn't find a parking space, but that was only to be expected at this time on a Friday evening. It was 8:20 pm – she was running late.

Finally, she managed to nip in front of everyone else to a space that was being vacated in Golden Square, just around the corner from the rendezvous on Brewer Street. Would Mia still be there? Gabby phoned and texted but got no response. She began to run, dodging through the throng, until she arrived outside the Mele e Pere Italian restaurant.

Gabby could see Mia's elegant outline as soon as she entered the informal establishment. The girl was seated at the back, with a view across the restaurant, and she waved when she saw Gabby coming through the door. She was sipping a glass of Prosecco and she called the waiter and ordered two more before Gabby got to the table.

'Gabby, how nice to see you again. Have you been practising your zouk?

'I should, shouldn't I? But no.'

'Yes you should. I've ordered you wine, is that OK?'

'Thank you, but just one. I'm driving.'

Mia's voice was low and refined. She had an adorable girl-like facial expression, with bright blue eyes and beautiful teeth. She was wearing a short-sleeved playsuit that exhibited her voluptuous cleavage, which immediately drew Gabby's gaze.

Not since before Valéria had a beautiful woman made her lose her concentration so easily and so completely. She tried to say something witty and scintillating, but the words came out all wrong and sounded ridiculous. Attractive women had always had that effect on her when she was younger – they made her lose control. She had difficulty keeping track of what Mia was saying, all she could concentrate on were the red lips, the slim figure, the glowing hair, no longer in a ponytail. Gabby had brought along a bottle of wine as a gift.

'It's a Châteauneuf-du-Pape … from France.'

'Now you've made me feel bad, Gabby.'

'Why?'

'I didn't bring you anything.'

'That's alright. Don't worry about it.'

Gabby tried to gauge Mia's age – with difficulty. She looked young, maybe early twenties, but somehow she seemed older.

'How old are you, Mia?'

The words blurted themselves out before Gabby could stop them. She blushed again.

'I'm so sorry … so sorry … I never should …'

'It's OK. I'm thirty. You?'

'Thirty-five.'

The same age difference as between Gabby and Valéria – déjà vu? Their knees touched as Mia turned to catch the waiter's attention. She ordered salt cod carpaccio with dill in orange sauce for starters.

'Gabby?'

'I'll have the same.'

Everyone in the restaurant seemed relaxed – talking, smiling, gesturing, eating, drinking – everyone except Gabby. She sat with her neck rigid, palms moist, breathing irregular. She was so coiled, she almost jumped when Mia asked the question that had been hanging in the air since they met.

'So, what are you looking for?'

Gabby wondered what the girl meant and how she should answer. She could have said some more wine or the food or death or the meaning of life or the answer to why, but instead she said, 'I've just come out of a ten-year marriage to someone I thought I'd be with for the rest of my life. But it didn't work out that way.'

In essence, Gabby wanted a relationship like her grandparents had had, not because it was perfect, it hadn't been, but because they'd been together for many years and could always count on each other. She was beginning to think that wasn't possible in the gay world – the role models weren't around. In any case, it was too late for that now, she only had two years left.

Mia looked thoughtful, as she sipped her Prosecco. She licked her lips slowly and sensuously before speaking in that almost hoarse, aesthetic manner of hers.

'I just want to enjoy my life while I'm young enough. I'm not twenty anymore and forty will creep up on me before I know it.'

'Have you ever thought about children, Mia?'

'About having them? No.'

Was it too early in the relationship for Gabby to tell Mia about her diagnosis? Gabby believed it was, so she was glad when the girl indicated she didn't want to get into anything serious.

That was what the girl was saying, wasn't it? Gabby was good at picking up those little innuendos in what people said, the small inflections in their speech that meant a lot. Yet she didn't want to deceive Mia now and maybe hurt her later, if things got complicated. But what was she thinking? They weren't even in a relationship yet, just out for dinner together – if that's what this really was.

The waiter came with the starters, interrupting her thoughts. They ate in silence, then Mia ordered pappardelle with wild mushrooms for the main course and tiramisu for afters. Gabby had the same, not because she didn't have a mind of her own, but because it suited her. While they waited for the pasta, Mia disclosed that she wanted to travel, to meet new people, before settling down and deciding on a mid-life orbit. That seemed fair to Gabby, it was always good to meet new people and putting off a stable métier for the later years was always the prerogative of the young, or relatively young – as long as there were later years to come.

Maybe that's what Gabby needed to do herself – forget about the narrow future and live for today. She'd been over-romantic and conservative in the past, preferring to know fewer people, but ones who left her with lasting memories – she'd move mountains for the ones she loved. Now there was a new reality.

There was a hint of mockery in Mia's voice when she replied to the thoughts Gabby had voiced.

'I also move mountains for people I love … I just don't love very often.'

The main course arrived. Again, they ate in silence. Mia was the first to speak, continuing from where she left off, as if there'd been no break in the conversation.

'I suppose you could say I'm emotionally detached.'

It was a statement that came out of the blue for Gabby, who thought the topic had been concluded, whereas it was a simple extension of the thought process for Mia. The two were turning out to be very different.

Mia was staring at Gabby as she spoke, who had to glance at the floor to break the intensity of that look.

'You're lucky, Mia, I wish I could be like that.'

'It comes from having a dysfunctional attachment style. It's actually a bad thing, but it would be a dull world if we were all the same, wouldn't it, Gabby?'

Knowing Mia was emotionally unavailable had an opposing effect on Gabby – it made her desire the girl even more intensely and it suited the short-term future that faced her. Maybe she was attracted to Mia's emotional flaws as much as to her physical attributes?

At that moment, the bustling restaurant became muffled and blurred and she went into one of her altered reality flashes. A strange bedroom – blood – death – not hers, someone else's. It only lasted a few seconds and, afterwards, Mia's face and body seemed closer to her than before. A shiver passed over Gabby's soul, her heart fluttered like a frightened butterfly and she wanted to run from the restaurant.

'Can we go somewhere else?'

'Sure.'

It seemed to Gabby that, up to now, she'd been borrowing someone else's dreams, someone she didn't know, and making them her own. That alter ego was filling up the massive empty space inside her and she needed something else to fill it with.

Mia paid the bill and suggested the nearby Ham Yard Hotel – a discreet establishment in a quiet cul-de-sac. Perfect. The air outside was cool when they emerged into the crowds on Brewer Street. Mia held her hand as they negotiated their way toward Lachesis.

CHAPTER 10

LOVERS

It was less than a five-minute walk to Ham Yard, a small piazza with tables and chairs scattered around the abstract sculpture, *Rational Beings*. Gabby hadn't known this place existed and it was refreshing not to have to make decisions, to allow herself to be led into the unknown by this girl who danced so evocatively and who was a complete enigma. Mia made her way into a room dominated by four large stone Balinese mirrors. They sat at a small table with white candles whose diffuse light cast a curious spell – ominous but appealing. It was much less crowded than Mele e Pere, which pleased Gabby.

'How do you like it here?'

'Better.'

'Shall we get a drink?'

'I'm driving.'

'I don't think so.'

Mia picked up the cocktail menu and ordered a couple of smoke 'n' bubbles. She said it was her favourite drink from this place. So she'd been here before – maybe many times. A smoke 'n' bubbles consisted of mezcal, agave, lime and champagne – it had a strong bitter punch, softened by a sweet bubbly champagne aftertaste. It wasn't as potent as her headkick, but after a few of them, Gabby felt her words becoming more fluent. The ambient light-classical music was a satisfying background for her growing feeling of well-being.

'You seem to be really far away, Gabby.'

'Sorry … is this better?'

Gabby pulled her chair closer to Mia and leant forward until the space between them was excruciating, causing

Gabby's thoughts to dissipate, her mouth to desiccate and her heartbeat to accelerate.

In the background Debussy's 'Clair de Lune' started. Mia rose to her feet and walked to the centre of the room. She stretched out her hands toward Gabby.

'Would you care to dance?'

'Is it allowed?'

'Of course, if that's what you want.'

Gabby tried not to think about what she wanted – tried to keep it at bay, even though she knew she wouldn't. Couldn't. Her father had taught her that the mind should control the body and not the other way around. But, at a time like this –

Gabby joined her on the floor and felt Mia's arm go around her waist. Her hands rested lightly on the girl's shoulders. Mia squeezed a little, to test the temperature. Gabby squeezed back, smelling her hair. It smelled of peaches. Mia's thigh eased between Gabby's legs as the girl moved her round the room. They responded well to each other's touch, dancing slower and slower, moving closer and closer. Gabby could feel the pressure of Mia's breasts against her own. Her lips touched Mia's cheek and the girl's hand moved beneath the waistband of her skirt and to the base of her spine. Gabby could feel the heat of her, smell the scent of her. Mia could sense something was happening and leant in even tighter. They weren't dancing any more, they were being sexually delinquent.

The music finished, but they kept swaying from side to side in a sensual rhythm. When Gabby opened her eyes, she could see the others in the room watching them. She tried to form a picture in her mind of what exactly was happening, but it was distorted, like the faces of the people watching. Gabby didn't care, because whatever was happening was rather glorious.

'How do you like your women?'

Mia whispered the question, even though there was nobody within earshot. Gabby didn't really know how to answer.

'Intelligent, I think … aesthetic … witty, I suppose.'

'How very conservative. I meant intimately, Gabby, how do you like them in bed?'

'Is that not a very personal question to be asking on a first date?'

Mia laughed, that mocking intonation again.

'A date? Is that what this is?'

Gabby didn't know. She was out of practice and confused. She could normally read a situation and deal with it accordingly, but this girl was breaking all the rules. She decided to fight fire with fire – or sassy with sassy.

'And how do you like your women, Mia?'

Mia began to walk toward reception.

'Shall we find out?'

After getting a room key, Mia picked up a candle from one of the tables and started to ascend the stairs. She looked back at Gabby, who was standing there motionless. This was a new thing to her. She didn't know how to handle the situation, whether to follow or not. If she'd had more experience, she'd have known what to do, but she'd been sheltered by her long relationship with Valéria and unfamiliar situations could confuse her. Without consciously deciding, Gabby found herself climbing the stairs after Mia. Anticipation filled her, gave an edge to her senses. She was alive now and tomorrow didn't matter. Desire surged through her like a tsunami – she was no longer herself, so she could no longer explain herself. There was nothing to explain – no logic in the liquid night. Gabby forgot who she was – what she was – and every step became its own little lifetime. Birth and life and death. And again. And again.

When she reached the first level, Gabby could see the candlelight disappear into a room and she followed. The door was ajar and the interior shimmered. The curtains were open and a gibbous moon glowed against an altar cloth of stars. The room was ornate – baroque even. Rococo and chinoiserie and filigree and champlevé – yet cool. Not cool exactly – tranquille, reposant, spirituel. It was a milieu Gabby had never experienced and she was a little unnerved. A scent of celandine filled the air and the sound of a violin came from the piazza. Gabby thought it might be the allegro non troppo from the *Symphonie Espagñole*, or the 'Fandango Asturiano' from the capriccio, or even 'Scena e canto gitano' – or it could have been something she'd never heard before.

She wasn't sure.

Gabby felt uneasy – guilty even. She felt this was reckless, even though she was separated from Valéria, both emotionally and physically. Yet the sense of hazard was palpable, like a heartbeat, a separate entity there in the room with them. Her brain was full of white noise and she didn't know if it was the smoke 'n' bubbles she'd drunk, or the fact that Mia's features had grown obscure, except for her eyes – wild eyes – dangerous eyes. They came up close and Gabby could see her own reflection in them, feel the breath warm and sultry on her neck. Mia's voice was like rough velvet and her words meant everything and nothing simultaneously.

This wasn't what she'd expected when she came out this evening. Actually, Gabby didn't know what she'd expected and, while this might have seemed like a thoroughly instinctual and spontaneous occurrence to anyone else, it was subliminal to her, a powerful force that expected something from her. Maybe it was right for her to be here, in accordance with the poetry of nature, with the shadows and strangely-hued chiaroscuros and dancing silhouettes in the guilty room.

It was.

As it was.

And there were three ways of knowing a flame: to be told of it; to see it; and to be burnt by it.

Mia came at her out of the shadows, kissing her face and pulling at her clothes, like they do in the movies. Gabby didn't really like that kind of thing, it was far too frantic for her. She preferred to take things a little easier, which Mia instinctively understood and slowed down. She manoeuvred Gabby toward the bed – her moving forward, Gabby going backward – slowly – all the time in an embrace. The pale moonlight glowed on Mia's hair and in her eyes as she discarded her playsuit. The buttons of Gabby's blouse opened all by themselves and the zipper of her skirt slid down noiselessly and unaided. Mia's hands moved inside her bra, which unhooked itself from behind and, by the time they reached the bed, they were both naked.

Starlight glinted on Gabby's skin as Mia touched her breasts, and everything became acceptable within the context of the night. She made a sound – not human, not her, not Gabby – a small unreal sound.

Mia's hands moved across her body. Searching. The girl kissed her and eased her legs apart. Gabby continued to make little noises like a lost puppy that had just been found. She could feel Mia's body responding as she moved her fingers across the girl's back. Breath came faster from her mouth. Their naked bodies perspired, even in the night's coolness, as they came together in a scissors embrace.

Gabby was surprised at her own indiscretion. She'd never acted this loosely with anyone before, not even Valéria, and she wondered why she was doing it now. Was it Mia herself, the easy way she felt with the girl, her words that resembled a sound she'd never heard before, coming from somewhere she'd never known? Was it because her eyes caressed an essential part of Gabby's inner being that believed intrinsically in the old ways of earth and essence? Or maybe she'd just drunk too much alcohol. Whatever it was, Gabby felt an overwhelming emotion for this girl she'd only known for a very short while and whose body was moving gently in rhythm with her own.

All thoughts of tomorrow flowed away on a river of passion that pulled her down until she was drowning and the sound of her own voice was a distant echo and her breath came in short gasps that floated like kisses through the open window and stayed as little stars in the night sky.

Their breasts caressed and Mia's lips covered her ears and eyes and the moon turned to rainbow as candy-coloured nails scraped on skin and Gabby orgasmed in a burst of starbright light, muscles convulsing and hands holding on to the bed to prevent her from levitating to the ceiling. Then she relaxed – slowly. Slowly, with a heavy heaving of her lungs and her mouth snatching at the steamy air. Slowly. Calmness crept back and sanity returned, slowly.

They lay together in the shimmering room.

A clock in the distance struck midnight. The candle had burnt most of the way down and Mia left the bed to open the mini-bar. Light flooded the room. She stood back to let Gabby see the display of bottles.

'What's your poison?'

'Is there any beer?'

'Just Peroni.'

'That's not beer.'

'There's brandy.'

They drank from the glasses provided. Mia kissed her again and brandy from the girl's lips wet her mouth.

The dying candle flame grew larger once the mini-bar was closed and Gabby remembered being told that Judas had hanged himself from an elder tree and the burning of that wood unleashed the devil.

She felt slightly hypnotised, with the candle flame blazing at her from Mia's eyes and the girl's blood-red lips pouting. Her mind was moulting and it felt as if she was in a time machine that began to whirl, slowly at first, but with increasing speed.

Mia's face was sensuous and wild, her hair glowing with light from both the moon and the stars, and her skin almost luminous in the gloom of the room. Soon the girl was all over Gabby again. Her candyfloss hands and white teeth and luscious lips, writhing like a lizard with the moonlight licking at her silver thighs, urging Gabby's face up into the secrets of her body to taste the juice of Genesis. Mia inched her way across Gabby's chest and stomach, down to the design-shaven vagina and her tongue quickly found the right spot. They moaned together in a synchronicity of pleasure and, at that moment, Gabby believed there couldn't be more to life than lust or more to marriage than madness.

Gabby was close to orgasm again when Mia suddenly got off the bed and stood there, looking down at her.

'Do you like to experiment, Gabby?'

'Experiment?'

'With sex.'

She didn't wait for an answer, just walked to the mini-bar and filled a glass with ice cubes. She took a pair of silk stockings from the pocket of her jacket and put them on, then walked back to the bed and moved her face right up close to Gabby's. She blew gently across Gabby's eyes and nose while guiding her hand to the tops of the stockings. The insides of her thighs were warm and moist.

Gabby tried to kiss her, but she pulled her mouth away, keeping her lips very close and running her tongue across them. Then she removed the stockings, slowly, and draped them across Gabby's nipples.

Mia was at the foot of the bed and she began to crawl forward, like a snake. Coiling herself over Gabby's body until her eyes were directly above and full of something Gabby didn't recognise – something she hadn't seen before. The girl wrapped one of the stockings around Gabby's wrist and tied it to the bedframe. Then the other one. Gabby was about to say something, but Mia clamped a hand over her mouth. A dribble of spit emerged from between the girl's lips and Gabby saw it fall in slow motion. She removed her hand in time for it to strike Gabby's mouth, like an exploding bomb.

Gabby felt like a sacrifice on a slab as Mia assumed the sixty-nine position and her tongue began to manipulate Gabby's clitoris. She was so light – so light. Almost weightless. It was like being made love to by an invisible person. The experience was translucent. Hazy. Dreamlike. Soft sounds of pleasure. Strange words. Heat.

Mia threw her head back as her fingers went deep inside Gabby's vagina and, before long, she could feel herself reaching climax. Mia felt it too. She reached for an ice cube from the glass and placed it on Gabby's clitoris. The cold shock had the effect of halting orgasm and Mia continued to fuck her until all the ice in the glass was melted.

Then she moved herself into position on Gabby's face and, before long, they could feel each other tense up and grow

rigid. Savage animals outside the window howled to get in
– birds screeched in the trees – Valéria was at the other side
of the world and Gabby was here, at the centre of the earth
and the street corner of the universe, as the glorious ecstasy
reached climax and they came together in a convulsion of
high-pitched yeses and then subsided into a rolling ball of soft
sweat and sighs.

They drank most of the mini-bar through what was left
of the night. Mia showed her things, did things to what was
inside her – not just sexual things, more than that.

She played music for Gabby – Rameau's *Les Indes galantes*
made her feel like dancing – a Grieg piano concerto made her
weep with emotion – a waltz from a Shostakovich jazz suite
made her believe she was in a different, long ago time – a
feeling she couldn't explain when she heard *Trois morceaux en
forme de poire* – and the finale to the *Firebird* that gave her
so much hope and made her feel so alive. More than alive.
Eternal. Part of everything. With her – Mia.

Mia spoke hoarsely to her while they lay naked on the bed
and her words were like kisses on Gabby's ears. The girl made
her laugh at things other people didn't laugh at – didn't think
about. Things Gabby didn't think about, until Mia told her –
and then she knew she'd think about them all the time. Was all
this something Gabby had to learn? Or was it something she
already knew but had discarded, and now had to relearn? How
to be a real woman, not a fake sterile cypher – a woman with a
deeper light – a more profound identity. And would Mia also
teach her how to cry?

Would that be the next lesson?

Gabby felt as if the girl had killed her and she'd been
reborn – a phoenix from the old ashes. There was something
in Mia's voice – something in the way she looked at Gabby –
something in the way she held her glass – something in the
colour of her hair – the way the light struck her naked profile
– the whiteness of her teeth – the redolence she left behind
her when she moved. The girl filled her body and soul and
she understood at last how the union of two people, the lover

and beloved, became love itself and ordinary life faded away and they were transported to a place where the impossible happens.

Morning came and they parted. The memory of Mia's velvet body still vibrating the strings of Gabby's soul.

CHAPTER 11

ITALY

Back at work at last after the long period of sick leave, Gabby's next assignment was in Italy. Palexion had a client with a factory in Emilia-Romagna and she had to go to Spiazzi, near Verona, to work on a product video shoot. She'd been up since 6:00 am to pack the photo and film equipment before catching her flight to Bologna. She thought about Mia on the twenty-minute drive to Heathrow Airport. They'd met three times and being with her gave Gabby a thrilling sense of danger, as if anything was possible, including having her heart torn to pieces again. But her heart was already dying, so it was a risk she was willing to take.

'Open your mind and let the world pour in' – that's what Mia had said to her during their last meeting at Mimi's Hotel on Frith Street. The words echoed in her head because she'd always kept the world at bay, not engaging with people unless there was a real need. She'd always chosen to keep her feelings to herself, never going off-limits, staying compulsively committed to Valéria. Like, she lived in London, a city full of art and culture, there to be enjoyed. But she'd never really made the most of it because her marriage to Valéria kept her restrained. Even now she was compelled to react in the same way to the strange relationship she had with Mia, as if she needed to belong to one person only.

Her flight departed on time and the journey was uneventful. She tried to concentrate on the job she had to do but fell asleep and dreamt she was at the Uffizi Gallery in Florence. Mia appeared before her, naked and standing in a shell, with her long red wavy hair covering her womanhood. She'd become Sandro Botticelli's Venus, emerging fully grown from the sea at her birth. Mia was no longer flesh and bone to Gabby, she was a goddess, beautiful and erotic, bringing all the emotional storms that come with that kind of adoration. Mia on a pedestal could only look down at Gabby. Despite her rational understanding of such a situation, Gabby was paralysed by its inevitability. She could only watch herself moving inexorably toward a predestined fate, unable to alter that destiny.

Gabby woke when the plane was on its descent to Guglielmo Marconi Airport. The terminal was packed with students returning to college and tourists queuing to collect their hire cars. It was all very disorganised, Gabby thought.

By the time she'd loaded her luggage and equipment into the Fiat MPW rental and left the airport, it was already past midday and she decided to stop in Bologna city centre for lunch.

She found a nice osteria off the tourist track, near the Palazzo della Mercanzia, where she ordered a very chilled glass of Aperol spritz and a Bolognese pasta. After a second glass, Gabby took a stroll around the town centre, admiring the leaning Due Torri, the Piazza Maggiore and the Neptune Fountain, wondering what it would be like to live a bohemian life here with Mia, who was from Italian parents, even though she was born in London. There was even a villa in her family name – Idoni, although the girl never said where.

One hour later, Gabby was continuing her journey to Gonzaga, where the local office of Palexion was situated and where she'd be staying for the next three days to work on the product photo shoot.

Next morning, Gabby met with Gianluca, a marketing manager from the client's bus company who was to take her to Spiazzi, about an hour's drive from Verona. Gianluca had proposed that the photo shoot should take place in that picturesque location, with a mountain backdrop that was famous for having a Catholic church carved into it.

As he drove along the Strada Provinciale, she could admire the outstanding beauty of the many vineyards, the cypress trees, the dogs lazing in the road, the slow pace of life. Overwhelmed by such sublime splendour, she daydreamed about an alternative reality, where everybody understood their natural relationship with rocks and rivers, where life was as it should be on this planet, not as it was.

It was difficult for Gabby to concentrate on Gianluca, as he tried to converse with her in English, reverting to his native northern Italian when he couldn't translate certain words and phrases. But she managed to get the gist of what he was saying about a wine event called Vinitaly, that was happening in Verona that week.

It was an international exposition, held annually in late September and usually for wine professionals. It featured about 3,000 brands from several dozen countries and was rated as the largest and most important wine show in the world. Gabby wanted to get Mia a rare vintage that didn't cost the earth, and Vinitaly might just be the place to find it.

The job was to work on a shoot of the lifting platforms the client manufactured. It sounded a bit boring at first, but Gabby was pleased to do it because of Mia's Italian background and she imagined she might even be able to find the Idoni village while she was here.

In Spiazzi they linked up with Gianluca's colleague, Antonio, who would drive them around the region. On every corner of the road, various phases in the life of Jesus were depicted in bronze statues. Gabby remembered her childhood, attending Mass on Sundays, eating fish on Fridays, making confession, taking communion – all the trappings of Catholicism. Its intensity was one of the factors that turned Gabby to something more somnolent – Buddhism. She was twenty-six and had a longing to be part of something bigger than her small self, something the priests didn't give her. But she never really engaged fully with the new practice of transcendentalism, simply believing in the principles of cause and effect without fully committing to all the dogma.

What put her off a bit was a Buddhist failure to explain the true concept of reincarnation. How could it be fair that some people were born rich, healthy, intelligent, with access to education and an opportunity to become enlightened, while others were born into poverty, had terrible physical handicaps, suffered mental problems and even died as infants. Was it because the universal entity that Buddhists aspired to be part of was unfair? Was it flawed? Could it be flawed? What would make it fair, so that everybody had the same opportunities to achieve it – to get there? Nirvana.

The Buddhists said a series of lives but, even then, no two series of lives would be exactly the same – they'd have to be identical to be utterly fair, wouldn't they? So, how could that be? How could every individual experience identical series of lives? There was only one answer as far as Gabby was concerned –experiencing every life! So, according to her logic, she was everybody who had ever lived and who ever would live. When she looked at somebody, she should see herself in a separate perception of the universal entity. When she helped somebody, she helped herself. When she hurt somebody –

It was what Jesus Christ taught, but what nobody understood – or didn't want to understand – was terrified of.

This was the meaning of life that Gabby subscribed to but, while she believed it completely, she had problems practising it. And it didn't answer the why question for her.

They finished the shoot and returned to the small village of Spiazzi where a single, stone-walled, corner restaurant was open. The owner, a heavy bald man with a thick black moustache, welcomed them at the door, then started an animated discussion with Gianluca and Antonio, gesticulating so vehemently that Gabby thought they were having an argument. His daughter was short, with straight black hair, bushy eyebrows, and a thin line of hair under her nose that reminded Gabby of Frida Kahlo. Moustache smiled at her – it was a smile that could have been used at a funeral.

'Would the signora take a photo of our ristorante … per favore?'

Gabby smiled back.

'Si, naturalmente, signore.'

Moustache saw that Gabby had a professional camera and wanted a good picture that he could hang in a frame on the wall. Gabby prepared the tripod, lenses and a translucent flag panel to protect the camera from the harsh sunlight, while the Italian family posed proudly outside their establishment.

It didn't take long and Gabby was happy to oblige.

'Grazie mille bella. Ora mangeremo.'

She'd later understand that the photo would be payment for their meal.

Gianluca and Antonio were already seated in the round, cavernous room, filled with family treasures and a large selection of local wines, some of which her escorts were already sampling. It was always a pleasure to dine with Italians. The respect they paid to their meals was almost a ritual, a sacred ceremony – the importance attributed to conversation – the relish with which they drank their wine – as if they had invented and owned time itself.

Despite being Brazilian by birth and spending the first two decades of her life in Brazil, Gabby was already used to the British and German lifestyle and work ethic – eating a rushed sandwich in front of a computer screen or during a meeting. So, although she admired their ability to feast leisurely on local produce, she had to force herself not to keep track of time and not to covertly check her phone for messages.

Two hours later, after banqueting on prosciutto, melone bianco, pasta and litres of red wine, Gianluca and Antonio were too inebriated to drive back to Verona. This caused anxiety for Gabby, until she eventually resigned herself to the knowledge that there was nothing she could do about it. Moustache and Daughter Moustache had ample room to put them up for one night and more red wine was produced and the singing started. As dusk began to fall, Gabby'd had enough of colourful conversation and she knew the intermittent renditions of 'Faccip Quello Che Voglio' and 'Non Ti Dico No' would keep her awake, so she decided to go for a walk, hoping the country air would help her get some shut-eye.

The village was small and she soon found herself outside

its confines. It became chilly when the sun fell behind the horizon and Gabby wished she'd brought her jacket. Spectres played hide and seek along the narrow, bush-lined lane – ghostly hands touched her with cold fingers. Ghostly sounds and smells and fleeting shadows that disappeared when she turned her head. Gabby wasn't frightened, it was the kind of magic realism she'd grown used to with her flashbacks. She knew they were just figments of her imagination. She sometimes wished they'd leave her alone, keep away from her – especially the buried memories of long ago. She'd come to terms with her childhood and wanted to leave things where they belonged – in the past. Or the future.

Gabby shivered as she walked. The ghosts screamed at her from the trees, they ran around her and away across the vineyards to wherever they lived. She shouted at them to go away, but they kept coming back. And back. She should have turned around, but she was being pulled by some absurd umbilical cord that refused to be severed. It was dark now and no moon or stars were visible in the night sky. A strange wind played among the branches of the trees and whispered terms of endearment in her ear – words she didn't want to hear – words that reminded her of the time – the time –

She was about to go back when she saw a light shining up ahead. As she got closer, she realised it was an old church and her curiosity took her inside. The lights were dim, but she could see candles flickering up near an altar. They cast an eerie light over a coffin on a bier, standing motionless in the gloom. The sight startled her and she wanted to leave, but she told herself it was ridiculous to be scared, she was a woman of the world – she'd seen many things – experienced many things. She knew the what and the when and the how – even if not the why. She didn't have to be scared, but she was. The anxiety wouldn't leave her. Despite it, she moved slowly forward, lighting a cigarette as she went. She took each step as if she'd have to turn and run at any moment. She came level with the coffin. It was closed, with wreaths and cards resting on the lid.

'Non sei autorizzato a fumare qui.'

Gabby turned to see a black-frocked priest standing behind her. He was young, maybe thirty or so, and very handsome – if you liked that sort of thing.

'I'm sorry, I don't speak buon Italiano.'

'You cannot smoke here.'

'Why not?'

'It is against the law.'

'Who's law?'

His English was very good. Gabby stubbed out the cigarette.

The priest sat in the front pew. He asked her what she was doing here and she said she was a tourist. She wanted to know who was in the coffin.

'A local farmer.'

'How did he die'

'In a fire on his land.'

How strange. Her father had worked on farms, and he had also died in a fire. She moved toward the coffin and placed her hands on the brass handles, gripping them so tightly her knuckles turned white. She tried to read the cards and the messages on the wreaths, but they were all in an Italian dialect she couldn't translate. She stayed there for what seemed like hours, but was really only seconds. The priest spoke from behind her back.

'Do you want to see him?'

'No!'

'Why not?'

'It would remind me of my father.'

'Did you love him … your father?'

'Of course.'

Suddenly, the priest pushed past her and brushed all the cards and wreaths off the coffin lid, scattering them across the nave. Flowers cascaded everywhere. Gabby was alarmed, but said nothing. The priest opened the coffin and looked inside, beckoning Gabby to come forward. She hesitated, apprehension almost choking her, but something made her move. There was nothing to be scared of – was there? They'd done a good job on the corpse and he had a half smile on his lips, as if there was a joke only he was getting. He still looked alive, except for the black marks from the fire that they couldn't cover up. The priest took her hand and placed it inside the coffin. Her fingers touched the body and Gabby told herself it was only a shell, the mechanical bit. There was no soul, no emotion, no pain, no love, no hate, no recriminations. No life.

Gabby wanted to ask the priest why he'd done that, but she didn't. In a way, she knew – to show that death was a part of life. Nowadays people hid death, they put it where it couldn't be seen and didn't speak about it. Yet it was as much a part of life as breathing. It was the only inevitable and universal thing that linked all life on this planet.

The priest sat back down in the pew, leaving the coffin open. Gabby was uneasy.

'I'd better go … '

'Not yet. Come sit with me.'

She did, keeping her distance.

'Can I have one of your cigarettes?'

'I thought it was against the law?'

'Laws are made to be broken.'

She lit two cigarettes and handed one to him. They were strangers sitting there, but in a way they weren't. They were linked by the body in the coffin, even if they didn't know it. They were unconsciously relying on each other, for strength and comfort and hope and forgiveness. The priest spoke first.

'I am sorry.'

'For what?'

'For making you stay.

'You're not making me stay, father.'

'Call me Francesco.'

What an unusual request. Gabby had never heard of a priest wanting to be called by his first name. She felt uneasy about doing it, it went against all the conventions of her Catholic upbringing. When he finished his cigarette, Francesco got up and replaced the coffin lid and began to pick up the cards and flowers. Gabby helped him and they arranged everything as best they could. Gabby had forgotten about the world outside the church – the world of reality, the real world. Everything had faded away except for Francesco and the coffin and the night. A sudden wind blew up and Gabby heard the loud slamming of a heavy door.

'I think I'd better go now.'

'Not yet, let me have another cigarette.'

'Don't you have any of your own, father?'

'I do not smoke.'

Suddenly all the lights went out and the church was plunged into darkness, except for the flickering candleflames up by the altar, casting grotesque shadows up the walls. It reminded Gabby of her first night with Mia in the Ham Yard Hotel in London. But this situation was entirely different. She moved quickly to the main door, but she was unable to open it. Francesco tried.

'No good, it is jammed tight. The wind …'

'What am I going to do?'

'Do not worry, there is another exit near the chancel.'

Francesco took hold of Gabby's hand and led her toward the chancel door. He turned the metal handle but the door didn't open. He tried again. Gabby helped him to pull, but the door was locked from the other side. The priest took a candle from the altar and went back to the main door to try again. Gabby stumbled after him, not wanting to be left alone. The main door wouldn't budge, no matter how hard they tried. Francesco walked back up the aisle, past the altar to the sacristy, but there was no way out. Gabby looked for her phone, to call Gianluca or Antonio or the Moustache and his daughter, but she'd left her phone behind in her jacket pocket. She'd put it away during the meal so as not to be tempted to keep looking at it.

'What are we going to do, father?'

'Protect ourselves.'

The priest began to light more candles, placing them in a ring so they were encircled by the flickering light. It seemed to Gabby that she'd be safe within the circle. Outside was

darkness, but she was protected within the ring of light –
protected from what, she didn't know. Time meant nothing
in that place, so it stood still. Every time a candle burnt down,
the priest replaced it with a fresh one. He'd go to the altar
each time because Gabby was scared to step outside the circle.
It was as if she couldn't move, as if she'd been petrified by a
sorcerer's spell and was condemned to stay motionless forever.

After a while, she started to sob. Francesco watched
her, but didn't try to comfort her. He looked up at the high,
narrow, stained-glass windows, but they were unreachable
without a ladder.

'Why don't you do something, father?'

'What do you want me to do?'

'Get us out of here.'

'I cannot … you know that. Have another cigarette.'

Gabby knew he wanted to help her, but that there was
nothing he could do. They stayed inside the circle of light as
the temperature fell. Gabby's voice shook when she spoke.

'I have to get out of here.'

'Will your friends not come for you?'

'They've drank a lot of wine. They probably think I've
gone to bed.'

Francesco took off his black cape and put it around her
shoulders. She was quiet for a while – reflective.

The circle of light flickered violently as a breeze blew at
the candle flames. They sat close to each other. Gabby rocked
to and fro and hummed a tune that she remembered from
long ago. The darkness outside the circle was filled with
ghosts. They moved around the ring of light and asked to be
let in. Francesco told them to go away, but they wouldn't. He
shouted at them and they disappeared for a time, but came
back again and again. He kept the candles lit and she rocked
and hummed.

As the night wore on, there were no more candles on the
altar to keep the circle intact. The ghosts were getting in!

'No!'

Gabby sank to her knees, rocking to and fro, to and fro.

Then she collapsed on the floor and started to convulse. The priest tried to help her. He rolled up the cape and put it under her head for a pillow, but she kept shaking. More candles were burning out and more ghosts were getting in. Francesco had to do something. He stepped outside the circle and went to the coffin. He brushed all the cards and wreaths off the lid again and opened it. Then he reached inside and lifted out the body. He carried it over and laid it beside Gabby. She stopped shaking and the convulsions left her.

Then she slept.

The candles flickered out one by one, but an inner peace glowed through the darkness of the old church until the first streaks of morning light came through the stained glass of the small high windows. Ravens circled outside the church, searching for an early breakfast. Their harsh cawing woke Gabby and she sat up, rubbing sleep from her eyes, trying to remember where she was and how she'd got there. Rainbow light shone through the windows and struck the bier. The coffin was closed and the cards and wreaths arranged on the lid. For a few seconds it was surrounded by a bluish luminescence.

Gabby heard a heavy bolt being drawn back and a key turning in a lock. An old priest emerged from the sacristy. He stared in disbelief at her for a moment, his mouth opened but it took time for any words to emerge.

'Tu chi sei? Cosa stai facendo qui?'

'I got locked in.'

'I am so sorry … how could this have happened?'

'The wind jammed the door.'

The old priest rushed to the main door and pulled at it. It swung open without any effort. Gabby was puzzled.

'It must have unjammed during the night. But don't worry, Father Francesco took care of me.'

'Father Francesco?'

'Yes, the young priest. Where is he?'

'There is only one priest … me, father Lorenzo.'

'Are you sure?'

'Of course.'

Outside, Gabby turned her collar up against the early morning chill. She thought she heard a sound behind her as she walked away from the old church and she looked around quickly. But it was nothing – just her imagination.

CHAPTER 12

DANCING

They were all still asleep when Gabby got back to the little corner restaurant. Just as she suspected, they were in a wine-sodden slumber and nobody had missed her.

Later, Gabby didn't mention her experience in the church to Gianluca or Antonio because they probably wouldn't have believed her. In any case, she wasn't sure herself if it had actually happened or if she'd just dreamt it – if it was another of her flashbacks.

They said goodbye and grazie to Moustache and Daughter Moustache and Gianluca drove to Verona, where Gabby decided to take a break before collecting her rental car to return to the office in Gonzaga.

Gianluca was eager to show her around the city he was so proud of and she humoured him, despite being tired from lack of sleep.

'How well do you know Verona, Gabby?'

He pointed toward the Castelvecchio Bridge, coming up on the right-hand side.

'I've been here before, but just for a day. My partner and I were touring through a lot of Italian cities at the time.'

'So, you did not see much, then?'

'I saw the House of Juliet.'

Gianluca laughed.

'And did you believe it was where Juliet stood waiting for Romeo?'

'Why not?'

'Because it never happened. William Shakespeare made it all up, Gabby. Then Verona invented the location for the tourists.'

Gabby knew, of course, that Shakespeare's play was a work of fiction and that the House of Juliet was an invention, just like the Sherlock Holmes apartment in Baker Street in London. But she didn't want to deprive Gianluca of his triumphant exposé.

'Lake Garda is not far from here, Gabby. You should visit.'

After picking up a bottle of Amarone della Valpolicella for a reasonable price at Vinitaly, Gabby decided to take his advice. The weather was pleasant at Lake Garda and the waning tourist season meant that many restaurants and bars were almost empty. Gabby decided she needed a little pampering and she fell into a deep slumber as she lay in the relaxation room after soaking in the hot whirlpools of the Thermal Park. She felt refreshed when she woke and went for dinner at a restaurant with a beautiful view of Lake Garda. The romantic vista make her think of Mia – despite the fact that the girl was five years younger, she came across as being more mature and confident, and those personality traits impressed Gabby.

Being single again after so long in a deep relationship could be scary, but it could also be empowering. Mia told her it was important to know herself and to be comfortable with herself, which was difficult for Gabby, because she mostly thought of herself as some slightly neurotic character from a Woody Allen movie. Mia said everyone was neurotic in their own particular way, and female psychologists like herself were crazier than most. But it was important to have a positive mental attitude, or PMA as Mia called it. Gabby's PMA had always been limited to aspirations of being settled with a partner, children, dog, nice home, occasional holidays in the sun – nothing too ambitious. But that wasn't going to happen – not now. She didn't have enough time left.

Of course, there was always going to be more to life than that – and there it was, her ever-present misfiring cognitive incoherence, making unrelated associations and demonstrating her chronic emotional vulnerability. It was difficult to make predictions about a non-existent future. Wasn't it? She laughed out loud at her own ambiguity, alone at the restaurant table.

People looked at her, then looked away, as if she wasn't there – as if she was just a disembodied voice. A ghost.

Her thoughts turned to Valéria. They were still married. No one had mentioned divorce and now she had no way of contacting her ex-wife. So, as they were still spliced, did it mean that she was cheating on Valéria with Mia? It was just like her to be thinking that. She needed to put a label on everything – to put things into boxes – to determine, to establish, to frame, to confine, to suffocate – so she could eventually possess. Gabby decided the best thing to do was to stop thinking altogether and just look forward to taking Brazilian zouk classes with Mia when she got back to London.

The next day was Gabby's last in Italy. She spent it with Leo, the local managing director at the office in Gonzaga. Her Italian colleagues were friendly, but a little reserved, except for Leo, who was invariably a hands-on person, touching arms and backs and shoulders as he spoke. Being touched by people she didn't know well was anathema for Gabby, but Leo's universally friendly personality and consistency of approach with everyone around him reassured her that he wasn't hitting on her. She finished editing the video and Leo's feedback was complimentary, making her feel proud of the end result. It needed to be perfect for Günther Engels, after what had happened in Qatar and her subsequent extended sick leave.

That night, she had dinner with Leo and his family. The managing director was a Brazilian national with an Italian background and they spent the entire time talking about Brazil and how things in that country would never change when it came to political corruption and slum squalor. Leo's Italian wife served the most delicious pizza with fresh vegetables and a very elegant Lambrusco with plenty of structure and a vibrant aftertaste. Next morning, Gabby showered at her hotel, then packed up and drove to Bologna to catch her return flight to London. It was a bright, sunny day and the memory of her night in the old church faded into the distant landscape.

The following week, Gabby made her way through pouring rain to Shoreditch in east London. She'd arranged a rendezvous with Mia to attend a dance school and learn more about Brazilian zouk. She was running late as usual as she parked up and made a dash for the dingy club door on Brick Lane. She shook rain from her shoulders and found herself on the threshold of a group of eager dance students of varying ages, already going through their routines. A slim woman in her mid-thirties approached Gabby.

'Are you here for the class?'

'Yes, but I'm waiting for a friend.'

'Which friend?'

'Mia Idoni.'

'Mia's not coming. She rang.'

Gabby wondered why the girl hadn't called her. The thought of dancing with complete strangers, when she'd barely been able to dance with members of her own family, filled her with horror. She only agreed to come so she could dance with Mia.

She was about to leave when the slim woman caught her by the hand and drew her inside.

'I'm Samantha, your instructor.'

'I don't think …'

'Take off your coat.'

Samantha was already opening the buttons and helping Gabby out of her Bonmarché suedette biker jacket and pointing to the place she wanted her to start from. The others had stopped dancing and were watching the newcomer as Samantha took both Gabby's reluctant hands in hers, pushing and guiding her to move from left to right, twisting her feet in a pretzel-like move she'd never attempted before, even with Mia. Once the instructor was convinced that Gabby had mastered the first basic steps, she released her to dance with the daunting strangers.

They came closer. Gabby could smell them, the redolence of them coming at her. She wanted to run, but felt that Samantha would come after her and drag her back. The instructor was watching, waiting to see if Gabby tried to make a break for it. She had to stay. There was no other way. At that moment, facing a room full of strangers, death seemed preferable to Gabby than having to touch and be touched by them.

The instructor paired her with a tall man from Martinique called David. He wrapped Gabby in his long thin arms and flashed her a big white smile.

'Don't worry, girl, you've got this.'

Was it so obvious she was worried? Then she realised she was shaking. David steadied her and began to move her around the floor. She was awkward at first, clumsy even, but the man guided her with soft touches on her shoulders and back and hips. She followed his steps and was soon moving from side to side in twists and turns that almost made her dizzy – and she realised how fabulously sexy this dance could be when performed correctly with the right person.

That person would be Mia. Soon.

The thought inspired Gabby and she kept getting told off by Samantha for being too impatient and not waiting for the male lead. It was the whole point of the zouk, the lead was insanely hard to follow and took a lot of concentration. Gabby had led on the few occasions when she'd danced with Mia – now it was alien to her to be led. An hour and a half later it was over. Samantha asked if Gabby was staying for the social club.

'What's that?'

'A kind of impromptu nightclub where zouk students get together. It's fun, you'll see.'

Gabby declined. She couldn't wait to get out the door. She called Mia from the car.

'Where were you?'

'Something came up.'

'Why didn't you call me?'

'I wanted you to go, Gabby. I knew if I told you I wasn't going to be there you wouldn't have showed.'

'You know what I'm like with strangers touching me, Mia.'

'That's exactly why I wanted you to go … on your own. You have to get over this phobia, Gabby.'

Gabby knew the girl was right. She had to rid herself of her fear of human proximity. What about when the end came – when her heart gave out? Would it be sudden or would strangers have to care for her? Or would she just take another overdose before it happened, to save time? Anyway, tonight was a milestone, a barrier broken. She was proud of having pushed herself to her limit – and even of extending that limit. Mia's voice resumed.

'How was the class?'

'It was good, I have to admit … once I got past the paranoia. The people were OK, and I like Samantha.'

'Will you go again?'

'Will you come with me?'

'Maybe.'

'We can dance together. I kept getting told off for not waiting to be led by the guy. Can you lead, Mia?'

'No, I wish I could. It's much harder.'

'OK, I'll learn how to lead, then.'

Mia said she believed Gabby would do just that, and be an even better dancer than she was.

She told Gabby the Brick Lane class was the best venue in London and she knew most of the people there, so there was nothing for Gabby to be scared of. It was just the men Gabby didn't like, the rest of it was fine, but that was a price she had to pay if she wanted to be part of Mia's life.

'Mia … did you tell Samantha to make me stay?'

'Of course. I knew you'd try to bolt, so I told her not to let you.'

Bit by bit, one day at a time, Mia's influence on Gabby began to shift her vision of the world around her, broadening her thinking, deepening her perception of herself and who she really was. For the first time since her teenage years, she started to engage with people. She felt years younger, filled with a kind of adolescent expectation and slowly letting go of her old stand-offish self – the girl always sitting by herself at parties while others danced and enjoyed themselves; the girl whose mother complained that her investment in ballet and jazz classes was going to waste. It made Gabby smile inwardly, imagining herself at family get togethers doing a grand jeté or dancing to forró on the improvised dance floor in the garage.

She would have to revisit those memories to liberate herself from them. And she realised that the strangers she'd always feared and barricaded herself against could be the means of giving her a real retrospection, turning her black-and-white world into a transcendence of colour.

After her fourth zouk class, Gabby ended up staying for the socialising. She had dinner with the feared strangers and even made some friends – all without drinking any alcohol, which was some achievement. It wasn't easy, but if it meant having something in common with Mia, it was simply what she had to do.

Being single was an opportunity to do new things and reinvent herself, to broaden her horizons. She changed quite a bit over those two months, but sometimes she worried she'd lose her balance because thoughts roamed inside her head like feral cats – from getting a motorbike, something she'd always wanted to do and had even taken the test some years back, to quitting her job, to simply giving up on everything and going travelling for a year. It was a constant battle between rationality and emotion. Mia told her to do what felt right.

'Would you come with me … if I gave up on everything and went travelling?'

'Maybe.'

'Maybe isn't enough, Mia.'

'It's all I can give right now.'

CHAPTER 13

THE HUNGARIANS

Gabby and Mia were becoming a regular item on the London scene. Mia was taking her places she never got to go to with Valéria. They went to an exhibition of Queer British Art at Tate Britain. Gabby wore a short black Alexander Wang dress with long sleeves, black stilettos and oversized designer sunglasses. She was going for the Audrey Hepburn *Breakfast at Tiffany's* look, but without the wide-brimmed hat. Mia was late and ran up the white spiral steps to place an apologetic kiss on Gabby's cheek. She wore grey skinny jeans, a tight black top and a long beige jacket by Ralph Lauren.

Although she identified as lesbian, Mia'd had brief relationships with men in the past – unlike Gabby, she had no problem with alternating sexuality. The amazing number of different denominations for being queer, or simply not straight, was their topic of conversation as they walked through the exhibition. Gabby was amused to see all the different types of sexual identity that people used to define themselves – terms like fluid, pansexual, polysexual, binary and many more. Things weren't as complicated when she was growing up and she wondered how kids today coped with it all. It must be really confusing for them, it was bad enough for her, growing up gay in a Catholic society in Brazil.

'They say there are thirty-five different gender identities.'
Mia's words forced their way into her thoughts.
'Really? That many?'
'And more being identified all the time.'
'Where will it end?'
'When everybody's hermaphrodite, I expect.'
Mia's last remark made Gabby smile as she imagined a

world full of people equipped with dual sexual organs and identities, like a species of echinoderm.

The exhibition halls were crowded, which indicated the level of interest in homosexuality. At times the two women were wedged close together, other times they lost each other in the swell of human bodies, waves ebbing and flowing on a gender-bender beach. They stood for what seemed like hours in front of a watercolour of Sappho by Simeon Solomon – the painting depicted the archaic Greek poet from the Island of Lesbos sitting side by side with Erinna, one of her lovers, in long classic dresses. The androgynous Sappho had her arms around the feminine Erinna, who had part of her breasts exposed, while Sappho kissed her tenderly.

Mia talked about ladies like Virginia Woolf and Pulitzer Prize winner Willa Carter, like Florence Nightingale and Emily Dickinson and Eleanor Roosevelt whose sexuality was never discussed with students of their work. Gabby regretted that throughout history gay people had had to hide their true selves and appreciated how lucky they were to have been born into more enlightened times, even if much still remained to be done in countries that openly discriminated. Mia thought it was illuminating that sex between two men was outlawed, but sex between two women was not, simply because Victorian society didn't believe, or refused to believe, that there was such a thing as sex between women.

'When did you come out?'

Gabby's question made Mia think back for a moment.

'It wasn't as straightforward as that, Gabby.'

'How so?'

'Well, I knew I was gay at the age of sixteen, gay friends knew when I was about eighteen and I came out officially when I was about twenty-two.'

'How did your parents take it, Mia?'

'My father was dead by then and my mother thought I was going to tell her I was autistic, so she was actually relieved.'

Gabby remembered her own experiences, which were totally different to Mia's. She was just eight or nine when she had her first realisations that she liked girls. She remembered having dinner with her godparents and saying she wanted to marry a beautiful blonde actress from one of the television soaps. Her godmother had smacked her about the head and told her never to say anything like that again. From then on she hid her inclinations, until it became impossible.

'I never actually told my half-brothers and sisters.'

'Why not?'

'They never told me they were straight.'

That remark made Mia laugh out loud, causing people to look round.

'What about your parents, Gabby?'

'I told my mother I was bisexual, I thought it would be easier for her to understand.'

'And was it?'

'No, she took it really hard.'

In fact, Gabby's mother said she'd rather see her daughter dead, had cried every day and didn't speak to Gabby for two months. She believed Gabby would suffer because of the way society in Brazil viewed gay people and she hoped she would die before that happened.

Gabby's workplace in Brazil was quite homophobic. People passed disparaging comments about gays and lesbians and sometimes it took all Gabby had not to lose her temper. But she kept quiet, remembering her mother's prophesy about suffering and not wanting to cause embarrassment to anyone. It was one of the reasons Gabby moved to the UK, to be respected for who she was and not to be harassed by people who invariably attacked anything and anyone who was different to themselves, out of a deep-seated insecurity and self-consciousness.

They left the museum in the early evening, taking Gabby's car to Belgravia where Mia had booked a table at Olivomare for dinner. The restaurant boasted a Sardinian take on its menu and was part of Mauro Sanna's Olivo Group, whose low-key style made it a popular place for the chi-chi crowd.

'What about some oysters to start with?'

Mia was surprised to learn that Gabby had never eaten oysters before.

'Never?'

'I think the sensation of them sliding down my throat would make me heave.'

'Good job you're not straight, then.'

They both laughed. Mia ordered fried oysters with red chillies, along with a bottle of Pinot Grigio.

'Don't they say you should only drink champagne with oysters?'

'And since when do you care what *they* say, Gabby?'

Actually, she didn't care, when she really thought about it.

'Drink what you like, when you like.'

And that was Mia's philosophy on most things. Gabby wanted to ask her about jealousy. Mia had said she was never jealous and didn't accept demonstrations of jealousy in others. Loving someone and allowing them to be free at the same time was as incomprehensible to Gabby as quantum physics. But Mia believed jealousy, although natural, was irrational behaviour and it wasn't healthy to act on it without good justification.

'And what's good justification, Mia?'

'That's a grey area, Gabby.'

Mia offered an example. One night, at a party, some guy was flirting with her girlfriend, who seemed to be encouraging him. He eventually grabbed the woman's waist from behind and she leaned back into him.

'What did you do?'

'I punched both of them in the face and walked out.'

Gabby was surprised. It was the first time she'd heard Mia talk about irrational behaviour and it shocked her slightly, in a heart-warming way. She was relieved to know the girl was capable of violence when provoked. It meant that Mia was capable of losing her super-cool – that there were things in life that could bring out the human in her.

The main course of prawn curry arrived, along with more wine – this time a more traditional Sauvignon Blanc.

'Have you dated many women, Gabby?'

'None since Valéria … apart from you.'

'And before that?'

'A few.'

'You were very faithful to Valéria, weren't you?'

'It's the way I like it … a relationship, I mean.'

'Would you be faithful to me, Gabby … if we were in a relationship?'

'Would you want me to be?'

Mia laughed without answering.

Directness was very high on Mia's priority list – as were her own opinions. She didn't like people who ate their steak well done, almost a criminal offence in her eyes, or who believed all wines tasted the same, or who disagreed with her about anything, so Gabby was constantly having to backtrack if she said the wrong thing. Everything had to be the "best quality" – food, clothes, company – as if she'd decided long ago that she only deserved the best and everyone else should think so too.

This kind of superiority complex grated a bit on Gabby, but she was prepared to overlook the irritation because she wanted to possess every aspect of Mia but knew that, instead, the girl was beginning to possess her.

Gabby realised long ago that getting hurt was part of life. She knew people got hurt and hurt others unintentionally on a daily basis, not because they were necessarily bad people, but because they involuntarily created unreasonable expectations – they couldn't help it. She knew she'd have to fundamentally change who she was if she wanted to stay with Mia for what was left of her life. She'd have to conceal the real Gabby, hide the neediness and restrain her very thoughts – stop being an irreparable, compulsive caregiver who was scarcely able to ask for anything in return.

It was Gabby's turn to pay the bill and afterwards Mia took her to a members-only cocktail bar a few blocks away. Mia whispered to the door security, who let them in, almost as if they'd been given a secret password.

The club ambience was dark and degenerate, very Berlin in the 1920s. Gabby half expected a grotesque and face-painted Joel Grey to usher them to the small table with black suede seats. A young blonde couple sat close by. Mia gave the attractive woman a look.

'I bet she's high maintenance.'

'We've just walked in and you've noticed that blonde!'

Gabby tried to check her pique, but it was showing.

'I have a radar for beautiful women, Gabby.'

'I know why you do it, Mia … to reinforce the message, "I'm single and I do what I want, deal with it".'

'I do it because it's human nature.'

Gabby didn't agree. At least, not with the ostentation of that comment. She, too, could spot a beautiful woman from a distance, but she chose not to comment or act on it when she was with someone she cared for. It was all about interaction. Her approach was always to make whoever she was with feel comfortable and respected. She didn't think that was a sign of insecurity, just common courtesy.

They ordered Asbach Manhattans, in keeping with the Germanic mise en scène, from a waitress in black-seamed stockings and French knickers.

After a while, Gabby noticed the blonde woman Mia had commented upon, looking over at them. When Gabby looked back, she smiled, displaying a gleaming set of even white teeth. Without taking her eyes off Gabby, she leant over and spoke to her male companion, who turned and looked in Gabby's direction. He smiled, then turned back to the blonde woman and nodded his head.

Gabby tapped Mia on the shoulder.

'They're looking at us.'

'Really? How exciting.'

The waitress returned with more cocktails and indicated that they'd been sent over by the blondes. Mia lifted her glass in acknowledgement. Encouraged by Mia's smile and undaunted by Gabby's frown, the blond man came across to their table.

'My sister wants to know if you would like to join us.'

His accent was slightly foreign – perhaps Hungarian, Gabby thought. Mia turned to her.

'Shall we?'

'I don't know, Mia.'

'Oh, come on Gabby. Where's your sense of adventure?'

Mia was already on her feet and crossing to the smiling blonde woman. The man waited and escorted Gabby by the arm. He introduced himself as Andras and his sister as Ramona.

They drank till late and talked about things Gabby couldn't remember. They laughed and seemed strangely animated and the club grew more surreal as time went by. Gabby realised she was too drunk to drive and she'd have to get a taxi, but Andras wouldn't hear of it.

'Ramona and I have a suite at the Halkin Hotel nearby. You can stay there until morning.'

Gabby was too out of it to resist. She was more than drunk, it was as if she'd been drugged. Mia wanted to keep the night going and Andras said there was champagne in the suite. So they all went back there.

The Halkin Hotel was a six-star luxury boutique establishment and Gabby felt disorientated as they travelled up in the spacious lift to the top floor. The suite was large and dazzlingly white in a minimalist style, with an enormous bed covered in white satin.

Andras poured champagne, then busied himself with some kind of equipment. It looked like a camera on a tripod, but Gabby couldn't be sure because it kept coming into focus then blurring again. Ramona seemed to be stripped to her underwear but Gabby couldn't remember her taking her clothes off. She was circling Gabby and Mia like a she-wolf with blonde hair and big breasts and a laugh licking at them like streaks of lightning.

It began to seem like a macabre ritual and Gabby wanted to go home, but Mia wanted to stay but only if Gabby stayed too. Ramona seemed to glide about the room on a cushion of air, with no movement except for her lips, that drew back across her teeth in a threatening smile. She rubbed herself against Gabby, then caught her hand with surprising strength and drew her reluctantly toward the white bed. Gabby felt hypnotised with fear and called out for Mia, who didn't answer. Her date seemed to have disappeared into the suite – absorbed into its ambiguity. Ramona began to undress her, until she finally stood naked in front of the Hungarian, then the blonde woman pushed her down on to the bed, her light eyes blazing and her lips blood-red and pouting.

Ramona was on top of her and she could hear distant mocking laughter, ebbing and flowing on the tide of this strange and surreal scene. Ramona's voice was like velvet and her soft mouth sucked at Gabby's tongue, while her strong thighs writhed in a sensual scissors embrace. Her fingers caressed Gabby's hair, then moved to the third eye – caressing, manipulating, mesmerising. Suddenly, she bent her head and sank her teeth into Gabby's shoulder, eyes rolling in her head. She laughed and slid gracefully from the bed, her hair in a fury around her crazy face.

Ramona glided across the room and disappeared into the surrounding ether, after her brother and Mia. Gabby tried to get off the bed, but couldn't. She rolled over and over, hoping she'd come to the edge and fall on the floor so the impact would bring her back to reality. But the bed went on and on – it had no dimensions, no beginning and no end, and Gabby was lost in its vastness. Her eyes began to close, even though she tried to keep them open. She didn't want to succumb to sleep, or whatever trance she was falling into. But the pull was too strong and she was unable to resist.

It was morning when she woke. Light illuminated the room and amplified its whiteness. Everything was white – except for a small red stain of blood on the bed. She rose and searched the suite for the others, but nobody was there. She called out, 'Mia! Andras! Ramona!'

Silence answered her. She went to the bathroom and looked in the mirror. There was a bruise on her shoulder – more than a bruise, a small wound with broken skin and congealed blood. She splashed water on her face, then went back to the bedroom and dressed.

Downstairs, reception was busy and she slipped out through the revolving doors without being noticed.

CHAPTER 14

A HAPPY ENDING

Up until now Gabby had believed, like most people, that there was a formula for happiness – usually a committed relationship, good job, house, kids, new kitchen and an annual trip to find the sun and drink cheap booze. Then the relationship gets old, the job is lost in a business merger, the house needs constant maintenance, the kids' demands lead to extreme stress and drinking cheap booze becomes an addiction. Dream to nightmare. On the other hand, pseudo independence was illusory – everybody needed to connect and most people lived their lives in quiet desperation.

Of course, role-model norms all broke down in the gay and lesbian world, just as established laws of physics collapsed at sub-atomic level. Gabby wondered if it was better to live for others, and in that way to live for herself – in accordance with her philosophical beliefs and the teachings of Jesus Christ. In the end, the only thing she could count on was the fact that things change – life turns to death, turns to life, turns to death and goes on until the why question is answered.

She conjured up a vision of Valéria and the book, *Maktub*, that her ex-wife had bought her when they first met in São Paulo – maktub means it is written, and Valéria meant it as a prophesy that they were destined to be together.

So, was everything to be considered in the context of a fate that was already written? If that was the case, what was the point of anything – of working, striving, planning, living? According to the concept of maktub, given certain initial conditions, everything that ensues is bound to happen as it does and in no other way and therefore nothing in nature was contingent and there was no room for human freedom. Fate was the major determinant of one's destiny and no outer force could disrupt it. In other words, you can't change your destiny, no matter what you do. It had sounded like a contradiction to Gabby when she first read about it – if she chose to go down one street, that was her destiny and, if she chose to go down another street, that was also her destiny. Until she realised that, at the sub-atomic level, an infinite number of variations of a particular situation can exist at the same time.

Although maktub stood for certainty, in actual fact it just made everything more uncertain. Gabby wondered why she'd ever wanted children, why she wanted to bring kids into a world of such uncertainty. Then, it was probably for that very reason that she'd wanted them, as a form of certainty, a focal point in an ever-shifting landscape.

But that was before Doha. Now –

Gabby knew that what she had with Mia would be brief, one way or the other, but there was no turning back. She had to let go of her anxiety and enjoy the ride, for as long as it lasted.

It was a time of extremes, a trepidatious dimension of reality, filled with seduction, surrealism and strangeness. A kind of sweet-and-sour endgame in a dreamlike world where the price of entry was all her previous conceptions. Gabby wondered if it was more than she'd be able to handle. Her heart was already splintering like glass at the prospect of finality – not just ending with Mia, but ending with everything. But, of course, everything had to end, sooner or later, and she'd clung on to the illusion of permanence for too long.

Gabby drove through the October wind and found a parking space near Wilton Crescent. She changed into a high-necked Caroline Constas top, which complemented her Ganni culottes and red stilettos, and did her make-up in the car, before throwing on an oversized jacquard coat and walking the few hundred yards to her rendezvous with Mia. She blended in with the elegant denizens of Knightsbridge who were all trying to stop the wind from destroying their carefully coiffured hair.

She climbed the spiral steps to the upper level at Mr Chow in Knightsbridge – a chic, arch-ceilinged restaurant that had been serving classic and creative Mandarin dishes for six decades. She saw that Mia had already arrived and was seated and sipping a Martini. It was two weeks since the Halkin Hotel and Gabby had been trying to contact her, without success – until she got a text earlier in the day to meet Mia at Mr Chow.

'Where have you been? I've been trying to contact you.'

'I've been to Amsterdam, Gabby.'

'Why didn't you answer my messages?'

'I forgot my phone.'

Gabby sat down heavily and pulled the neck of her top to one side, revealing a yellowing bruise on her shoulder.

'What happened at that hotel, Mia?'

'Don't you remember?'

'Vaguely.'

Mia explained that Gabby was on the bed with Ramona, so she went into the lounge with Andras. Gabby then fell asleep and they couldn't wake her, so they went back out to an all-night club in Soho.

'She bit me, Mia.'

'Did you get a tetanus jab?'

'No.'

'You should.'

The waiter came and Mia ordered two more Martinis, along with starters of glazed prawns with walnuts. She seemed quite blasé about the episode at the Halkin and this irritated Gabby. An awkward silence pervaded the space between them. Mia noticed Gabby's discomfort and reached over and took her hand and held it tightly. Love was like dance and Gabby needed to anticipate Mia's moves, to avoid being trodden on. The silence remained through the main course of Emperor crab with Chinese broccoli and sautéed brown rice, along with more Martinis. Gabby felt she was in a vacuum, with no sense of anything outside the hollowness around her own personal space. Mia finally broke the impasse.

'Let's go.'

'Where?'

'You'll see.'

Mia was a little drunk after all the Martinis, as she'd started drinking long before Gabby. She staggered a little as they approached the entrance to the Sanderson Hotel in Fitzrovia and Gabby had to catch her arm to steady her. They went through the long bar to the lobby and waited for the elevator to the first floor.

Gabby was surprised and a little alarmed when they reached their destination – a spa.

'It's a spa, Mia.'

'I know. Consider it treatment for your illogical aversion to being touched by strangers.'

Mia gave their names to the receptionist, who handed them forms to fill out in the waiting area. A lady of Thai descent asked if they wanted anything to drink. Mia ordered another Martini, while Gabby just had water, as she wasn't sure why she was even here and didn't want to get in the same state she'd been in at the Halpin, just in case this was another one of Mia's "adventures".

Once the forms were filled out, they were taken through a maze of ethereal white curtains until they finally reached the changing rooms, where they stripped. Mia came close and touched Gabby's naked body, who shuddered and put on the white robe and slippers that had been laid out for her.

The Thai lady escorted them to a white chaise longue which faced a tall, narrow, silver water fountain that cast shimmering reflected light across the ceiling.

Mia broke the silence between them.

'I think we could both do with a massage, don't you?'

'You could have told me we were coming here.'

'And spoil the surprise? You can't deny it, Gabby, you do seem stressed.'

The dreamlike atmosphere of the interior had been designed by Philippe Starck, who also designed Bon and Le Paradis du Fruit in France, Katsuya in Los Angeles and Quadri in Venice – the Thai lady's voice floated over Gabby and faded away in diminishing echoes that resembled the fading from memory of a nostalgic song.

Two young women escorted them to the massage room, where they were placed in separate cubicles. Gabby's mind wandered to unrecognisable places as the woman's hands manipulated her body, then returned to reality for a brief moment, before drifting into the ether of some astral plane where spirits existed and all consciousness resided. The three subdivisions of her instinctive mind ceased to exist and were supplanted by her intellect which, sharpened, was the gateway to the spiritual essence of everything. She let go of her attachment to the physical world of illusion and went to where all was visible and known – the abode of the archangels. All her past karma circled her as she spun toward final unification.

'Would you like a happy ending?'

The voice of the masseuse brought her back to earth.

'What?'

'A happy ending. It's paid for.'

Gabby didn't know what a happy ending was but, if it was already paid for – why not? To Gabby's surprise, the masseuse began to rub her finger up and down one side of her clitoris. Gabby tried to sit up, but the girl gently pushed her back down.

'It's OK … just enjoy.'

Gabby was disorientated for a moment, but her body began to react to the girl's stimulation and a feeling of warmth and well-being came over her. After the initial manipulation, the girl, very lightly and softly, began to glide her fingers over the middle of Gabby's vagina, from top to bottom. The stroking was slow at first, then faster, then slow again, using varying degrees of pressure and switching direction. Gabby could hear her own low moans of pleasure as if they were coming from someone else. She wondered if Mia was experiencing the same happy ending. The girl smiled down at Gabby as she rubbed in small circular motions, focusing mostly on the clitoris, then larger circles to stimulate the rest of the vagina.

'You know what your U Spot is?'

Gabby didn't. She shook her head.

'I'll show you.

The masseuse began to stimulate the area just above the urethral opening and to the sides of it by gently stroking with the tip of her finger. Gabby found this to be super pleasurable, as the girl's fingers moved from the U Spot up to the clitoris and back down again. By now, Gabby was coming close to reaching orgasm and the girl knew it. She stopped using her fingers and produced a small portable vaporiser and began to spray a jet of warm moisture over and into the vagina.

The vapour treatment only lasted for a few moments and, afterwards, the masseuse began to stroke the upper left quadrant of Gabby's clitoris with one finger, very slowly and very lightly – barely touching. It was a teasing sensation and Gabby found it slightly frustrating, which the girl sensed and placed her thumb and index finger either side of the clitoris, then pressed down and inwards, squeezing on the clitoral bulb and rolling it between her thumb and index finger.

By now Gabby's time was almost up, so the masseuse produced a vibrator, which she began to rub all over Gabby's body, starting with her breasts and nipples. She placed a light, wet towel between the sex toy and Gabby's clitoris, then ran the vibrator up and down the labia, penetrating Gabby's vagina, before bringing her to a stupendous orgasm with clitoral stimulation over the towel. Gabby gasped for breath when it was over and it took a few moments for the masseuse to get her off the table and into her white robe and slippers.

The Thai lady came and escorted her back to the changing room. Mia was already there, a grin spreading across her face.

'How was it for you, Gabby?'

'Surprising.'

'No need to thank me.'

'I won't, then.'

They showered and dressed and Mia insisted on taking a cab to the Looking Glass Cocktail Club in east London. They entered through an unimposing door, into a small bar with mismatched furnishings and exposed brick walls. They were presented with a cocktail menu that told the story of each drink and the character it was named after. Mia ordered a Mad Hatter, which came as a delicate teapot and cups on a tray but, instead of tea, the pot was full of Sipsmith VSOP gin, laced with Pedro Ximénez sherry.

They played flamingo croquet and had their fortunes told in the surreal setting of the club. The gypsy fortune teller told Gabby she had a short lifeline, which she already knew, but that she'd take a trip that would make things right for her.

'And what trip would that be?'

'We're not meant to know everything, young lady.'

'Give me a clue.'

'You'll know the answer to the question you've been asking.'

'The answer to why?'

'That's all I can say.'

Mia was very drunk after the gin teapot and the cocktails she'd already consumed. Gabby wanted her to go home, but she insisted on finishing the night at the Purple Bar in Holborn. Had she been a little less inebriated, Gabby would have let her go on alone, but she didn't want to leave Mia in case something bad happened to her.

The bar was a symphony of purples, lavenders and violets – chic and intimate and draped in violet silk opera curtains. It was furnished with lavender Queen Anne chairs, purple etched Venetian mirrors and a bar that looked like a long coffin, with brass handles to hold on to if you were too drunk. It was straight from the pages of *Interview With The Vampire* and the clientele looked a little like pale-skinned bloodsuckers, which unnerved Gabby when she remembered Ramona and the Halkin Hotel. Mia ordered two blood-and-brandy cocktails and they sat and took in their surroundings.

That particular night a magician was performing in the centre of the room. He completed a few, not very spectacular, illusions, then called for a female volunteer. Nobody was forthcoming. Mia gave Gabby a drunken nudge, then raised her hand.

'Over here, she'll do it.'

All eyes looked Gabby's way.

'No, I can't … '

'Go on, Gabby, don't be such a sissy.'

Mia pulled Gabby to her feet and pushed her out into the centre of the room. The magician, who looked a little like Lestat, took her hands and bowed slightly to her.

'What is your name?'

'Gabby.'

'Gabby, I am Girondo. I am going to lie on the floor, and I want you to lie directly on top of me … fully clothed, of course.'

Gabby didn't want to do it. It'd been a long evening and she wasn't interested in taking part in parlour tricks. She glared at Mia for getting her into this.

Girondo lay on his back, with his arms outstretched, and beckoned for Gabby to flop face down on top of him. She hesitated. Her aversion to being touched by strangers was screaming at her to run from the bar and keep going, but she didn't. Slowly, she descended to her knees, then lay on top of the magician. As if through instinct, she spread her arms and her hands touched his. Their fingers entwined and her hair fell across his face, so she could no longer see his features. She closed her eyes. They remained in that position for several moments, without anything happening. Then, almost imperceptibly at first, they began to levitate. Higher. Higher. The audience gasped. They floated to halfway between floor and ceiling, then hovered there, unmoving.

Gabby noticed her surroundings begin to change. The walls of the bar fell away and the ceiling opened up. There was no longer a floor underneath them and they seemed to be suspended in a void – purple at first, then changing colour over and over, colours that Gabby had never seen before and didn't have the words to describe. She could see grass – a vast prairie or steppe – deep waving grass as far as the eye could see. Her feet touched the solid ground of grass – green, waving, waist-high. There didn't seem to be any temperature or atmosphere. She tried to remember where she was – knew she'd been here before, but couldn't remember when – or why. She walked, exploring the featureless grassland. There should have been more than that – but what?

Gabby saw something distant on the grass plain – something solitary and still. She moved toward it and saw an oak tree, in full leaf, with 7^2 carved into the bark. She sat under it. There was no wind to move the leaves. She touched the trunk and it was as if she'd never touched a tree before – a living, dying tree. She created some wind. It blew the branches into waving leaf arms. She began to see the potential. Anything was possible here. Everything existed in the astral quantum, just for the making – for the taking – part of the eternal non-being of probability. Hovering between nothingness and eternity. Unexplainable in the mortal mental landscape of words. The tree sang in the breeze.

Gabby lay flat in the long grass, a subject for examination – a patient – a criterion. She heard the faint hiss of the cosmos, the microwave of background radiation which was the sibilant after-echo of Genesis. But it was distant, moving further and further away. Fading forever. Then an old familiar feeling returned, a feeling of claustrophobia, a longing to go somewhere else, away from the endless expanse of grass and the solitary tree. She needed somewhere real – a cocktail bar, a city street, a bed. She concentrated. The tree disappeared. There was movement around the grass steppe – comings and goings – shapes – sounds.

Gabby felt a slight bump and she opened her eyes to find herself on the floor, lying face down on top of Girondo the magician.

She stood up.

The crowd applauded.

CHAPTER 15

THE VINEYARD

Nobody really cared how anyone else felt. It was a harsh reality, but it was true. People made empty gestures about being concerned, but those overtures were nothing more than facile demonstrations of what they believed was expected of them. Gabby listened to a mixtape of Petit Biscuit as she drove along the empty dual carriageway in the early hours of the morning, trying to find a solution to the unsolvable equation that was Mia. She knew she couldn't let the girl go, even though she'd told Gabby that their relationship had to be open and casual – that was all it could ever be. No deep feelings could be allowed between them, only sex and superficiality.

It was now November and the days were shortening. Gabby hadn't seen Mia for a couple of weeks and she was missing her, more than she should have been.

Gabby was returning from a trade show where she'd met her boss, Günther Engels, again. She still felt uncomfortable about their encounter in the Swissôtel room in Bremen two-and-a-half years ago. It was strange because initially she'd felt that the whole incident was somehow her fault. But her attitude had changed since then. In an industry surrounded by men, she no longer made such an effort to disguise her femininity in order to fit in. She wore what she wanted, when she wanted and if they didn't like it, tough.

Engels didn't seem to have said anything about her being lesbian – maybe it would've damaged his reputation if people found out he'd raped a dyke rather than a damsel. Whatever. Gabby didn't care about it anymore. She'd definitely moved on, she believed the more we cling on to bad memories, the more negative stress it causes. It was pointless. Life was all about impermanence, so it was best just to embrace the present and not to look back.

Cutting through a thick fog, she noticed a small shadow in the middle of the road. It was a deer that had been hit but was still standing, bleeding from a deep gash in its flank. She immediately stopped and got out of her car, slowly so as not to spook the animal. She approached the deer with an outstretched hand, not really knowing what she could do to help. Maybe if she could somehow get it into the car, she could take it to a vet? As she came close, the deer's wide frightened eyes looked directly into hers, as if it could read her mind. Then it staggered off the road and into the undergrowth and disappeared. Gabby stood there, wondering if it would live or die, then walked slowly back to her car and drove away.

As she continued her journey, she thought about that deer, hurt and alone in the bushes. And she thought of herself, enduring her own private agony. Would her pain seem more real if she bled like the deer? Maybe that's all there was to life – a constant stream of affliction as one decayed from the inside. Perhaps certain kinds of love were not meant to be real, only to be imagined, kept hidden away at the back of the mind, protected from the damaging effects of a true relationship – an eternal memory, love as an embodiment of some divine splendour that mere humans should never experience.

Yet part of her was willing to compromise, to change from being an emotional zombie, as she was with Valéria, and to take chances. Risk peace of mind for a few rare, blissful moments with Mia. Sex with Mia was more than just sex, it was sacrifice – it was an offering to the gods. But when they made love Gabby was sometimes offended by the girl's eyes. They behaved as though they belonged to someone else – someone watching. Everything about her intimidated Gabby – her clothes, her hair, her voice, the way she walked, the way she laughed – it was all a beautiful and irresistible torture.

They'd arranged to meet the following Saturday and, as it was her turn to organise where they went, Gabby wanted to make it a special occasion.

It was 10:00 am when Gabby pulled up outside Mia's apartment in Notting Hill. She was wearing light-blue ripped jeans by Jacquemus, a black short-sleeved Bardot top under a Balmain leather jacket, with beige suede boots. She waited in the car until Mia came running with her typical agitated smile, quickly opening the door, kissing Gabby briefly on the lips, before settling back into her seat. She was wearing an ivory slim-fit dress under an open Iris & Ink trench coat, with black sequined, eight-hole Doc Marten boots.

As they joined the motorway Mia was on the lookout for clues as to where they were going.

'You must tell me where you're taking me, Gabby.'

'I don't think so. You'll have to wait.'

'I hope you're not kidnapping me.'

'Would you call for help if I was?'

'Maybe … maybe not.'

The journey took them south on the M25 for just over an hour, until they arrived in the Low Weald area of Kent, past late-medieval houses to the charming village of Headcorn and their final destination – the local aerodrome. Mia looked perplexed when she emerged from the car.

'What's this, Gabby?'

Gabby didn't reply, just made her way to the small office, where they were greeted by James, a young pilot. As he gave them a flight briefing, Mia's eyes opened wider.

'Oh my god …'

Then they made their way to a Robinson R44, four-seater, light helicopter.

'You should go up front with James, Mia, as you'll be helping him to fly it.'

'Oh my god … I've never even been in a helicopter.'

James helped Mia into the cockpit, while Gabby climbed into the back. With headphones in place, they hovered over the ground, gradually lifting into the air. A few seconds later, they were high above the autumnal countryside, with its many dying hues of red and brown and amber. The day was calm, with a milky sun illuminating the fields and hedgerows. After a while, James allowed Mia to fly the helicopter, while he monitored her through a set of dual controls. Every so often, she turned back to smile excitedly at Gabby, who was equally excited to see she was enjoying it so much.

They reached the chalk downs of Dover, then turned back.

The flight took about an hour and, after they landed, they thanked James and made their way, high on adrenaline, back to the car.

'Wow! What made you think of that, Gabby?'

'It's something I enjoyed doing, and I thought you would too.'

'You've been in a helicopter before, then?'

'I took some lessons in Brazil a few years back, when I went there for a holiday with Valéria.'

'That's so cool. Can you fly one?'

'Not alone. I never finished the course.'

'Why?'

That question kept popping up – Gabby still didn't have the answer.

It was after midday when they arrived at Chapel Down Vineyard in Tenterden, just a few miles from the aerodrome They held hands as they were taken on a private tour Gabby had booked. Their guide was a lady in her fifties called Janet.

'Welcome to Chapel Down.'

It was the dormant season, so they had the place mostly to themselves. Janet took them first to a modern processing plant with enormous stainless steel machines for pressing and processing the wine. She reeled off all sorts of information about the English winemaking world that mostly went over Gabby's head, but Mia, because of her interest in the subject, listened intently and even made notes on her phone. They were both pleased to learn that the UK was the biggest importer of champagne in the world, despite producing five million bottles a year, one million of which came from the Chapel Down vineyard.

The second stop was the barrel storage room, with thousands of bottles in metal cages, mostly covered in dust.

Gabby was curious.

'Why would anyone choose English wine over French?'

Janet smiled in an exasperated way, to indicate she'd answered that question many times over the years.

'The chalk scarps of Kent, my dear. And we're less than 250 miles from the champagne region of France, so the soil isn't much different … and climate change gives us the sun we need in summer.'

Next stop was the vineyards themselves. As all the grapes had been harvested, pruning was taking place and Janet explained the Guyot system, where the fruiting arms of the vines were trained along metal wires. In the distance, they could see three beige alpacas, which seemed very out of place among the Chardonnay and Bacchus vines. Gabby turned to Janet.

'Thank you so much, Janet, I'll take the tour from here.'

Mia was a bit perplexed.

'What, no tasting?'

'Patience.'

When Janet had receded toward the gift shop, Gabby pulled Mia close and kissed her, moving her lips down along the girl's neck to her shoulder, inhaling her perfume, which was a mixture of raspberry and pomegranate. Mia moved her head to one side, exposing her neck to the kiss. It was turning out to be a good day.

Gabby took Mia by the hand and led her through the bare vines to a small hut in the field populated by the three alpacas. Mia patted the animals on the head and Gabby told her she wanted it to be a South American experience.

'Imagine you're high in the Andes, Mia.'

'Wouldn't it be a lot colder?'

'Not necessarily.'

There was a low table inside the hut, laden with a picnic hamper that contained freshly baked yuca bread, brigadeiro truffles, jamón del país, queso fresco cheese, Black River caviar, passion fruit and sweet granadilla.

'The only thing that's not South American is the wine.'

'My god, Gabby … how did you arrange this?'

'Not so difficult, really. There's a South American store close to where I live in Kensington. I got them to ship the stuff down this morning. Janet did the rest.'

'And the alpacas, did you import them?'

'No, they belong to a farm up the road.'

They sat cross-legged on a mat on the floor and opened up a vintage bottle of Kit's Coty Blanc de Blancs 2013. They drank out of crystal glasses and ate off china plates provided by Janet. Mia swirled the wine around in her glass before tasting it – to release the bouquet she said. According to her, the mouth only tasted basic flavours, like sweet, sour, salty and so on, but it was actually the nose that picked up the nuances. There were actually more taste buds in the septum of the nose than in the mouth. She put her hand behind Gabby's neck and pulled her close, then she transferred the wine in her mouth across to Gabby's, making her lose her breath for a second or two. It was the most delicious mouthful of wine Gabby had ever tasted.

Mia talked about the different aromas and flavours of wines while they ate. She'd tried many varieties of vintage wine, always taking notes to help her remember the ones she liked best. She had to have those flavours in her repertoire so she could recognise them. Gabby wondered if there was a direct analogy with the girl herself – how her distinctiveness should be perceived. Could it be that Mia was unable to recognise and value affection easily? Was that the reason she was unable to open up fully to Gabby?

'Seriously, Gabby, it must have cost you a fortune.'

'Not exactly a fortune, Mia.'

'A lot, then.'

'How much did the happy ending cost you?'

'Touché.'

Mia continued to talk about wine and her laughter echoed around the small wooden hut and sounded like the music of a piano sonata or a contralto voice in a cathedral. Gabby was in love with her, with her face and ears and hair and hands and words – and also with her flaws and aloofness. When the meal was over, Mia leant over and kissed Gabby.

'Wait, there's one more thing … you know you said you wanted your own vineyard?'

'Gabby …'

'Well, I couldn't afford a vineyard, but those Bacchus vines outside are yours … a hundred of them. You'll take part in the harvest and have your personalised bottles of wine.'

Mia was speechless. She opened her mouth, but Gabby put a finger up to her lips to indicate that words were not required.

Outside, they interlaced hands and watched a fiery red sun sink below the horizon. Time stood still again. It was the most beautiful moment Gabby had ever experienced. It only lasted a short while, but it created something – something new was born in Gabby at that moment and nothing after it would ever be the same. Because she could no longer endure the uncertainty of not having Mia completely, at that moment she came to the decision that she preferred the certainty of not having her at all. Mia would never fully comprehend the enormity of the impact she'd had on Gabby's life and how she came into it at just the right time and saved it, if only for a limited period. That didn't matter, because she'd also changed its course so very fundamentally. Gabby didn't want her to know that because it would have forged a shackle that eventually would have caused resentment. She tried to remind herself that real love wasn't selfish – wasn't owning someone – wasn't partisan. It was the coming together of two free spirits and the ebb and flow of those spirits as they drifted away from each other and came back together again. But that kind of love was beyond Gabby – at least in this life. She had to set Mia free from her feelings, even if it meant being left in emotional despair.

Gabby would not do what she did when Valéria left. She was past that – Mia had taken her past that. Now she existed in the negative space between dream and reality and she'd have the knowing of Mia harvesting the Bacchus vines the following autumn, when she herself might have less than a year left to live – if, of course, the DNA prophesy of the fourth of July came to pass. The knowledge that she'd still have a part of Mia, long after the girl was physically gone took away some of the fear. She'd have that mirage with her when the time came. And the freedom from obsessive love would give Gabby the opportunity to see what else she could achieve – what else she should have achieved a long time ago.

That evening, watching the sunset, She decided to say goodbye to Mia.

CHAPTER 16
BRAZIL

It was her first trip in the newly acquired family car – a beige Volkswagen Fusca with matching leather seats. Gabby sat in the back with her cocker spaniel puppy, watching the never-ending winding roads passing the window. Her father had given her the little dog a couple of months earlier to make up for the horses she missed so much.

They were on their way to Ouro Preto in the Serra do Espinhaço mountains of Minas Gerais, in eastern Brazil. 'Malandragem Dá Um Tempo', by the samba musician Bezerra da Silva, was playing on the radio. It was one of her father's favourites and he sang along, making up his own lyrics when he ran out of the ones he knew and tapping the steering wheel to the beat, as if it was a tambourine.

'We are nearly there.'

Her mother's voice broke into the music as the first buildings began to peep out from behind the green mountain forest. They descended steeply in the almost unbearable humidity of early April, after an eight-hour drive from São Paulo. Her father drove slowly and carefully, to avoid the thousands of pilgrims who had travelled to the colourful town of Ouro Preto for the Semana Santa, the festivities in celebration of the holy week of Easter.

People thronged everywhere through the cobblestone streets and baroque rococo buildings, reminders of the town's opulent past, when gold was mined to accommodate the spread of Brazil's peculiar interpretation of Renaissance opulence. It was known as "rich village" back then, with impressive palaces, churches, bridges, fountains and white buildings with multi-coloured doors and window frames.

They reached their final destination, a street-party area with magnificent depictions of crosses and chalices and Cor Jesu Sacratissimum, with many varieties of traditional Easter decorations made from fabrics and flowers and a kilometre-long carpet of colourful sawdust for the processions in celebration of the resurrection of Christ.

Not taking any time to rest, Gabby's parents began setting up their market stall, displaying the clothing they'd managed to bring with them in the small vehicle and hoped to sell. More stock had been sent ahead in boxes to the local coach garage.

Gabby did her best to help with her small, eight-year-old hands passing the lighter packs to her mother, who was distracted by a brown owl with black eyes and a rotating head.

'José, do something about this owl!'

'It is not doing any harm, Maria.'

'I do not like it. It is bad luck.'

And they needed all the luck they could get. Before moving to São Paulo, their house in the bustling city of Vitória da Conquista, where Gabby was born and lived for the first five years of her life, had been burgled. The large green box where they kept her mother's jewellery, money and important documents had been broken into and everything stolen. With very little support from the local police, Gabby's mother had decided to take charge of the investigation herself.

She found out that the burglar was actually a cousin of one of the Bahia policemen and that's why no progress was being made in the case. Once she had the name of the culprit, Maria marched straight to the police station, pulling Gabby by the hand with her.

When they got there, they were confronted by a big, burly officer who turned out to be the robber's cousin. Maria demanded that the thief's house be searched for the stolen items. The policeman took her outside and told her it would be best if she let the matter drop.

'Best for who?'

'Best for your daughter.'

It was a blatant threat, but Maria knew he had the power to carry it out. Like most police forces in Brazil, the Bahia station was corrupt and had links to organised crime and drug dealing. For a favour, the big policeman could have anyone in Gabby's family killed. Even though she was very young, Gabby would always remember the look of defeat on her mother's face as they trudged the two kilometres home.

The incident left Gabby with an irreversible lack of respect for the police, making her more scared of them than of any criminal. Maria asked Gabby not to tell her father about what had happened, because he'd just go down there with the Colt revolver he always carried and get himself shot. The fact that Maria knew the name of the thief put the safety of the family in jeopardy and they needed to move. The final decision was made when Gabby's health deteriorated, due to her kidney problems. They had to move to São Paulo. A call was made to Gabby's godmother, Carmen, who was already living in that city. Then they sold everything, including the little shop that had Gabby's name – Gabriela's Fashions – over the door. That was three years ago.

A couple of hours after setting up the stall, it was time to go to the coach station to retrieve the stock that had been sent there. Gabby's father wanted to go and take a handcart with him.

'No, José. I will go. You should fetch water and set up the gas for cooking. We will be living and sleeping here for the next few days and we need everything to be done properly.'

'The handcart will be too heavy for you, Maria.'

'I will take Gabby, she can help me push it.'

José rarely argued with Maria. She was a feisty woman and what she said was usually what they did.

And so Maria and Gabby went to the coach station with the handcart. On the way, Gabby wanted to see the splendour of some of the many churches in Ouro Preto. Taking her mother by the hand, she led Maria through the procession that had already started. Girls of mixed ages paraded in handcrafted angel costumes of white, pink and lilac. They had large wings made of real bird feathers, artificial flowers and halo-like tiaras. Gabby wished she could have been one of them, but visiting the churches came in a good second best. Slow, melancholic music played the procession along and the religious aroma of incense filled the air, with the whole spectacle wrapped in the pealing of church bells. They passed a group of Roman soldiers bashing their short swords against their shields, in time with the music. Catholic saints led priests carrying the body of Christ in a coffin, while artisan shops sold religious sculptures made of wood and soapstone.

They reached the church of St Francis of Assisi as a cool evening breeze provided some respite from the earlier heat of the day. Then a fog fell suddenly, shrouding the town in a sinister cloak of fine moisture. A medallion above the church entrance depicted St Francis receiving his stigmata from heaven, as the heads of three chubby angels looked on with eyes wide. The interior was dim and Gabby seemed awed by its delicacy and grace, even though she was too young to fully appreciate the sculptures of Aleijadinho or the paintings of Mestre Ataíde. It was the first time in her little life that she'd seen a black saint, at the centre of the mural of the *Assunção da Virgem*, on the ceiling.

'What does pardo mean, mammy?'

'It means someone who is part black and part white … a mixture.'

'Am I parda, mammy?'

'No, do not be so silly. You are white, with green eyes like your grandmother and great-grandmother.'

Maria sank to her knees to pray, while Gabby continued to be overwhelmed by the monotheistic terrorism of it all.

'And what is written on the ceiling next to the skull and pen and candle, mammy?'

'I do not know, Gabby. It is in Latin.'

A woman kneeling nearby offered an interpretation.

'Vanitus, vanitatum memento mori translates as vanity of vanities, remember you must die.'

'But, what does it mean?'

'It means, young girl, that we should not place too much importance on this life, it is only a preparation for heaven or hell.'

Hell. That word made Gabby's young heart skip a beat. The concept of heaven or hell had not been fully developed in her child's mind, but she'd seen the pictures of people burning in fire. The image put her off exploring the church any further and she asked her mother if they could go.

They collected the stock from the coach station and struggled to get the handcart through the crowds on the main street, so Maria decided to take a longer route through the backstreets. It seemed like an eternity to Gabby and, when they finally emerged and approached the stall, where they'd left her father and the dog, she knew something was wrong.

Even though there were crowds everywhere, the crowd gathered round the area where the stall was located seemed different – more animated – more excited and gesticulatory. Plumes of fiery smoke rose into the air from the centre of the ring of people. Firefighters tried to keep the crowd back and put out the flames at the same time.

Gabby looked up at her mother's face, which was now pale, as if all the blood had drained from it. Maria let go of the handcart and rushed toward the scene, screaming at the top of her voice, while the firefighters held her back.

'José! José! Where are you? Please … nossa senhora aparecida, do not let this happen!'

Nobody seemed to notice Gabby being lifted up above the melee. The young girl drifted higher and higher, until she could see down through the mushroom of smoke and fire. She could see her mother crying and being held back, the surrounding crowd, the firefighters, the ongoing procession, Jesus in his coffin, the church and the town glowing in red light, the smell of burning, the blackened bodies of her father and the little dog.

When she was brought back down, she ran to her mother, who was sitting by the kerb with two other women trying to console her with sugared water. An old man was reciting what happened. He'd noticed a strong smell of gas as José was setting up the stove for cooking. He heard a loud bang and saw the lids of saucepans fly up into the canvas top of the stall. Oil spewed out and spread all over José as the fire erupted. The old man tried to pull him out, but the blaze was sudden and intense, it engulfed everything so quickly – the stall, the clothing, even the car parked nearby. There was nothing left. Gabby held onto her mother.

'Did papa go to hell?'

'No, minha filha … no!'

'But … he burned.'

Maria held her daughter, rocked her in her arms, kissed the top of her head. They both tried to shut out the whole world, never to be part of it again. All the pain, the tears, the guilt, the loss – everything that was important to them was gone. There was no more world – only hell.

The women began to lift Maria from the kerb, praying all the time. An ambulance arrived and Gabby and her mother were taken to the back of it. Maria was given a sedative, which she didn't want to take but they made her, and the mayor turned up to offer his support, eventually taking them away in his car to a hotel for some food, which neither of them could eat. People they'd never met tried to help them, calling and offering money and emotional support and they stayed at the hotel that night.

The next day, however, everything was different and Maria had to face an inquisition. It was as if people around them had changed their minds overnight. They were saying José was negligent for cooking so close to a vehicle and the adjacent stallholders wanted to be paid for their losses and damaged goods. Gabby, totally helpless, had to watch all the arguments and finger pointing and accusations and her mother was summoned to the police station to provide an explanation and to organise what needed to be done about José's burnt body.

It required a superhuman effort, so soon after the accident, but Maria wasn't an average woman, she had amazing qualities, capable of overcoming any obstacle that life threw in her path.

Her world had been turned into a nightmare in a matter of minutes, but she had to stay strong for her daughter.

Gabby didn't eat, drink or speak for the next two days, despite her mother's persistence. When all the arrangements to transport José's body back to Bahia for burial had been made, they boarded the afternoon coach to São Paulo. Even though she had her own seat, Gabby sat on her mother's lap for most of the eleven-hour journey, with her arms wrapped around Maria's neck. Maria said very little during that long trip, as Gabby herself tried to make sense of it all. She'd tried to understand what dying really meant when she heard the words of the stranger in the church – now she knew.

In the end, Gabby concluded that there could not be a god – there was no divine saviour. From then on, life would be up to her and she would set its course. Losing her faith at such an early age would place the heavy burden of unobstructed free will on her inexperienced shoulders, making her grow emotionally old before her time. She had nothing to believe in, except her own concepts, whether right or wrong.

Finally, the mountains of Minas Gerais disappeared into the distance as the flatness of São Paulo State imposed itself on the landscape in front of them and the skyscraper skyline of the city appeared on the horizon.

CHAPTER 17

MARIA AND JOSÉ

Maria and José were both born in the municipality of Maetinga in the north-eastern state of Bahia and were friends from a very young age. Maria's family was considered to be one of the richest in town. They owned a dairy farm, a hotel, a butcher's shop, a restaurant, a small pharmacy and a petrol station and it was rumoured that their wealth originally came from the use of slaves on their sugar plantation. Nevertheless, the Bento family name always carried good value in that region and was respected in the way that rich people are often admired by the poor they control.

José, on the other hand, came from a humble family called Pereira, who had a small farm not far from town where they trained horses. José always loved horses and that's why Gabby did too. José's father had died when the boy was only nine and his uncle cheated his mother out of the farm, so the family was displaced with nowhere to go. They found an empty shack to live in, on the edge of a plantation, and José worked every day at the local market doing all kinds of jobs – shoe shiner, delivery boy, porter, horse handler, as well as working for the Bento family delivering milk.

And that's how he and Maria met.

He was such a good worker that the family gave him other jobs in the restaurant and the hotel and he and Maria became close. There was one occasion when José turned up for work at the restaurant and picked up a cheese pastel, which he loved, for breakfast. Maria's father kept a shotgun under the counter which he used to scare off the drunks who came looking for a free meal. On this morning, Maria was the only one serving, as her older brother Jonas was wiping down tables. She decided to play a prank on her friend José and picked up the shotgun and aimed it at him.

'Put down that cheese pastel!'

'Woah … stop, Maria. I was going to pay.'

'Hands up. Give me your money.'

José held out the coins and, as Maria reached forward for them, her finger accidentally tightened on the trigger. Just in time, Jonas threw himself at José and they both hit the floor before the gun went off and blew a hole in the door. It was lucky no one was walking past outside. Maria's laughter was soon curtailed when her father came running and took the gun away from her.

'What are you doing, Maria? You could have killed someone.'

'It was just a game, papa.'

'Guns are not play-toys, never forget that!'

She was severely chastised and made to wash the hotel linen for a whole month, as well as helping with the cooking and cleaning.

At the age of fourteen, Maria was taken from primary school to marry a man who was eight years older. His name was Edson and the family believed he had excellent prospects and that it would be a good match.

'But I want to marry José!'

'Do not be ridiculous, Maria, José is a poor menino negro.'

'He is not … he is white, just like us.'

'His grandmother was an escravo Africano.'

Which, of course, was not true. It was his great-grandmother who was an African slave.

Edson was good to Maria at first, but things changed when she became pregnant. They moved to the outskirts of Maetinga and she lost contact with José. Edson travelled a lot in his job as a salesman and Maria was left alone for long periods. Her parents moved to the southern state of Paraná to buy another farm and she only had Gabby's great-grandmother, Vovó Magdalena for company. Magdalena's husband Orlando was killed in a gunfight with the Revoltosos when they came marauding and plundering. Maria's mother, Esther, had seen it from a pit covered in bushes which the children used to hide in when the Revoltosos raided. Vovó Magdalena was very old and obese and she died shortly after Maria's parents moved away, so Maria had nobody when she gave birth to her first son, João.

When João was four months old, Maria travelled to Paraná to visit her parents and show them their grandson. They wanted her to stay, but she found it too cold there and, anyway, Edson insisted that they go home as soon as possible. On the way back, they had to change trains at Luz station in São Paulo. The train was crowded and Edson boarded first with the luggage. Outside on the platform, Maria was pushed away from the train by the avalanche of people trying to board. She began to panic in case the train pulled off and left her and João behind. She became desperate, trying to get on the train without hurting the baby, when she saw a pair of arms outstretched through an open window. She passed João into the waiting hands, which withdrew into the train, then she managed to get herself on board. She found Edson trying to store the luggage, but João wasn't with him.

'Edson … where is João?'

'He is with you, is he not?'

'No, I passed him to you, through the window.'

'What are you talking about, Maria?'

Maria was panic-stricken and she went from carriage to carriage looking for her son, but couldn't find him among so many people.

'João! João! Where is my son? Where is my bébé?'

The train was so packed with people, she couldn't move forward, so she collapsed on the floor, crying and sobbing, while Edson tried to force his way through the throng to search the remaining carriages. That's when Maria saw José – he was like a mirage, with his black hair and white shirt and high-waist trousers and black leather boots, coming toward her in slow motion like a handsome cavaleiro. He had João in his arms and he placed the baby on Maria's lap.

'Where did you find him?'

'With a woman who got off the train and was about to leave the station with him. I heard your voice and I knew it was you, Maria. Do you remember me?'

'José Pereira, of course I remember you. I almost killed you with my father's shotgun once … and now you have saved my son. I can never thank you enough.'

'No thanks needed, Maria. Perhaps we will meet again.'

With that, he tipped his wide-brimmed hat and left the train. Maria didn't want him to go. She wanted to know what he was doing at Luz station and how he had been since they last saw each other. She wanted him to sit beside her and put his arms around her. She wanted him to kiss her. But he was gone, and it was like he'd never been there. Maria didn't speak much to Edson during the rest of their journey back to Bahia. He, of course, wanted to know who found João and she told him it was a stranger.

During the years that followed, Edson proved himself to be a violent and unfaithful husband and Maria often considered leaving him. But in those days, in north-eastern Brazil, options were limited for a young single mother without a formal education, not to mention the moral judgements she would have to face. So, they carried on their lives in Maetinga, with Maria staying at home to look after João and the other three children she had for Edson by the time she was twenty. He carried on travelling, sometimes spending months at a time away. When he was back in town he was unpredictable, drinking in the bars and arguing when he came home.

One evening he became very violent, smashing things and frightening the children. He accused Maria of having an affair, even though it was he who was seeing other women on his sales route. When she denied it, he hit her in the face, knocking her across the room. At that moment, she decided she didn't want her children growing up in the shadow of violence and she began to formulate a plan to leave Edson.

Apart from death, the only other thing you could be sure of in life was that people change, that's what Maria told herself

– it was just a matter of whether they changed for better or worse. Once she'd made her decision, the first thing she had to do was get herself financially independent.

She began to design and sew her own brand of clothing and to sell them from catalogues. She based her designs on what she saw in popular magazines and, gradually, her reputation grew. She was becoming quite successful in the region and some of the more influential women began to call on her to order bespoke evening dresses that they could be sure no one else would be wearing.

Then one day José turned up at the family restaurant run by Maria's older brother Jonas. He was dressed all in white and carrying a guitar. The two men greeted each other warmly and laughed when they recalled the shotgun incident.

'Does Maria know you are here, José?'

'Probably not.'

'I will call her.'

Which Jonas did. Maria came quickly and she and José embraced. She thanked him again for saving João from abduction five years earlier.

'What were you doing in Sao Paulo, José?'

'I was working as a porter at Luz station.'

Since then he'd made some money buying and selling horses and had come back to Maetinga to build a small house for his family. He'd never been to school, but he was very good at business. They ate and drank and talked late into the evening and he played the guitar and sang 'Trem das Onze', a samba written by Demônios da Garoa that he liked very much. People in the restaurant gathered round him because they thought he was a star from one of the soap operas.

José stayed in Maetinga while his family's house was being built and he and Maria saw a lot of each other when Edson was away, which was most of the time. Very few families in the town had a television set, except for the Bentos. Jonas kept a large colour TV in the restaurant, where the town gathered to watch the news or soap operas, to which most of the women were addicted, and also whenever Brazil played football. After one particular match which Brazil won against the old foe, Argentina, everybody moved the chairs and tables back and a group of musicians, including José, played forró and baião and the crowd danced wildly. During the evening, the musicians took a break and someone put 'Taça Vazia' by Tibaqib and Miltinho on the record player. It was a slow tempo and José asked Maria to dance. He danced well and she leant in close to him. Had it been any other occasion, people would have talked but, on that evening, anything was possible.

That's when the restaurant door opened and Edson staggered through, drunk. He took one look at Maria dancing with José.

'I knew it! So this is the man you are fucking.'

'Edson … no!'

Edson staggered over to Maria and slapped her across the face. With that, José punched him and knocked him clean out on the floor. Police were called and José was arrested for assault, but released the next morning when Jonas gave evidence about what had happened. By then Maria was gone. She took the children by bus to the nearby town of Aracatu, where she rented a house and continued with her garment business.

Maria wanted a divorce and Edson wanted the children. Divorce was difficult to come by in a rural Catholic community, but the Bento family was very influential. A phone call to a local judge got the jeitinho brasileiro network moving and everything was taken care of. But there was a price to pay – as a divorced woman, Maria was shunned by her family, her friends and even strangers in Maetinga, where she was regularly reminded that she'd brought shame on the family. Attending Mass on Sundays or just walking on the street attracted all sorts of judgemental looks from men and women, in a place where Maria was once highly regarded. So she stopped going there altogether and remained in Aracatu.

Maria was stronger than anyone imagined and being away from Edson was a great relief. It meant she could begin again, this time wiser and with money of her own. During all the upheaval, she forgot about José Pereira but, as time went by, she found herself thinking about him again. Edson had put her off men, but José was different – he was gallant and kind and charismatic. And one day he turned up in Aracatu, with his guitar and his songs, to serenade her. They spent a lot of time together and José moved in with Maria and her four children and the kids accepted him as their new father. He asked Maria to marry him, but she was wary of marriage after Edson and didn't want to rush into anything. She was in a position to choose who she wanted, a privilege unheard of in her family up till then, and she wanted to choose wisely – with her head instead of her heart.

It was only after Maria became pregnant with Gabby that she finally said yes.

Not one of her family attended the small ceremony that took place in a little chapel in Aracatu. And José had an ex-girlfriend who was enraged when he left her for Maria. She placed dead flowers on the doorstep of their house and a headless black chicken as a despacho. In the end, they moved to Vitória da Conquista, where Gabby was born.

Of course, Gabby knew none of this.

CHAPTER 18

ALONE IN A CROWD

Once they'd been back in São Paulo for a while, Maria realised that, without José, it would be difficult to take care of an eight-year-old and carry on travelling to expand her garment business, so Gabby was sent to live with her godmother, Carmen. There were tears and tantrums for hours, but it was the way it had to be.

'Why, mammy? I don't want to. I want to be with you.'

She was taken to a large, cold house in the northern zone of the city where her godmother and two cousins, Marco and Michele, waited by the stairs. Marco was thirteen and Michele was nine, just a year older than Gabby.

After a brief conversation between Maria and Carmen, Gabby was left at her new home, along with a small silver suitcase that had been given to her by her father. Inside was a pink dress with matching pink shoes, a pair of shorts and three tee shirts – and a small, soft, toy dog.

She wouldn't see Maria again for six months.

Gabby didn't go to her father's funeral because Maria didn't want her to remember him like that. Of course, Maria didn't know that Gabby had already seen him like that from the air above Ouro Preto.

Carmen sent her to a private school, one that her cousin was also attending. And Michele became her only friend and protected her from the older girls who threatened to poke out her green eyes with a pencil, because they didn't like the way she stared at them. Those were lonely days for Gabby, even though she was surrounded by people. Time was still a strange concept to her and there seemed to be too little of it in the mornings and too much in the evenings.

It was a time of unrest in Brazil, with hyperinflation and empty shelves in the supermarkets and economic instability and protests on the streets that turned into riots. Gabby's godmother didn't seem overly concerned because she made a good living from a supermarket she owned in the northern zone. She bought produce directly from farmers out in the countryside when she needed to, even though it was illegal to do so, and her biggest problem was having to change the price tags every day. Opening the doors of the supermarket was like opening the gates of a stadium to a crowd of excited football fans. People queued for milk and rice and beans and bread and other basics.

Gabby got paid a cruzado for helping out and it was always spent on books. Jules Verne was her favourite because the writing took her away to fantastic places, from where she'd only come back with the greatest reluctance.

In the evenings, she'd join the others to watch the soap operas on TV. One night she experienced a sudden rush of blood through her veins and an exhalation of air from her lungs when she saw a tall, blonde, blue-eyed woman on the screen. Gabby had never seen anyone so beautiful.

'Who is she, Michele?'

'That's Jocasta.'

Marcos chipped in.

'Jocasta is her soap name, her real name is Vera Fischer.'

'When I grow up. I'm going to marry her.'

The room fell silent and everyone looked at Gabby. She'd obviously said something wrong, but she didn't know what. Next thing she knew, her godmother's hand struck her a heavy blow to the back of her head which almost knocked her off her feet.

'Never say that again, Gabriela! Never, ever! Do you understand me?'

Gabby was sent to her room for the rest of the night, where she realised for the first time that being in love with a woman would be an agonising experience, both physically and emotionally.

Maria kept on working away, leaving Gabby without her guidance, her care, her life experience, her love – yet she kept herself in the present by turning up unexpectedly from time to time and sending Gabby lavish gifts to remind the girl why she did what she did – for her future. But it was that future which Gabby feared the most – a constant stream of strange-familiar houses of other family members, spending around a year at each. Being passed to grandparents, aunts and uncles, older half-brothers and half-sisters, who'd all welcomed Maria back into the fold now that José was dead.

She lost all longing for her mother's presence in that constant stream of strange-familiar people she knew but didn't really know and with whom she had nothing in common. From once being best friends, they grew apart and didn't have much to say to each other when they met. Gabby called her Maria instead of mammy and the once unbreakable relationship died a slow death.

Gabby's only reminder of her father was a small black-and-white photo of him in his cavaleiro outfit and holding his guitar, which she kissed each night before she went asleep.

Maria's promised "short while" turned into ten years and Gabby was expected to be grateful for her absence.

'You would not want to be travelling with me, Gabby.'

Not knowing that was what her daughter wanted more than anything else – to be next to her mother, no matter what.

Gabby was also expected to be grateful for the hospitality shown to her by the extended family, and she was – or, at least, she wasn't ungrateful. But it was a colourless thing and, in a country like Brazil, various kinds of unhappiness competed with each other. Personal unhappiness could never be important enough to matter much, because worse things were happening. Personal unhappiness climbed into Gabby's eyes and became a forlorn expression.

Maria considered herself something of a clairvoyant and, when Gabby was fifteen, she had a terrible nightmare – a 'premonition' she called it. 'I felt it on my skin, as if it actually happened to me.'

She dreamt she was hit over the head with a piece of metal and knocked unconscious. When she came to, she was bound and gagged in the boot of a car which was travelling at speed. When the car stopped, she was dragged out of the boot by two men with black eyes and stabbed many times, everywhere – in her body and head and eyes. Then she was thrown into the Aguapeí river. While she was dying, she could feel the hatred as if it was in the water with her – tangible – a living thing.

Next morning, Maria found out that her cousin Tomás had disappeared. Tomás was a bit of a playboy – tall, blond, handsome and with a successful car dealership. He was flash, drove a Porsche 911 turbo, was popular with the ladies and many men envied him. The police were notified, but there were no clues to his whereabouts and it was assumed that he'd taken off somewhere with some woman – maybe someone else's wife, which he'd done before. Weeks passed and then, one afternoon, Gabby's half-brother João announced that a body had been found in the river. It was Tomás. He had been killed in exactly the way Maria had experienced in her dream. It confirmed to Gabby, once again, that there was no god and she was living in a world of pain.

Such was the vulnerability of life in Brazil.

Such was the lingering mysticism of dreams and premonitions.

The life that's left behind when someone dies goes on and things eventually got back to normal. Gabby was living in a large, five-bedroom home owned by her grandparents. Also living there was Jonas, who was now an alcoholic and infatuated with Olivia, a mulatto maid. One night Gabby was woken by loud screams coming from the laundry room. When she went to investigate, she found a drunken Jonas trying to force Olivia into one of the washing machines, so he could "clean the blackness off her and be able to marry her". Shortly after, Jonas had a stroke which paralysed him and Olivia's job was to take care of him, which she did without any sign of contempt or malice. Olivia's composure and grace reassured Gabby that there was at least some goodness left in the world.

At sixteen, Gabby was being noticed by the opposite sex. People at school teased her because she'd never kissed a boy. Her disinterest and even disgust was sometimes apparent and she had to try to disguise it on occasion because it was beginning to be rumoured that she might be gay. Gabby wasn't ready to come out yet, so she began a plan of action to dispel the rumours. She had to kiss a boy and it had to be witnessed, so the entire school would accept her "normality" once and for all. A victim had to be found and he'd have to look the part, someone whose kiss would make all the straight girls envious. She chose Bernardo, a blond, fair-skinned boy from the second high-school year. Many of the girls drooled over him and he was the perfect target.

But how was Gabby going to make him kiss her?

She chose a shopping area on Avenida Paulista, where a lot of the kids hung out after school. Bernardo was there, surrounded by his admirers. Gabby arrived with her friend Juliana and went over to him and whispered in his ear.

'I've heard that you're gay.'

Bernardo stared at her in disbelief for a moment, with a perplexed smile on his face, as if he was trying to figure out what to do. Then he grabbed her and kissed her full on the lips – the kiss lasted for at least a minute and it was gross for Gabby, like kissing a wet fish. The only way she could get through it was to imagine she was kissing the blonde woman she'd seen on the TV soap when she was nine. When she managed to get her lips back, she looked around at the other girls and the open-mouthed expressions of surprise and envy on their faces. Then she winked, patted Bernardo on the butt and walked away, swinging her hips from side to side. Mission accomplished!

That night, Gabby fell into a deep sleep and it felt as though she'd been taken out of this world. She dreamt about her father – memories came and went – many memories. He was larger than life for her, a hero, an Itabira, rescuing her from the circumstances of the world many times when she was very young. Apart from giving her his kidney, he'd found her lying in an open coffin in a local funeral parlour, then with snakes around her neck from a visiting circus, and he'd pulled her out of a stream she'd fallen into when she was four. Whenever she got into trouble, he was always there to rescue her. But what would he think of her now, if he was still alive? Would he help her overcome her struggles with her sexuality? Would he still love her as much as he did back then, when she was his beautiful little girl?

Gabby woke with beads of cold sweat on her forehead.

Her eighteenth birthday was just around the corner – the transition from girl to woman. A significant milestone in her life. Her heart overflowed with expectation for the new experiences that were waiting for her outside that claustrophobic environment. With a misguided sense of obligation, meant to compensate for her continued absence, Maria insisted on celebrating the occasion in the most extravagant way, by organising a party in one of the region's most prestigious venues. A sit-down meal, live musicians and even security guards to keep out the drug mules and thieves and muggers and aviãozinhos. It was the last thing Gabby wanted, she'd rather have had a motorbike to get her away from the bairro as quickly as possible. Maria told her a motorbike wasn't for young ladies and she'd never attract a husband by being so overtly Amazonian. Her mother knew nothing of Gabby's total disinterest in males and Carmen never mentioned the soap opera incident to her.

Invitations went out to everyone – to all the most popular students at school, most of whom Gabby didn't even know, to all the cousins and aunts and uncles, and to remote family members that Gabby had never even met and never wanted to meet. Dresses were specially designed by Maria – one short satin in a light salmon colour for the reception and another long tulle in champagne for the second part of the party, where she'd be dancing with carefully chosen young men in blue tuxedos.

On the evening itself, Gabby looked the way she felt, like she didn't want to be there. Camouflage was usually her most effective trait – but not on this occasion. People asked why she wasn't happy and did she always look so dejected? Her mother took her to one side.

'At least make an effort to smile, Gabby. I have spent a fortune on this for you.'

'You know I wanted a Yamaha Road Star Silverado, Maria.'

'Do not be ridiculous. If your father was still alive …'

'If he was, I wouldn't need anything else.'

If Gabby refused to comply with something it was always Maria's tactic to turn guilt away from herself and onto her daughter, by insisting that it was what José would have wanted. Thinking of her father at that moment made Gabby even sadder, but Maria was determined not to let her ruin the party.

The pièce de résistance came at midnight, when Gabby officially became eighteen. All the guests assembled along a red carpet as Gabby emerged in tragicomic Cinderella style, through dry-ice smoke and a matching fanfare. She was greeted by her cousin Marco who, in the absence of a boyfriend, played the part of Prince Charming. Everything was carefully choreographed in advance by the buffet manager and Gabby had been allowed to choose the music she was expected to dance to. She chose the waltz from Act 1 of *Swan Lake*, much to Marco's chagrin. He complained as they walked the length of the red carpet and out on to the dance floor.

'Could you not have chosen something worse, Gabby?'

'Not my fault you have no taste, cousin.'

The guests formed a circle around them as they spent the seven minutes of music rotating gracefully round, covering the space in a manner that allowed Gabby to blow out the eighteen candles held in the hands of a shimmering orb of girls in the same champagne tulle dresses. At the end of the night, which was really the next morning, Maria seemed satisfied with Gabby's performance and, for weeks afterwards, the party

was the favourite topic of conversation with the family, which
Gabby tried her best to keep out of.

CHAPTER 19

COMING OUT

By the time she was twenty-one, Gabby was working for a large American computer company and in her third year at university, where she was studying publicity. She decided it was time she told her mother what she wanted to do with her future and, more importantly, what she didn't want. By then, Maria was in her fifties and travelling less and less, spending more time in São Paulo. Gabby had moved out of her grandparents' house as soon as she began working and had a small apartment in Praça da República. Despite her mother's almost permanent presence in the city, after so many years apart Gabby no longer needed or wanted to be close to her. Their meetings became more and more infrequent and the topics of their conversations increasingly superficial – never about what either of them really felt.

However, Gabby decided that she owed herself the gift of truth so, one afternoon, she screwed up her courage and went to see her mother. When she arrived, it seemed as if Maria's clairvoyance was already working and she could read Gabby's mind.

'I need to talk to you about something important, Maria.'

Her mother continued flicking through the TV channels without making eye contact with Gabby, who kept talking, even though she wasn't getting any response.

'I don't expect you to like, or even understand, what I have to say.'

Maria began banging the remote control against her leg, pretending there was something wrong with it.

'You said I could always tell you the truth, regardless of what it was … right?'

Maria stopped fidgeting and looked directly at her daughter.

'Get to the point, Gabby.'

'Why do you think I've never had a boyfriend?'

'Because you are too demanding.'

'No, Maria, it's because I'm bisexual. I like women more than men.'

Maria blessed herself, but showed no other outward sign of surprise, as if she knew what was coming, but refused to accept it until it was actually spoken. She remained silent. Gabby waited – and waited.

'Say something, mother.'

'I would rather see you dead, Gabby … or die myself, rather than live to see what will become of you.'

After these words, Gabby could no longer bear to look at her mother, so she ran from the house with her heart in her hands. There was no point in telling the truth – the truth hurt, both the teller and the told.

After brooding for a few days on the encounter with her mother, Gabby strengthened her resolve to be honest about her sexuality. That didn't mean going around waving a banner declaring that she was a lesbian, but it did mean not avoiding the issue if and when it presented itself. But Gabby needed to understand on a deeper level, so she could accept herself as she was. She went to the university library, gathered as many books and articles on homosexuality as she could find, then retreated to a private room where she could carry out her research without judgemental interruption. She needed to convince herself that she was neither crazy nor sick, contrary to the established viewpoint of the Catholic hierarchy in Brazil.

In search of that reassurance, she devoured the literature for days on end, without much inspiration, until she came across an article that caught her attention. It referred to a 1935 letter from Sigmund Freud to the mother of a homosexual young man who wanted her son to be "cured" through psychoanalysis. Freud replied, listing various geniuses throughout history who were homosexuals – Leonardo da

Vinci, Plato, Michelangelo, to name but a few – and told the anxious mother that homosexuality was nothing to be ashamed of. Gabby wished her own mother could've gotten that same reassurance from someone she respected. But that hadn't happened and Maria would call Gabby's mobile crying, then hang up. Other times she'd say how disappointed she was and how selfish Gabby was for not giving her grandkids, even though her other children by Edson had given her eight.

Nevertheless, it was one thing for Gabby to come out at home, yet another thing entirely to do the same at work – running the risk of losing her job in a homophobic culture. She kept to herself at the office, but it sometimes seemed as if certain people could sense that there was something different about her – or maybe it was just her imagination? To counteract that possibility as much as possible and to avoid unnecessary controversy, Gabby hung out with Daniel, a male colleague from her class at the university. Daniel was tall and slim, with dark spiky hair and freckles across his nose. He was an artist who could draw the most wonderful portraits and landscapes she'd ever seen. His intelligence and caustic sense of humour were what she found most attractive, not his physicality. Spending time with him was always fun and unpredictable.

Daniel came from a middle-class background – he went to law school in the mornings and studied publicity in the evenings. He and Gabby would meet up at weekends and go to the arcade, or to the cinema to watch art-house movies, or to galleries, or to drink, or just to hang out in the large apartment in the south of the city where he lived with his mother. Despite the absence of physical attraction, Gabby enjoyed his company and always felt comfortable around him, as he never tried to push her into doing anything she didn't want to do. In fact, she sometimes wondered if he might actually be gay himself.

Her twenty-first birthday arrived and the memory of her eighteenth compelled her to avoid a party, so she made herself scarce and spent the day with Daniel. That evening, after a few drinks, Gabby came out to Daniel and told him about her interest in women. He didn't seem surprised or appalled in any way, neither did he reciprocate with an admission that he might be gay himself.

'I'd like to go to a gay club this weekend, Daniel.'

'Alright. I'll come with you.'

'You don't mind?'

'Of course not.'

They met at the Vila Madalena metro station and took a short taxi ride to the discreet Ipsis Club that Gabby had found on the internet.

The club interior was almost entirely blue and Gabby had never seen so many dazzling women in a single space. She hadn't realised how many lesbians and bisexuals there actually were, she'd believed there were only a few people like her, but now she realised that wasn't the case. Watching them dance so close together, caressing and kissing each other so intimately, made her jaw drop, her palms tingle and her knees go weak. Daniel seemed more interested in Gabby's reaction than in all the stunning women around them. He was wearing a pair of knee-length, baggy shorts, with a Che Guevara tee shirt and Converse trainers, and he looked out of place among the gay men wearing trendy designer clothes.

'So, what do you think of the place, Gabby?'

She could hardly speak with excitement.

'Maybe … maybe we should get a drink?'

They went to the bar and mixed absinthe with guarana, an energy drink, then retreated to a quieter area upstairs where they could watch the dance floor and the small stage where semi-naked go-go boys and girls excited the audience. And the excitement was contagious. A sense of unbridled daring came over Gabby. She went back downstairs without Daniel and began to dance by herself. Soon she was absorbed into the throbbing crowd and found herself beside a group of girls who were dancing wildly. They were all about Gabby's age and one of them caught her attention. She tried to make eye contact with the girl, which was difficult because of the way she was gyrating round the floor. Eventually, Gabby managed to elicit a sexy smile from her – it was the strongest signal she'd ever received from a woman and it made her heart beat like a time bomb in her chest. It was time to act or she'd miss the opportunity.

Gabby glanced up to where Daniel was still sitting, sipping his absinthe and guarana – he didn't seem to be missing her so she manoeuvred herself across to where the girl was dancing.

'Hi, I'm Gabby.'

'Nice to meet you, Gabby. I'm Carolina.'

It was difficult to be heard above the noise of the tribal house music, but Carol, as she liked to be called, was due to graduate as a veterinarian from a university in Ribeirão Preto. Her family lived in São Paulo and she came to the city as often as she could.

'I haven't seen you here before, Gabby. What are you looking for?'

The question took Gabby by surprise and she didn't know how to answer it.

'It's my first time here, and I'm not actually sure what I'm looking for.'

'Have you been with a woman before?'

Again, the forwardness of the question took Gabby by surprise and she could feel the blush rising up her neck to her face.

'No … have you?'

'Yes, I'm bisexual.'

The dance ended and they sat together, close to the other women in the group who were all lesbian, according to Carol. Gabby was a little unnerved by the candid way in which Carol spoke about the group's sexuality. Yet it was refreshing and not all that surprising really, seeing as they were in a gay club. Some of the women in the group were there with their lovers and everything seemed as normal as in the heterosexual world where Gabby had been brought up – the world that made her feel like a freak and whose social conditioning and conformity she now wanted so desperately to escape from, to experience the new and exciting reality she'd just discovered.

Carol was beautiful, with full red lips, bright hazel eyes, straight blonde hair and a sensuous figure. She was wearing a revealing white top, jeans by Jaeger and high heels,

'Your boyfriend is watching us, Gabby.'

Gabby looked toward the balcony. Daniel was looking down.

'He's not my boyfriend.'

'I know he's not. He's with you for moral support, as it's your first time in a gay club and you didn't know what to expect.'

Gabby laughed self-consciously. The girl was right.

'And he's not gay. You should have come with a gay man, Gabby.'

'How do you know he's not gay?'

'By the way he's looking at us.'

Gabby wondered what that meant – and how Carol knew Daniel wasn't gay. Gabby herself wasn't sure, and she'd known Daniel for some time.

'I don't know any gay men.'

Carol touched the small scar on Gabby's chin.

'How did you get that sexy scar?'

It was a distant memory now. It happened when Gabby was three and living in Bahia. Every night her father would take her into the garden and they'd count the stars and give them names. He used to take her in his arms and swing her from side to side, saying she was like a little bird and he was helping her to fly. One night she woke up and sneaked out into the garden on her own. She climbed up on a metre-high wall and jumped, flapping her arms as she fell to the ground. She landed on asphalt and cut her chin badly and had to be taken to the hospital for stitches. The scar was a reminder that she couldn't fly.

Carol kissed the scar on Gabby's chin, then moved her lips up to her mouth. For the first time in her life, Gabby felt true desire as a result of kissing someone. It was a feeling of being in the moment – with a woman, not a man – no rough beard, the softness of her lips, the smell of her skin, the brush of her hair, the gentleness of her touch, the subtlety of the seduction. It was what Gabby had been waiting for all her life – like she'd suddenly stumbled upon a well-kept secret. Her whole life assumed a new meaning as she kissed Carol back – all the time she'd wasted – all the future risks she faced became irrelevant in that blue room full of wonder. She no longer wished to fit into the heteronormative code, just to please her mother, her family, her friends, her work colleagues, the church, the neighbours and every other bigot on the planet. For the first time, she knew who she was – truly, and not who she thought she was. She was immediately addicted, forever lost in the alternative – and she could never go back.

They kissed as if they'd been lovers for all eternity, lost in the intimacy of each other. The next thing Gabby knew, Daniel was tapping her on the shoulder.

'Can we go now?'

'Daniel … what's the matter?'

'I want to go.

Carol shook her head and gave Gabby a rueful look.

'I said you should have come with a gay man.'

Gabby didn't want to go, she wanted to stay in the new reality of Carol's kiss.

'You go Daniel, I want to stay.'

'We came together, Gabby, we should leave together.'

The mood was shattered. Carol had already broken away from Gabby and joined the other women who were preparing to get back out on the dance floor.

In the taxi on the way home, Gabby tried to understand. It wasn't as if Daniel didn't know she was interested in women – it was the whole point of going to a gay club in the first place.

'Why, Daniel?'

He didn't answer for a while. Gabby didn't know it then, but she'd learn as she went through life that straight people resented gays and lesbians, especially beautiful ones. They used terms like "what a waste" and "I bet I could turn her (or him)", as if it was their right for being born heterosexual to have the privilege of having sex with people of a different inclination, whether those people wanted it or not. Daniel thought he could handle seeing Gabby with another woman, maybe even like it, but because it excluded him, because he wasn't invited to be part of it, he reverted to type and became surly.

The next morning Gabby had made up her mind to leave Brazil for good. She daydreamed about it at work, smiling absently at her colleagues for no reason, not hungry or thirsty, feeling none of the usual stress or anxiety. She felt liberated, taken over by a sense of inner bliss at the endless possibilities of a different kind of life. The simple act of kissing a woman had opened up her mind and given her the strength to implement a plan that she'd been considering for some time. It was no longer enough to slide through life as her family and friends did. There was no longer a limit to what she could do – like leaving the country to look for a better life somewhere very far away, where she would be respected, despite being gay. It would be a quest for meaning, to find the reason she was on this earth, to answer the question – why.

Maria had finally decided to retire and stay permanently in São Paulo. Now it was Gabby's turn to leave her, to find out if people were different in other countries. She would go to Europe and reinvent herself. She'd become relevant, be whoever she wanted to be, before it was too late and she became enveloped by Brazil, sucked into the quicksand of its conservative mediocrity and unable to escape. She didn't tell anyone about her plans because she believed someone would jinx them and ruin everything. She was taking no chances.

Three months after her graduation, a ticket to London, via Paris, was secretly purchased and, at a family gathering during the Easter period – the time when her father was killed so many years earlier – she made her announcement.

'I'm going away and I don't know when I'll be back, if ever.'

Her mother cried, her half-sisters and brothers laughed and said she'll be back in a month. Others asked what she was going to do so far from home – to which she replied, 'live a new life'. She didn't show any emotion, or regret, or empathy. None of them had travelled abroad or even had passports for that matter. Venturing into the unknown was far too risky for any of them to consider.

The following week, after taking pleasure in quitting her job, she caught the coach to Guarulhos Airport with a rucksack containing her first passport, a copy of *Civilisation and its Discontents* by Freud, a Canon camera, maps of Paris and London, a few basic changes of clothes and one pair of trainers. Nobody came with her. She didn't feel the discomfort of the economy seat on the Aigle Azur Airbus – to her it was like floating on a cloud that was taking her to her new dreamworld. She couldn't eat or sleep during the twelve-hour flight because of the adrenaline being generated by a mixture of trepidation and excitement.

Paris was everything Gabby imagined it to be – sophisticated, bustling, chic, recherché. She made her way open-mouthed to the Montclair student hostel in the bohemian Montmartre area of the city and settled down for the night. Next morning, leaving her rucksack by her bunkbed, she took her passport, camera and some euros and stepped out into the late-spring morning of her brave new world. With a small bottle of wine, a loaf of bread and a piece of Brie cheese, she found a spot on a park bench beneath the Sacré-Cœur basilica, where she could just glimpse la Tour Eiffel. The breathtaking sensation of leaving her one-dimensional existence and being part of the new beau monde overwhelmed her.

Getting lost in the Gallic mise en scène, she strolled for hours, down narrow alleyways and across wide boulevards and through a babel of voices and a dreamtime of sensation fantastique. The city had everything she could imagine – art, culture, unique architecture, exquisite cuisine, fine wine and elegant women and Gabby wanted to become part of it, to be absorbed into its ambience.

But that would have to wait – next day it was time to leave for her final destination.

London.

CHAPTER 20

OMENS

The annual Christmas Eve zouk party was in an underground club in Shoreditch. Gabby wore a black, tight-fitting flapper dress that accentuated her figure. She didn't know if Mia would be there. She'd tried to say goodbye to the girl, as she promised herself she'd do in the vineyard in November, but couldn't bring herself to go through with it – they just didn't see each other as frequently. She didn't answer Mia's calls a few times, even though she desperately wanted to, and then the calls stopped. But the thought kept coming back to Gabby – Mia saved her life once, after Valéria left, could she save it again? And so, she eventually rang back, as she always knew she would.

'Why didn't you reply to my messages, Gabby? I was worried.'

'Worried?'

'You know … '

'Don't, I won't do that again.'

'Good!'

Gabby was disappointed that Mia was calling because she was worried she'd done something stupid, and not necessarily because she missed her. Now it was Christmas Eve and Gabby hadn't seen or heard from Mia for two weeks. The shoe was on the other foot and it was Gabby who was worried.

The theme of the evening was the prohibition era of 1920s America – gin-joints and gangsters – bobs, beads and high hemlines – speakeasys and shady silhouettes. Gabby was a little late arriving and the men in the room turned their heads when she entered. She immediately saw Mia at the other side of the club, sitting with Adriano Correia, an expert in

Brazilian zouk technique, but she pretended not to notice. Adriano was a famous dancer – he was tall and toned and had a reputation with beautiful women, who fell for his moves on and off the dance floor. Other men approached Gabby, kissing her three times in the carioca style and she smiled politely and made her way to the bar.

Gabby ordered champagne and was taking a sip when she felt a hand on her shoulder.

'I didn't know you were coming tonight, Gabby.'

It was Mia. Gabby turned and smiled.

'I didn't know you were either.'

'You going to get me a drink?'

'Sure. Champagne?'

'Why not?'

They exchanged small talk for a few minutes, avoiding the serious stuff. Then Mia invited her to come join them at Adriano's table.

'Have you met him before?'

'No.'

'You'll find him fabulous.'

'Will I?'

They crossed the room and Adriano stood and kissed Gabby's hand, while Mia introduced them to each other. Some media people also sat at the table, trying to interview a disinterested Adriano, to learn more about his upcoming performances. As the night wore on, Gabby danced with a variety of men, but not with Mia. She didn't know if she was doing this deliberately to provoke a tiny spark of jealousy, which Mia professed not to have. Of course, Mia would've known there was nothing to be jealous about, as Gabby had no interest in men. Maybe she should have danced with some of the women?

At that point, Adriano walked on to the floor and excused the guy who was dancing with Gabby. The man bowed and moved away.

'Do you mind, Gabby?'

'No … of course not.'

They danced, fast and sensuously. Adriano was a superb mover and Gabby tried her best to match him.

'You dance well, Gabby.'

'Not as well as you.'

'Do not underestimate yourself.'

Was that what she'd been doing all her life?

The music changed from zouk to forró, then to lambada, then bossa nova and back to zouk again. They stayed on the floor and most others in the club stopped dancing and formed a circle. They clapped in rhythm with the music and Adriano performed an exhibition of dancing perfection with Gabby.

When it finished, he and Gabby bowed to the cheering, whistling, clapping crowd. Adriano held Gabby's hand in the air and bowed to her. Cameras flashed and the cheering increased in volume. Suddenly, Mia walked through the circle of people and slapped Adriano hard across the face, then she retreated, disappearing into the coalescing crowd.

Adriano raised his hands in the air, as if he'd conquered Everest or won an Olympic gold medal and all the men in the room wolf-whistled and stamped their feet on the wooden floor. Gabby went after Mia and found her in the ladies' room.

'What was that, Mia? Were you jealous?'

'Of course not!'

'Then, why?'

'He was supposed to be with me, not you. I don't like being ignored.'

They stood there, facing each other in silence. Then Mia began to laugh.

'I've made him a homme hero by slapping him, haven't I?'

'Yes, their beloved bull-calf.'

They laughed louder, fell into each other's arms and embraced.

Christmas Day was spent at a luxury apartment in Mayfair with some friends of Mia's family.

Gabby brought red tulips as a gift, but it was an uneasy evening for her. They were all part of a cliquey London set and didn't seem to want to accept her into their circle as they accepted Mia. The apartment belonged to a middle-aged Englishman called Eugene and his twenty-something girlfriend, Samantha. He reminded Gabby of Günther Engels as he pompously carved the turkey while the caterers were busy dishing up the roast potatoes and Brussels sprouts. Eugene was a writer of risqué paperback fiction and Samantha was a "model".

Also at the long table were two very good-looking gay men in their early thirties, both called Trenton; a businesswoman of indeterminable age called Eve; and Pete, a black man who wore dark glasses indoors – Gabby wondered if he was blind, but discovered that he wasn't. The numbers were made up by two young women in their twenties who went by Victoria and Alexandra. Eugene introduced them as sisters and they were, apparently, "it girls" – whatever that meant.

Mia wore a scarlet midi-length dress by After Dark with matching heels. Her red hair was up, exposing a Van Cleef diamond necklace around her elegant neck, which sparkled below her crimson lipstick. Gabby wore black again – an evening dress by Pia Michi with a split up the left side and a sequinned Kayamiya bolero jacket, which responded to the sparkle from Mia's necklace.

Mia was glad to see her when she arrived and whispered in Gabby's ear.

'I'm so glad you've come.'

It was as if she'd been rescued from some unbearable kismet.

Eugene led the conversation while mutilating the turkey.

'So, Gabby … it is Gabby, isn't it?'

'Yes.'

'So, what do you do, Gabby?'

'I'm in marketing.'

'How very ersatz.'

Gabby wasn't letting him away with that remark.

'And you scribble soft porn, I believe.'

'Touché.'

How did Mia know these people, Gabby wondered?

Mia, who was so cool and classy – what was she doing with these cyphers?

The dinner seemed to go on forever, like a commercial for margarine where everybody had to pretend they were savouring the unpalatable. Knowing looks were exchanged across the table, and pretentious kisses blown, along with little winks and sly glances between the businesswoman and the black man. A Christmas pudding was then served, which Eugene set light to and everyone cheered. They were allowed to smoke in the apartment and the host puffed on a large cigar while Gabby couldn't wait to light up a cigarette to smoke with her brandy.

'What happened …'

'At the zouk party?'

The it girls had obviously heard about Mia's face-slapping and they bounced off each other in their glee. Mia was defensive.

'Nothing happened. Who said something happened?

'Adriano Correia …'

'Got his face slapped …'

'Dancing with …'

'Our guest …'

That was the problem with these people, they spoke in half-sentences – dealt in half-statements. Innuendos – so they couldn't be accused of saying anything directly. A hint. A vocal intonation.

'Gabby danced with Adriano. It was great. The crowd applauded. That's all.'

'I see …'

'It's just that …'

'Someone said …'

'Nothing fucking happened!'

Mia's outburst brought an end to the issue. The gay men gasped and the model looked anxiously at Eugene, who moved the brandy bottle out of Mia's reach. An awkward silence pervaded the room for a short while, until conversation resumed and the subject turned to a Natalia Goncharova exhibition at the Tate Modern. Gabby put her arm around Mia and kissed her, for the benefit of the others at the table.

They left early, to feigned protests from Eugene, who said the evening was young yet and couldn't they stay for another while? A short while? A little longer? Both Mia and Gabby had enough of the half-sentences and wanted to be able to drink some brandy back at Mia's place, without anyone making snide comments about it. Of course, the others were glad to see them go.

Mia was in a mood when they got to Notting Hill. Gabby couldn't understand why they'd had to go to Eugene's in the first place.

'Why do you associate with these people, Mia?'

'They're friends of my family.'

'Why weren't your family there?'

'Because they're in Italy for Christmas and I wanted to stay here with you. I had to go to Eugene's to represent them.'

'Thanks for inviting me.'

'Are you being facetious, Gabby?'

'Yes.'

They poured the brandy and decided to say no more about it. Outside the window, it began to snow, lightly at first, then heavier, until huge flakes were falling. Gabby pulled Mia's small waist close to her and began to undress the girl. She was wearing nothing underneath the scarlet dress and she lay on the bed with her red hair around her freckled face. They made love for a long time, stopping occasionally to drink more brandy. Afterwards, Gabby's eyes began to close, as she looked out on the carpet of soft whiteness covering the street, while the brandy and the warmth of the apartment took their effect on her tired body.

January and February came and went and they took some time off work in March and went to Alpbach for the skiing. On the second day, Mia said the weather looked threatening and decided to stay in the comfort of the resort. Gabby wasn't a great skier and she wanted to go out for some practice. There was a line at the ski lift – a group of tourists who'd come on a bus and who were sliding about clumsily, or propping themselves up on their poles, or resting their weight on their neighbours, leaning over to adjust their bindings and bringing the line to a halt. At the front of the line, they had to unzip every pocket to find their badges for the lift operator to punch, then climb the small slope to be ready for the T-bar.

Gabby was halfway along the line when she saw Mia passing by. The girl didn't get in the line, just kept moving uphill on her skis, as lightly as if she was walking.

'Mia!'

Gabby called out, but the girl didn't turn around. She was wearing climbing skins and she moved easily and rhythmically, her long legs lifting in her tight-fitting pants, snug at the ankles. The sun looked unreal, like a painting on the expanse of snow where Mia's moving figure cast no shadow. Gabby ended up on the same T-bar as a man from the tourist group and, halfway up, she saw Mia again. At that point, the lift skirted a hollow, where the trail advanced through high dunes and intermittent fir trees embroidered with ice. Mia was moving effortlessly, with that precise stride of hers.

'Mia!'

She seemed to be smiling when she looked over at Gabby, but didn't wave or make any kind of gesture. When she disappeared from sight, Gabby felt as if she'd been erased, somehow, from the face of the earth.

As soon as she reached the top, Gabby started down the slope, searching for a glimpse of Mia and hurtling faster and faster. The girl appeared out of nowhere, still moving up, and Gabby almost crashed into her, shooting past like an arrow, then losing her balance and ramming, face first, into fresh snow. At the bottom of the slope, breathless and dusted with a fine white icing, Gabby joined the line for the lift again – then back up to the top. On the way down, she saw Mia ahead of her, this time going in the same direction. The girl was skiing unhurriedly, making her turns with precision. The tourists from the bus, on the other hand, were plunging down like sacks of potatoes, shouting to one another.

Gabby was almost abreast of Mia when the sun, instead of getting stronger as midday approached, froze and disappeared. The air became full of sleet, flying slantwise and Gabby wasn't able to see much in front of her. She was skiing blindly, trying to avoid the tourists who were tumbling, skis crossed and bindings broken, head-over-heels around her. Air and snow were now the same colour, opaque white, and Gabby could only barely make out Mia's silhouette, suspended in the midst of it. When she came close, the girl's face was covered by a windbreaker and hood, so that only her nose and eyes were visible. Gabby was covered in snow, hair pasted to her temples and her cheekbones glowing red.

'Mia … '

The girl didn't turn her head. Gabby was partly glancing sideways at her, partly watching where she was going in the white-out.

Then the sleet stopped and there was a break in the blizzard. The sky appeared – blue behind the feathered peaks of the frozen mountains. The mouth and chin of the hooded girl revealed themselves.

'It's over.'

'You're not Mia.'

She smiled and skied away.

Easter came early that year and they decided to spend the rest of their holiday in Italy. Mia booked a castle she'd heard about and had always wanted to visit. It was in a remote region of Tuscany and Gabby hoped to be able to visit Florence while they were there. It was late afternoon when they arrived and the wind was blustering a bit – rustling through the leaves of trees, making the branches sway and swoop, as if telling Gabby to turn back. The coach had dropped them off at the bottom of a long driveway, with the outline of the castle looming in the distance. Triangular turrets cut into a hazy sky. Floodlights illuminated red and green ivy, climbing toward dozens of leaded windows, and a mile of stone steps led up to a flagged courtyard where huge double doors waited, with dark statues of angels flanking either side.

The castle grew larger and larger as they approached, until it lowered over them like a gothic giant. A labyrinth of tall thorn hedges appeared to the left as they crossed the courtyard. Gabby was drawn toward it.

'Come on Gabby, we haven't time for that.'

She was about to turn away and follow Mia when she saw what looked like a scrap of black silk on the ground. She picked it up and discovered it was a butterfly, which lay lifeless in her hand. A butterfly – at that time of year? Gabby looked closely at the creature, its wings were remarkable, dark crimson veins stretched to the silky tips, which suddenly twitched to the touch of her finger. It was still alive. Slowly, the dark wings stood upright and she was about to throw it into the air when it flew up and attached itself to her mouth – the butterfly liked her, it was trying to kiss her. Then she noticed tiny droplets of blood on her white top, it took her a moment to realise where they were coming from. She snatched the butterfly from her lips and stamped it into the ground.

'Gabby!'

Mia was directly behind her. She dabbed at the tiny puncture wound.

'What happened to your mouth? Did you prick it on those thorns?'

'No, I was bitten by a butterfly.'

Mia scowled.

'Being facetious again I see. Let's go in.'

They crossed the flagstones to the medieval door, with the words OMNIUM EST TERMINUS carved above it in Latin.

'All must end.'

'You know your Latin, Mia.'

'I am second-generation Italian, Gabby.'

Gabby felt a sense of foreboding as Mia crossed the threshold in front of her. She wondered why they'd come to a place like this – like some vampyre lair from a bad B movie. There was an air of impending disaster, along with a jangle of inevitability. Gabby took a deep breath, pulled open the heavy door, and followed Mia into the castle.

It was quiet in the huge reception hall and Mia was nowhere to be seen. There were doors off either side and a long hallway leading deep inside the edifice. Detailed red tapestries lined the walls, along with eccentric paintings of arrogant aristocrats long since dead. The floor was black marble with the sheen worn off from centuries of feet and the lighting was dim, but enough to see by. Gabby wondered where she was supposed to be and how she could get there.

'Mia …'

She listened and heard a distant rumbling – mumbling – somewhere down along the hallway. She followed the sound and it grew louder. And louder. She came to a door and could go no further. Gabby cautiously opened the door and the commotion inside assaulted her ears. The room was full of people, old and young, male and female, priests and nuns and even a bishop or two – Gabby was sure she saw a cardinal. Mia came out of nowhere and escorted her through the crowd.

'What kept you?'

'Sorry.'

'There are some people I want you to meet, Gabby.'

Mia took Gabby to a group in the centre of the large room. They all turned to look at the two women as they approached. Mia presented an elegant lady in her sixties.

'I'd like you to meet my mother, Gabby. This is Gabriela, mother, who I told you about.'

The woman kissed Gabby on both cheeks and said she was so glad to meet her at last. It took Gabby by surprise; this wasn't at all what she was expecting. Mia also introduced her to an uncle, an aunt, two cousins and other extended family members – about a dozen in all. Gabby pulled her to one side.

'Why didn't you tell me it was a family reunion?'

'I wanted it to be a surprise.'

Every Easter, the members of the Idoni family who could make it assembled at the castle for Mass and a dinner to celebrate the miracle of Christ rising from the tomb. It was a tradition – Mia was duty bound to come, having missed the Christmas gathering. Before Gabby could reproach the girl for putting her in such an awkward situation, a bell rang and everybody trooped off to an ornate chapel where the cardinal said Mass, assisted by several bishops. It was an eerily ritualistic ceremony, almost medieval in its intensity of incense smoke and incantation. Everyone took communion – except Gabby.

Afterwards they were shown to their rooms by a young man dressed in black and silver livery. He took Mia's bags, but Gabby insisted on carrying her own. They were led down another long silent hallway, then up a precarious staircase. The staircase had six posts, with a different face carved into each of them – screaming faces of fear. The young man saw Gabby's interest.

'Il castello fu costruito su un vecchio terreno ardente.'

'He says the castle was built …'

'… on an old burning ground. I can speak some Italian, Mia. What's a burning ground?'

'Where they burnt witches alive. The faces on the posts are …'

'I can imagine.'

At the top of the staircase, the porter accidentally dropped one of Mia's bags and it tumbled all the way back down. She flew into a rage, swearing at him and calling him a clumsy idiot in a variety of languages. This was the fourth time Gabby had experienced that side of Mia – once when she admitted punching two people in her exposition of when it was justifiable to act on anger, again when she slapped Adriano, then when she lost her temper at the Christmas dinner, and now. The young man retrieved the bag and they proceeded.

'Why are we in separate rooms?'

'Don't worry, I'll come to yours later, Gabby.'

'Do they know about your sexual … orientation?'

'Who?'

'Your family.'

'Of course.'

That evening, after showering and changing into a black two-piece by Faviana, with a plunging neckline and exposed midriff, Gabby came down to dinner. The dining room was huge, a sparkling gold chandelier showered the space with an enchanting aurora – it rainbowed round the walls, with diamonds of light like stars that had been plucked from the night sky and scattered across the high ceiling. There was a long table, covered in red and white linen, that seated about a hundred guests, while the aristocrats of old looked down from their paintings along the walls.

Gabby was seated next to Mia's mother, whose name was Ruth and whose husband had disappeared on a business trip when Mia was ten. The rest of the family were adjacent and the conversation centred for a while around Gabby – who she was and where she came from and they wanted to know all about Mia's "best friend". It was all very polite and courteous, until Ruth gave her an enigmatic look through squinting eyes.

'You didn't take communion today, Gabriela?'

'Please, call me Gabby. I hadn't been to confession.'

'And do you have sins to confess?'

'Doesn't everyone?'

The meal was an extravagant affair that went on for almost four hours. Speeches were made and prayers were recited and by the time they left the table it was midnight. Gabby excused herself, saying she was tired after their journey down from Austria, leaving Mia drinking champagne in the exalted company.

That night she dreamt of flames and burning flesh and woke with a start to find someone standing over her. It was Mia.

'I came, as I promised.'

They made love and it seemed to Gabby that, as she'd been introduced to the family, her relationship with Mia would now be long-term, or as long as the term she had left to live. So, there was no longer any reason for her to break up with the girl she loved.

Suddenly, the window flew open and cherry blossom showed their naked bodies like a scented pink snowstorm. It startled Gabby, but Mia continued to caress her, unconcerned.

'Don't worry, they planted cherry trees as a memorial to the women who were burnt.'

But surely it was too early in the year for those trees to blossom?

And for butterflies?

CHAPTER 21

THE BREAKUP

Gabby felt as if she'd finally come to her senses. Even if the DNA test proved correct, she still had a year to live, her job was more manageable than ever, she was intelligent and many considered her beautiful. So why did she think she deserved to be loved as well? Why not simply go with the flow and take life, and death, as they came? Then again, pretending she was fine was one of her more potent skills. She did continue dancing as if there was no tomorrow because, deep down, she believed there wasn't. There was no doubt the zouk classes had increased her enjoyment of life after Valéria, but was it all just for Mia's benefit – the girl who made her dance – the girl who saved her life?

'You're dancing like a pro, Gabby.'

'Thanks, but I still have a long way to go. I need more moves and styling.'

'You have good hip action.'

'Hip action is the key … but dancing with the men puts me off.'

'Try listening to zouk and kizomba on your own, feel the rhythm by yourself.'

'I've tried, but I need you to lead, Mia, I can't do it with anyone else.'

'You shouldn't depend on me so much, Gabby. It's not good for you.'

Instead of splitting up with Mia, as Gabby had intended in November, they were more closely connected than ever – or so it seemed. The last six months had gone by so quickly and the two women had shared a lot. Over the course of the past month or so, however, Mia had been a little reclusive, due to study pressure for her PhD she said, and tonight's zouk class was one of the rare occasions she made herself available to Gabby.

It was Friday night and, after the zouk session, Gabby took her to the Boundary Rooftop Bar in Shoreditch, which wasn't very far from the class venue. Mia had a butch look about her that night – tight black jeans by Miu, a loose grey top and black boots. To complement the butch effect, she wore bold make-up, which was maybe a bit punchy, but not ostentatious. She'd had her hair shortened and it was held back by a mother-of-pearl clip.

Gabby wore black heels with a light blue jeans and a black Simone Rocha top with long sleeves, cut to show off her collar bones.

They ordered Smokey Snow cocktails, which consisted of mezcal, Hystèrie liqueur, orgeat syrup, lime juice and egg whites. They talked about trivial things, as Mia generally tended to keep the conversation light and not get too heavily into the emotional stuff. She was a psychologist and she liked to leave her work at home when she came out to enjoy herself. That was, until she asked Gabby about the future.

'How long have we known each other, Gabby?'

'About a year, I think.'

Gabby knew exactly how long, to the day.

'And where do you think you'll be in a year's time?'

The question took Gabby by surprise. She'd never told Mia about the DNA test in Doha because she didn't want to lose the girl like she'd lost Valéria.

'Where I'll be? What about you, Mia?'

'I hope to have taken my PhD and be practising somewhere.'

'And us?'

Mia didn't answer, pretending not to hear the question and sipping her cocktail as she looked around the restaurant.

Their meal came and broke the tension as they looked out over the spectacular view of the City and east London. Gabby had sea bass with artichoke velouté and spring onions, while Mia selected lamb cutlets with crushed potatoes and black olives. Gabby wanted the meal to be over, so they could get back to Mia's place, which was where they generally went after zouk class, but Mia seemed to be lingering deliberately, postponing going home.

Finally they were finished and they took a taxi, which pulled up outside the apartment in Notting Hill. Gabby climbed out of the cab after Mia.

'Are you sure you want to come in, Gabby?'

'Don't I always?'

'Yes … yes, you do.'

She said that with resignation in her voice. Her earlier enthusiasm for conversation was gone and she was quiet, thoughtful, less self-assured than usual, as if something was playing on her mind. The taxi drove away and they walked across the street to Mia's apartment block. Inside, she poured two brandies and held one out. Gabby looked at the glass she'd been offered, then put it to one side.

She moved quickly and kissed Mia on the lips. It was an awkward moment. Mia pushed her away gently and she complied, a little perplexed by the girl's coolness.

'At least drink the brandy first, Gabby.'

Gabby sensed what was coming. If she was honest with herself, she knew it had to come some day and now it seemed that day was here. She should have said goodbye back in November after the vineyard tour, now it was too late. The impetus had been with her back then – the front foot. Now she'd being taken by surprise, ambushed, because they'd been getting on so well. Mia had given her no indication that tonight would be the night. Gabby should have been warned, given time to get used to the idea. This was wrong, she had to get the advantage back!

Gabby put the glass to her lips and drank the brandy down in one. Then she moved close to Mia again and removed the clip from her hair.

'Are we going to make love?'

'You should go, Gabby.'

'What?'

'I'm sorry …'

'Mia … please don't do this.'

'I'm sorry, Gabby.'

'But why?'

That question again. Silence held the room in a vice. Gabby knew Mia wouldn't be able to answer the question – there was no why, just an inevitability. Gabby was more physically and emotionally connected to Mia than ever, but it was evidently a one-way street. What about Christmas together – and Austria – and Italy with Mia's family? That event had reassured Gabby that their love was unbreakable. Was she a complete fool? Was it all some sick illusion? She struggled with the sudden realisation of what was happening, even though she'd really always known it was eventually going to. She didn't want Mia to leave her, but she didn't want to lose her dignity either.

Gabby remained silent while Mia tried to figure out the best way to handle the situation. She'd done it before, many times, and the women usually left quietly. She'd tried to hint at it for the past month or so, but Gabby hadn't taken the subtle warnings, either because she'd deliberately ignored them, or because she hadn't picked up on them – and Gabby usually picked up on everything, every change in tone of voice or body movement or nuanced gesture.

So she knew what was coming.

Or should have.

Something inside Gabby was telling her to go. This Mia was a complete stranger – not the woman she'd been in a relationship with for almost a year. She couldn't trust this new woman and trust was everything. Anything could be achieved with trust. Everything could be achieved with trust. But her feet were rooted to the floor. Her mind began to swirl. Thoughts came at Gabby out of the ether – strange thoughts – new thoughts – streams of consciousness. She wondered if this situation might be other than it seemed – a flashback – or a flashforward? Maybe she was dreaming and this encounter wasn't real at all. Maybe she'd wake up in a moment. Or maybe she wouldn't.

'Am I dead?'

Mia looked at Gabby, who'd sat down heavily on the couch.

'What?'

Then Gabby noticed something out of the corner of her eye. It was herself – at least, an image of herself in a photograph that was lying on top of a glass side table, along with some magazines. She picked it up – the picture was of her and Ramona on the big white bed in the Halkin Hotel.

'What is this, Mia?'

Mia tried to snatch the photo from Gabby, but Gabby held onto it.

'You know what it is.'

'Why have you got this?'

'Andras gave it to me.'

'Why?'

'Just a souvenir of the night, that's all.'

Gabby looked at herself in the photo – sprawled on the bed, semi-conscious, with her legs spread apart, blood oozing from the bite on her shoulder. Ramona was sitting beside her with false fangs and a bloody mouth. She stood up and moved toward the window, trying to see the image more clearly.

'Are there more of these?'

'I don't know.'

'You do, Mia. You set it up, didn't you?'

'Of course not!'

'Who were those people?'

'I don't know … part of some vampire club … I think.'

Gabby imagined the picture of her in that compromising position, and maybe others, being used in some weird perverted brochure in Hungary or Transylvania or somewhere. She was angry at Mia's compliance in the thing. Mia tried to placate her, moving to her and kissing her. She began to undress Gabby and Gabby let her, even though she knew she shouldn't. What kind of idiot was she, allowing herself to be manipulated? Had Mia been using her all along, and was now discarding her when she was tired of her – when Gabby had used up all her amusement value? And now, instead of leaving like she should, she hesitated.

Mia knew she wasn't going to storm out because she hesitated – and she rarely hesitated. But she also knew she'd hurt Gabby, who was standing still – halfway between the window and the couch. And she could almost see the blood running from the psychological wound she'd inflicted.

'Let's do it, then.'

'Like, one for the road?'

'No, not like that, Gabby.'

'Like what, then?'

'Like this.'

Mia tried to cajole Gabby because she was embarrassed after being found with one of the photographs Andras had taken that night. She shouldn't have left it lying around like that. She removed her own clothes and laid Gabby down on the couch. The leather was uncomfortable and cold on her body, but Gabby didn't complain. Mia's arms went around her neck and she kissed her face and eyes. Gabby wanted the truth.

'What do you really think of me, Mia?'

'I think you're beautiful, Gabby.'

'What was Italy about?'

'I needed someone to keep the family at bay.'

'A convenience? I don't understand … do you even like me?'

'Of course, Gabby. I loved you …'

'Loved? Past tense?'

'Yes.'

'Why?'

There was no answer to the why question. Mia was just trying to make amends in the only way she knew how – an easing of her conscience before the end.

'You knew I never stay in a relationship for long. In fact, we've been together longer than I've ever been with any other woman.'

'So, I should think myself lucky?'

'I didn't mean that.'

This was going all wrong. Mia just wanted to get it over and get Gabby out of there. She winced a little as Gabby pushed her fingers inside her and, after that, the sex became quick and rough and Mia could feel Gabby's anger being applied to her body. Even though they were supposed to be making love, Gabby was really attacking her. Brutalising her. Trying to damage her. Trying to give Mia back the hurt thing she'd given Gabby earlier. The rejection thing.

Gabby rolled over and lit a cigarette, which Mia didn't like her to do in the apartment. But she didn't care. She smoked it in silence, knowing she should get up, put her clothes on and leave. But she didn't. She felt cheated. Let down. Disappointed. Gabby felt as if she'd been singled out by Mia and used by her and now the girl didn't intend to take any personal responsibility for her actions.

Or was it the other way around?

They got dressed, each knowing it was the last time they'd make love. To Mia it was the end of another tryst and she'd go on to many more. To Gabby it was a watershed, a turning point that would define the time she had left in this world. Mia wouldn't save her life a second time.

'You have to go now, Gabby.'

'Is that all there is?'

'That's all.'

'I thought there would be more.'

'There never could be.'

Gabby didn't reply and Mia didn't know why she'd made that last remark. It could have remained unsaid, just understood. But now that she'd said it, Mia thought she needed to explain.

'I'm sorry.'

'For what?'

'For not being like you, Gabby. For being the reckless bitch that I am. But you knew that when you got involved with me.'

She did know. She'd known all along that she needed a life apart from Mia. She'd never planned for Valéria's going, she'd possessed her as though she was a gift, given to her in love – something beautiful and eternal, unbearably precious. Now she was gone – and Mia was going too.

'One more year, Mia, that's all I wanted.'

'After that it would've been another year, Gabby, then another.'

'No! One more is all I have.'

'What are you talking about?'

'I'm going to die on the fourth of July next year.'

Mia was dumbstruck for a moment. She drank her brandy and poured herself another. Then a sceptical look came over her face as she turned to Gabby with the bottle.

'Why say such a thing, Gabby? Don't humiliate yourself like this.'

'But it's true!'

'It's not true, and you know it.'

Gabby couldn't understand why Mia didn't believe her. Was it because she hadn't told her before and now she thought Gabby was lying in a desperate effort to postpone the inevitable? Mia couldn't understand why Gabby would say such a thing – was it a desperate effort to postpone the inevitable? Or was it true?

'How are you supposed to know this, Gabby?'

'I don't want to explain it. It doesn't matter now.'

'No, you can't do this. You want me to feel guilty and you're using this crazy lie to make me feel sorry for you.'

'It's not a lie.'

'Then explain it.'

'I don't want to … not now.'

Gabby put on her coat and made her way toward the door. Before she could reach it, the brandy bottle came whizzing past her head, missing her by inches. She turned, to see Mia standing by the window looking out at the street below and laughing.

'Why did you do that, Mia.'

'Because you're trying to hit me with your pitiful lie.'

Gabby had an in-built danger alarm from her early life in Jardim Brasília that went off when the noise got too loud and it was flashing red as Mia spun round from the window to face her, still laughing.

'You think it's funny that I'm going to die in a year?'

'If I'd known you were going to turn out like this I'd never have …'

'Turn out like what, Mia?'

'A whimpering little sissy.'

'You're right, you are a reckless bitch. I don't deserve this from you.'

'You deserve a punch in the face, Gabby … that's what you deserve.'

Mia came at her from across the room and tried to hit her. Gabby defended herself and struck back. Mia toppled backward, over the couch. She turned toward the door again, but Mia grabbed her from behind, pulling at her hair and scratching at her face. She threw the girl over her shoulder and she sailed across the room and struck the wall in an upside-down position, then slid to the floor. She knew about Mia's stormy side, but this was new, this violent craziness. Gabby couldn't believe it when Mia immediately jumped back to her feet and came at her again – blood running in a little rivulet from her nose. This was madness, but she couldn't stop it. Mia was young and fit, but Gabby had practised martial arts and the two women dodged around the room in a crazy pas de deux – hitting out at each other.

Mia snatched up the brandy bottle from the floor and Gabby picked up a cushion from the couch to defend herself with. She lunged as Mia came at her and managed to pin the girl against the wall. Gabby pushed the cushion over her mouth to stop her biting and tried to keep her still by pressing her knee into Mia's stomach. The girl struggled like a feral cat – kicked and clawed and tried to free her face from the cushion. Gabby could barely hold on to her and her strength was ebbing fast.

Then she felt the frenzy subsiding as Mia began to quieten down and stop struggling. Gabby removed the knee from her abdomen and slowly withdrew the pillow from the girl's face. Mia smiled at her. A strange smile, with traces of vomit emerging from between the lips, as she slumped to the floor – eyes wide open and staring. Gabby bent over her.

'Mia …'

No reply. She brushed back the girl's hair with the palm of her hand and lifted her on to the couch. She felt like a little rag doll. Nobody would have believed, looking at her lying there, that she had such virulence. Such vindictiveness.

'Mia …'

Gabby lay beside her, propped up on one elbow. She looked down at the young face and into the dead eyes that stared back at her. All the energy was gone from her. All the determination and ferocity. She was quiet now – like a lamb. And Gabby felt an overwhelming love for her that was almost unbearable.

Gabby saw that face in front of her again, the half-image-half-code face from the time after Doha, when she'd come back to the apartment in Kensington. Only this time the features were less distinct and the emotional sense of loss more acute. It was a beautiful face and intrinsically female in nature. Not beautiful in a humanistic way, but in an eternal, wave-like way – coming and going like an apparition in the mist. It was crying, not in a recognisable way, but in an all-encompassing way, as if the whole face was a teardrop – an anguished silent lamentation.

After a while, Gabby rose from the couch, washed her face and brushed her hair. Then she put her coat back on and left the apartment.

CHAPTER 22

HEDONISM

It was in her absence that Gabby felt Mia's presence more vigorously. She hadn't grasped how bad the aftermath of what had happened in the apartment in Notting Hill would be. For a while it was a problem she didn't think she could cope with alone and the urge to go back there, like people who long to go back to the scene of a crime, was overpowering at times. But she resisted the desire, despite the physical pain of losing the only person who had ever seen inside her soul and understood who she was, something even Valéria hadn't done.

Alright, Mia was egotistical and self-obsessed and even cold, to a certain extent, but at least she was honest. People didn't like honesty, even though they said they did all the time. As soon as someone was completely honest with them, they rejected that veracity and called it bias or bile.

Staring at the morning cereal bowl, her hands shook and it took a supreme effort to stop the tears from flowing. Tears that were for herself and not for Mia and, as such, were selfish. Mourning the loss of something was always a selfish thing – it was never for the person or thing that was lost, but always for what was left behind. Memories haunted Gabby like ghosts in the gloom. How she regretted what she'd done and wished she could take it all back. But that was impossible – even if she was able to and Mia could draw breath again, it would be a hazardous situation, because she'd know that Gabby couldn't live without her. That kind of power was dangerous.

After the body was discovered police came and interviewed Gabby, as the last person to see Mia.

An autopsy was conducted and the level of alcohol in her blood was discovered to be high. Vomit was also found in the larynx and the lungs and it was concluded that she'd suffocated in her sleep.

After an interminable time, the spirit presence that was the essence of Mia seemed to have seeped into Gabby, triggering the lure for new adventure, rupturing her certitudes, evaporating some of her more deeply held values. She no longer recognised herself in the actions of the new soul inside her, whether it was dancing closely with people she didn't know, or making new contacts without prejudgement, travelling to places she'd previously avoided, indulging herself, questioning the status quo of almost everything, embracing the new and discarding the old, or just feeling more alive than she'd ever felt before. Mia's ghost made her embrace life with an open mind and she was becoming more like that free-spirited girl. Mia was now an intrinsic part of Gabby.

The hardest thing was filling the void – interminable periods without the sound of her voice, the vibration of her laugh, the voltage of her eyes. Gabby had to accept that everything from now on would be less satisfying, substandard, and that she'd be fighting daily battles with herself to find meaning in other things, in other people.

She began to live as if every day would be her last, and not in an aesthetic way. She overcompensated for the loss of herself. She fabricated her feelings and she dated women in London, Paris, Milan – anywhere she was sent by Palexion Limited. She even returned to Ham Yard with a pretty young actress to try the smoke 'n' bubbles, but it didn't taste the same. Neither did the fried oysters at Olivomare or the teapots of gin and sherry at the Looking Glass Cocktail Club. She even took a trip to the Royal Academy of Arts to contemplate the works of Henri Matisse, but found them uninspiring. She was watching herself go through the motions of experience without truly being there, immersed in a world of shallowness and meaningless sex.

During her time with Valéria, Gabby had been invited to a gym by a Brazilian professional athlete called Anna, to try jiu-jitsu as a means of keeping fit, as her job meant long hours behind a desk or travelling on planes and trains. The thought of it had appalled Gabby because of her phobia about being touched by strangers. Anna convinced her to give it a try, to face up to her fear and defeat it. Eventually, Gabby conceded to pressure from Anna and Valéria and went along to the gym and dressed in the regulation kimono-like suit. She walked toward the mat where a mixed group of men and women were throwing each other about and laying on top of each other to practise force-and-surrender techniques.

Gabby reacted in horror and ran from the place without saying goodbye to Anna.

Three months after Mia, Gabby met Anna again, this time at a forró party in west London. Forró is another Brazilian dance, similar to zouk, only much faster. Anna couldn't believe it was the same Gabby, dancing cheek-to-cheek with several men.

'Gabby … it is you! I almost didn't recognise you.'

'Anna … sorry about that day at the gym. I was so nervous. I just couldn't bear to have close contact with people I didn't know.'

'You clearly don't have that problem anymore. Would you like to dance with me?'

'Sure, I'd love to.'

They danced, swirling round and round, coming close together, then back to arm's length, then close again.

'What made you change so much, Gabby?'

'I've been having zouk classes and I love it.'

'That's fantastic. What made you choose zouk instead of forró?'

'It's a long story … about a girl who made me dance.'

Anna smiled knowingly.

'I think I understand.'

'She made me change and do many things I never dreamed I would.'

They continued to dance together and Gabby could feel the woman's breath on her neck as she began to hum to the music. Her lips accidentally brushed against Gabby's and she pulled away, almost apologetically. Gabby pulled her back. The forró was fast and Anna whirled Gabby around. Her voice had a faraway sound as she hummed and held Gabby close, so she wouldn't fly away across the floor. It felt as though their bodies were one within the wild dance. Joined. Part of some inevitable primal force.

Afterwards, they went for a meal and a drink at Maggie James' restaurant in Old Court Place, which was like an old English barn with all sorts of paraphernalia, including a beehive. Gabby had roast rump of lamb with cauliflower cheese, while Anna chose venison with red cabbage and mashed potato – accompanied by a couple of bottles of Côtes du Rhône. They ended up in Gabby's apartment, which was closest. She poured Drambuie and they laughed together in the glowing room.

It wasn't long before items of clothing littered the floor in a trail to the bedroom, where Anna manoeuvred herself into the sixty-nine position and buried her face in Gabby's vulva, breathing hard, moving her pink tongue through little bubbles of liqueur in a way that Gabby hadn't experienced before. They rolled back into the missionary position and Gabby kissed her face and neck. She could feel the woman's eyes on hers, caressing, the stroke of her long eyelashes against her cheek, her breath in Gabby's ear, her fragrance assaulting Gabby's senses, the taste of her deep in Gabby's throat – the movement of her – strong, smooth – her fingers touching all the right places as they played the coquettish tune of love on each other's bodies.

But she wasn't Mia.

No matter how hard she tried, without Mia, London would never be the same place again. It had changed fundamentally. Gabby knew it – the restaurants and the nightclubs and the hotels and the humanity behind it all, if there was any humanity behind it. All had changed forever – even if she could still feel the essence of it in the air. The excitement, the intensity, the stark naked stimulus. But it was not for her anymore – never for Gabby again. It seemed alien to her now – the city that once was everything, her very lifeblood. It was a hostile place, hard and angry. Disillusioned. Dead.

She needed to get away from London, so she sold her apartment in Kensington and left in the early hours of one morning, without telling anyone, travelling to the rolling hills of Burgundy, where she was surrounded by the grape vines that reminded her of Mia. She wondered if the girl's ghost ever went back to Chapel Down vineyard to see how her Bacchus bushes were doing. She hoped so.

Gabby thought that in rural France she could get away from the world, the flesh and the devil and experience a more natural lifestyle. A simple life was what she needed after the excesses of the last few months – at least for a while. Time was moving on quickly and her time was running out. It was already September and the DNA prophesy left her only ten months to live. She needed some solace and solitude to be able to take stock and put a value on her life, to get away from the tyranny of her ever-changing moods and the persistent thoughts of Mia. She needed to find answers, not least to the enigma of her own personal inquisition. Almost her entire adult life had belonged to someone else, either as daughter, girlfriend, fiancée or wife, and this was a time to belong to herself alone.

Gabby rented a sprawling farmhouse near the timber-framed town of Auxerre, on the River Yonne, with a solemn, conservative population of about 20,000. She hired a Peugeot 205 GTI to get about in, as the place was so remote, and drove around the September roads and lanes to get the lie of the land. But solitude wasn't conducive to Gabby for very long and she soon needed company. So she went into town, but found the nightlife there to be non-existent. On the way back, she passed a tourist campsite which sounded lively, with music and singing, so she parked up and went in.

The campsite housed a transient mixture of families and single backpacker types – touring caravans and tents. The music and singing was coming from a gathering round a fire, people were playing guitars and accordions and drinking a mixture of home-made wine and absinthe. Gabby asked if she could join them and they said of course. She'd picked up a couple of bottles of Pinot Noir in town which she now donated as her entrance fee.

As the evening wore on, the open-air party became more raucous, marijuana and amphetamine were produced and the group got larger as passing travellers joined in. Gabby noticed one girl who kept looking in her direction – she was young, very young, wearing a short suede dress and nothing much else. Gabby did nothing to encourage her, as she might even have been a schoolgirl, wearing make-up and seductive clothes for the night. But the girl kept giving her unmistakable signals.

The night grew deep and dark, the fire cast surreal shadows on the surrounding faces. Gabby drank, smoked weed and even took some speed to keep herself awake. One by one, the revellers faded and fell asleep, until just a few of them were left. Gabby'd had enough, but she was in no fit state to drive. She staggered back to her car, intending to sleep in it for the night and drive back to the farmhouse in the morning.

Gabby climbed on to the back seat but, before she could close the door, the young girl from the campfire climbed in after her. She was pretty, with a smile full of white teeth and skin the colour of honey. Her voice was light and sing-songy.

'I saw you when you arrived.'

'Did you?'

'Yes, I kept looking over at you, hoping you'd come and say hello.'

'How old are you?'

'Old enough.'

Gabby didn't ask who she was with, even though she should have. But she'd drunk too much wine and absinthe and smoked too much marijuana and swallowed too much speed, which was now making her heart beat fast – or maybe that was the girl, who sat close to Gabby – close as a lover. She could feel her breath on her face – hear her heart beating. Or maybe that was her own.

'You got anything?'

'Anything?'

'You know ...'

Gabby didn't know. The girl had an eight of resin, which she heated on a spoon and flaked into some hand-rolling tobacco and skinned it up. They smoked a couple of joints together and laughed out loud at nothing much and talked complete bullshit. Then the girl slipped off her buckskin dress – and she was wearing nothing underneath. Her breasts squeezed themselves against Gabby's chest and they fell backward on to the car seat, still laughing at nothing.

'What's your name?'

'Gabby.'

'Hi Gabby, I'm Angel.'

And she was.

They lay close together on the cool leather and the cannabis made the whole car undulate up and down. The brand new smell of the girl broke over Gabby's senses like a wave and she couldn't resist any longer. Her tongue and lips caressed Angel's smoothness, who responded with a touch that was pure skill. And, as they bobbed about on their illusory ocean, Gabby wanted to take out her heart and fling it overboard. At the moment of orgasm, Angel's cool eyes burnt into hers and then began to roll. It felt as if she was weightless in the palpitating car, as their bodies became one and the pleasures of Philotes flowed back and forth, to and fro, from one to the other.

When Gabby woke the next morning, Angel was still lying beside her. Gabby nudged her awake, in case she had to get back to whoever she was with. Maybe one of them was her boyfriend, or her father, and was on the way over with a gun in his hand. The girl smiled and stretched like a cat.

She invited Gabby over to where some of the group from the previous night were cooking breakfast. There were six of them, including Angel, and they were a country/folk band calling themselves Tom-Tom. They were happy for Gabby to join them, even after spending the night with Angel. That didn't seem to matter – they were into free love and sharing everything and the commune spirit. They all had cool names like Rainbow and Wolf and Raine and Starlight and Bird. Gabby thanked them for their hospitality and invited them to come and spend some time at her rented farmhouse.

And that's how it all started.

Günther Engels and others at Palexion tried to find her – they called and tried to contact her. Gabby ignored them. Her mother tried too, and the police, even some of the zouk class. She threw her phone away and bought a new one. She didn't want to be found by anyone – not her work colleagues, not her family, not her friends – no one. She was a new person now and wanted to stay that way.

The farm consisted of a main building with a number of barns and outhouses scattered around it surrounded by a stone wall. The entrance was of a pair of high, wrought-iron gates. There was a rough track up to the main farmhouse and the land consisted of open areas and small copses of trees and brush. Tom-Tom stayed for two weeks and Gabby slept with Angel every night, after drinking wine and absinthe and smoking weed and snorting a variety of powders up her nose. When they left, Gabby gave them an open invitation to come again and they spread the word about the hospitable Brazilian/British woman who lived on her own in a big place close to the town of Auxerre.

Other people began to drop in once word got out about a woman who was looking for herself. With money. Independent means. Offering to share with anyone who had a philosophy on life to offer, no matter how bizarre it was. A gift horse, for the looking.

The farm soon achieved notoriety in the solemn conservative town of Auxerre and it was raided at intervals by the gendarmes, looking for drug dealers and bail jumpers and people traffickers. Subliminal stories began to appear in local newspapers, about orgies and black magic and child sacrifice going on inside the stone walls. The headlines screamed

FERMER LA COMMUNE DE L'ENFER!
Close the commune from hell!

Break it down! Scatter the layabouts to the wind – after first burning Gabby as a witch in the market square – because the whole evil thing was a blight on the vineyards and orchards de la belle Bourgogne. Gabby and her guests weren't concerned about the bigotry of the local paysans. It was difficult for her to know if these people were really interested in helping her find a new reality, or just in indulging themselves in the booze, drugs, sex and shelter she was providing free of charge. But she believed that, if anything came out of it, then she might be doing something positive.

Eventually, Gabby gave up on the conceptual side of things and just floated into the hedonism. Nobody wanted to get too heavy – even the chatterers and dedicated camp followers. They listened for a while, but eventually drifted away to the philosophy of pleasure. And Gabby really couldn't blame them – didn't blame them. The world outside the farm was devouring itself, just as it was inside the farm – there was no difference. And they were only human, they hadn't seen what she'd seen, hadn't been where she'd been. They didn't know what or how or where or when – never mind why. So how could they know anything? How could she realistically expect anyone to understand? It was too early in the evolutionary process. They still thought in terms of images that obsessed them. In terms of who they were – or who they thought they were. Identity – whatever that meant. They still clung to it, even though it meant nothing anymore.

But for now identity was still part of what made them human. So they could never understand, no matter how many words she spoke or how she explained what she was trying to find. They didn't really care about massive black holes lurking at the centre of every galaxy – gateways to eternity. Doors to the time before the beginning – and also after the end. If there was any beginning or end. The universe was an overwhelmingly hostile entity to them and its nature was obscure – writing its secrets in mathematical code that was only understandable to the very few. They didn't care that all objects had an influence over each other – even though those influences weren't apparent. That Time and Self were different sides of the same coin. Or that real happiness was always insignificant and never grand nor dramatic. Or that togetherness told the truth and separation spoke confusion. Or that the end was always implicit in the beginning.

Gabby had sex with as many women as possible, but she always looked forward to seeing Angel. She knew the sex was good for the girl too, because she responded to Gabby's touch in an eager way. Breath came fast from her mouth when Gabby moved her hand across Angel's back. Her eyes stayed open, staring into Gabby's. Her voice was like velvet when she spoke – words of love and longing. Her face was sensuous and serene. Her hair glowed with moonlight and her skin was almost luminous in the twilight. Their naked bodies entwined in the nights' coolness, in an embrace that had been waiting all the long months. And Gabby felt an overwhelming emotion for the girl she seemed to have known for so long but had only just recognised – whose body moved gently in rhythm with her own. All her searching flowed away on a river of passion that pulled her down until she was drowning and the sound of her desire was like a distant animal and her words floated like kisses up into the star-filled sky.

Hadn't it been like that with Mia?

But Angel came and went and Gabby became more and more disillusioned. She wondered if she'd done the right thing in leaving London and coming here. Her time was running out and she was achieving nothing. All the high living and loving left a hole where her heart should have been – it all seemed so futile – so pointless. Maybe things couldn't be changed. Maybe things just had to follow their own route and nobody could alter that – no matter how much they knew.

A feeling of being watched by somebody, or something came over her. Just a feeling. A sense of eyes on her. It was unnerving. There were always lots of people coming and going and she was never alone. Yet this was singular, not part of the whole. Separate. She couldn't think what it might be. Maybe people from Auxerre setting up surveillance, or the police, or

the local press. They all watched the farm from time to time –
until they got fed up and went away, only to come back again
when they had nothing better to do.

194

CHAPTER 23

THE GHOST

One night Gabby was woken by the phone ringing. She didn't want to answer it because it was so late and it could be anybody – some social media moron wanting to shout abuse and too cowardly to do it to her face. The phone rang for what seemed like a lifetime before she eventually answered it and heard a familiar voice on the other end. The voice sounded cold – dead – not as she remembered it.

'Who is it?'

'You know.'

'What do you want?'

Gabby wasn't alarmed, because she was used to strange happenings. This was just another enigma that defied explanation – another ghost – another emanation of the old emotions, the ones she knew she'd always have.

'I want you.'

'It's too late.'

'Too late for love, but not for death.'

'You didn't believe me.'

'Why do you think that was?'

'You were only human, I guess.'

There was silence on the phone. Gabby was almost afraid to breathe – as if the voice on the other end was a nervous animal and any sudden sound might scare it away. They listened to the silence, both of them. For ages. Forever. Just absorbing each other's presence as if they were lying together again. Then the spell broke.

'I don't want you to speak to me again.'

'No?'

'No. Goodbye.'

Gabby hung up, but held on to the phone for a long time. The farmhouse was still. Silent. Gabby could feel the world turning. Spinning. Around and around to its final destiny. She could feel the pulsing of positronium atoms, way out in the cosmos – she could hear the hiss of active radio galaxies – she could understand the mathematical language of possibility and the perfect gravitational balance of the void – she was conscious of approaching light waves, their speed and consistency – she absorbed the cosmic microwave background of the universe and saw the spiral of a galaxy toward its black hole as the DNA spiral of life. She saw everything.

But it wasn't enough.

The feeling of being watched grew stronger and stronger in the days and weeks that followed. She knew something was there on the farm, but she couldn't see it. Couldn't catch it – whatever it was. Sometimes she'd sense it behind her, but when she turned there was nothing. Nobody. Or across a room full of people. Staring. Fixed in its view. But she couldn't visualise it. It was invisible. Stalking her. Prowling. Waiting for the time to strike.

Gradually, the population of the farm thinned out. Natural selection of an unnatural collection – other things were contributing. People ultimately couldn't understand what Gabby was looking for – so the cabbalists and transcendentals took off to the next new phenomenon. The freeloaders weren't getting loads for free anymore and there was very little publicity for the camera cravers. A few psychedelics and schizophrenics hung around for a while longer, not really knowing where they were – or why they were there. And the fewer people occupying the farm, the stronger the feeling of being observed grew.

Gabby began to take notice of those still around – which became a lot easier. Some were long-termers who'd been there from the beginning. Others were recent comers and probably wouldn't stay for long. And a few she wasn't sure about – maybe they'd been there a long time or maybe they'd just turned up. Anonymous people you could see every day and still not recognise – not know anything about – or want to. All sexes and all ages blending into one another until everybody seemed androgynous and perpetual. Except for one. A young woman – maybe twenty-five, maybe a little older, it was difficult to tell, difficult to know precisely. Gabby noticed her more than the others, she stood out.

Gabby caught her watching her. Her eyes, watching her. Eyes she recognised from somewhere, even if she didn't recognise the young woman who owned them. She seemed like a wraith, an illusion, a mirage. A vision. Anamorphic. There but not there. There when observed, and disappearing into the fabric of the farm when concentration was distracted. Fading away when Gabby's mind-focus shifted – concentration on the individual bringing her into being and lapse of attention allowing her to return to the farm. But the eyes remained. Watching. Observing. Waiting. Looking inside Gabby's soul. She could feel them burning – dissecting and destructuring. Knowing everything. Being everything. Being the act. Being the guilt.

The guilt came like an old friend. Like a missing but essential part of the whole. Gabby knew this and felt a contentment in the knowledge. As if she was becoming part of the eyes watching her – knowing them and what they wanted.

'Mia?'

'You've recognised me, at last.'

'It is you …'

'It's me.'

Now that she'd said the name, it was as if Gabby had always known it was her. The admission sealed the fact.

'What are you doing here?'

'You knew I'd come back.'

'Why?'

'Because you killed me.'

'It was an accident … you attacked me first, Mia.'

'You provoked me.'

Gabby couldn't remember, it was such a long time ago – lifetimes ago. And she hadn't been in full control at the time.

Relationships went wrong for a variety of reasons all the time – like Valéria. That was the same thing, but not the same. Gabby hadn't wanted the pain to come back at the time – hadn't realised the pain was still there, had never gone away.

'We both got what we deserved, Mia, didn't we?'

'I didn't.'

'What did you deserve?'

Gabby knew what she'd deserved, the same thing Valéria had deserved. And maybe that's why she'd done what she'd done, maybe it was Valéria she'd accidentally suffocated with the cushion.

'You told me I was beautiful, Gabby.'

She didn't remember telling her that. Maybe she had – but she couldn't remember it. Maybe she'd just told her what she wanted to hear and that was a mistake. She'd told her because she knew she wouldn't be changed by saying it and assumed Mia wouldn't either.

'It was what you wanted to hear.'

'You killed what was beautiful.'

'I'm sorry.'

'No you're not. You're lying now, just as you were lying then.'

'I wasn't lying.'

Gabby knew there was nothing she could say now. It was too late. She should have been stronger, more aware of the other woman's state of mind. She should have known that, despite the outward signs, she was stronger than Mia, both physically and psychologically. Nothing could replace what she'd taken that night, but that was the way it was.

'You used me, Mia, for your amusement.'

'I used everyone, Gabby. You wanted to be used.'

'I wanted to be loved.'

'You thought you could change me, didn't you?'

'No. I thought you could change me … and you did.'

'But not enough.'

'Yes … enough. I didn't realise I could be you, Mia … if I tried.'

'You should have just walked away and not lied, Gabby.'

It wasn't a lie. It was what was foreseen. She'd have known that if she'd lived for another year. What happened wasn't only damaging to one of them, it killed them both – they both died that night.

'Why did you come back, Mia?'

'You took my life away, Gabby. You kept it for yourself and left me nothing. I can't move on until I have myself back. Only you can give that to me.'

She moved closer to Gabby, closer than Gabby wanted her to. Why was she here? Not her, not Mia – her ghost. Gabby didn't know if it was a ghost or not. It was something – some essence of what had been there before, tangible and intangible at the same time. A figment of her imagination? Maybe. A manifestation of guilt? Maybe not. In a way, deep down, Gabby knew she'd come back, or some shadow of her would come back, because it could never be over until she did.

Gabby backed away, looking for some place to hide inside herself. But there was nowhere – the hiding places had all gone. She was naked.

'I want myself back, Gabby.'

'I can't give that to you.'

'You have to, otherwise I'll take it.'

'I can't, Mia. I need to be you so that I can live. You saved me once and you can save me again. You had to die so I can live, don't you understand that?'

'You have to pay for what you take, Gabby.'

'I paid … I paid, Mia.'

'You didn't pay enough.'

'What is enough?'

'You'll find out.'

So that's what she came back for. Elimination. Maybe it was what Gabby wanted too? To give up the ghost. Become part of the – part of the – absorbed into – into – falling. Falling. Into the flames. She began to cry. Not audibly. On the inside. Tears rolled down her face. But the ghost was gone. Back. Somewhere out on the farm, Gabby didn't know where.

Maybe waiting in one of the barns for her to come, so she could take herself back.

And so it went on, with the spectre of Mia coming and going – appearing and disappearing. Haunting her, bringing back old feelings, old emotions, old desires she didn't want. Dragging her back to somewhere she didn't want to go – to feelings she didn't want to experience again. Guilt. Anger. Elation. Despair. Desire. And all the others. Coming at Gabby like light waves. She talked to the others on the farm for reassurance, the ones who were left. But they were no help.

'Get out!'

'What's the matter, Gabby?'

'Get out, all of you!'

'But, Gabby …'

Gabby went berserk. Shouting and ranting and raving like a lunatic.

'I don't want you here anymore.'

'What about your new reality?'

'Fuck my new reality!'

Because nobody wanted to listen, because it was all too confused and traumatised and neuroticised.

Gabby got violent – anger masking guilt. Hostility holding back humiliation. She threw furniture around the farmhouse and tossed things through windows and ripped down curtains and pictures from walls. The hangers-on gathered up their stuff and headed for the hills. Gabby drove them out, she followed them down to the big gates to make sure they went, shouting at them all the way.

Then she was alone again. Not quite alone, but it felt as if it was how it was meant to be. Always. And she'd only just realised it. There was nobody left but herself.

And the ghost.

Gabby searched the farmhouse and grounds for Mia. She searched the barns and the woods, but couldn't find her anywhere. She was always one step ahead, or one step behind. Gabby knew she was there – somewhere. She could feel her eyes. Watching. Waiting. Sometimes she could hear her voice.

Whispering. Saying how she'd taken her life away and now she would have to take Gabby's – was taking Gabby's – had already taken it. Gabby wanted her to leave like the others, wanted to get rid of her, to throw her out so she could get her mind right again, focus her thoughts on what was real and important – before she went insane.

She was starting to regress to that time when she'd tried to take her own life, after Valéria left. Now she was preoccupied with a ghost – if it was a ghost. Sometimes Gabby didn't know for sure. She seemed like a ghost – the way she could melt into the walls of the farmhouse. But Mia wouldn't go, no matter how much Gabby shouted or threatened or pleaded or ordered or asked.

The farmhouse was still and empty, except for eyes watching. No life. No feeling. No humanity. No warmth. Even though there was no cold. No right nor wrong. No words. No conflicts. Just concepts. Of what is. What was. What would be. Between one thing and another. Neither one thing nor the other. Gabby was tired. She drank some brandy straight from the bottle. Fatigued. Exhausted. She moved outside the farmhouse, where she couldn't tell if it was night or day. But she could hear the insects. She carried the bottle in her hand and felt the grass alive under her bare feet. The sky was mauve and there was no wind. She was unable to see the million stars she knew were overhead. More than a million. Billions. Beyond the mauve sky.

She moved instinctively toward the nearest barn, only a hundred feet away. Fear filled her, gave an extra edge to her senses. Tiredness left her body, evaporated into the heady air. She was alive, adrenaline rushed through her veins and the short hairs on the back of her neck stood up. She sensed the danger, the life-threatening jeopardy. Gabby knew again who she was – what she was – as she moved closer to the barn. Every step became its own little lifetime. Birth. Life. Death. Again. Again.

The barn was quiet. She listened. Quiet. The door was open and Gabby stepped inside. She moved silently across the hay-strewn floor, making no sound. She paused to take another deep drink from the brandy bottle, saw the ghost sitting on a bale of straw – looking away from her. The danger was palpable, like a heartbeat – a separate entity between them. Her brain was full of white noise. The features of the ghost were obscure as she turned her head to look at Gabby, holding the brandy bottle by the neck. Except for the eyes.

Wild eyes.

Dangerous eyes.

Was it waiting for her? Did it know she'd find it? Did it want her to find it? Now, after all the haunting? Gabby moved closer to the eyes that reflected her own face, her own eyes. There was no guilt in them. Everything was acceptable within the context of the eyes. Gabby touched the ghost and it didn't react. It lifted its face to her and she kissed it gently on the lips. The ghost was naked. She touched its breasts. It made a sound – not a human sound. Her hands moved across its body. Searching. Between its legs. It made another sound. Gabby couldn't hear it. A light reflected in the corner of its eye, glinting off the blade. Gabby ignored it – knew it was there but wanted it to come. To end it. End everything. It lifted the blade, high over its head, over Gabby's head. She knew it was there, she could see the glint of steel in the corner of her eye and she waited for the pain – to end it. End everything. She looked deep into the wild eyes – saw what had always been there.

Gabby jerked violently backward. Brandy spilled over the straw from the bottle as it dropped from her hand – stained the ground a golden colour. Her face was full of horror as she backed against the wall.

'I'm sorry!'

Gabby could feel the tears welling up in her eyes.

'I'm sorry!'

The barn echoed her words back at her.

'I'm sorry!'

Gabby crept away, back out into the insect night, across the wild grass, her head hurting and her heart on fire. The sky was black and infinite-, with a billion stars overhead. She quickened her pace until she was running. Running. Running. Away. Back to the farmhouse. Back to safety. Away from the primeval darkness.

After her breakdown and recovery, Gabby stayed on at a sanatorium in Burgundy for a while, until after Christmas, surrounded by quietude and tranquillity. But a vast sense of emptiness pervaded her and she knew it was time to move on again. It was time to forget about previous aspirations of education, career, relationships, children and the rest. All that was irrelevant now. There was nothing left but the prospect of a premature death and a short six months until then. That short time left would have to be utilised to overcome the things that terrified Gabby, used to push the final boundary, but not in the way she'd been doing it up to now.

Used to finally find the answer to why.

And where better to seek that answer than Tibet.

Or as near to Tibet as she could safely get.

CHAPTER 24
CLOSE TO WHY

Her destination was a Tibetan refugee community where she would be reunited with a long-time friend, Rafaello Bianchi, who she'd met a decade earlier in London, when they were both members of the Chelsea Arts Club. Raffaello was an incredibly intelligent lawyer from Rome who'd given up the luxury of his Knightsbridge town house for a primitive life in the remote mountains of Himachal Pradesh, where he spent his time praying, reading and writing at a Buddhist temple and working with a project to educate young children.

Gabby was able to trace his whereabouts through social media and she managed to get a message to him saying she'd like to visit. She'd almost given up on a reply, when an email arrived from a library laptop in Dharamshala. Raffaello, unlike his monk friends who had no nationality due to being displaced from their native country, could come and go as he pleased, but he chose to stay and only came to, what might euphemistically be called, civilisation to pick up messages, like the one from Gabby.

Gabby had to apply for a permit from the Indian government to reach the remote and restricted region where Raffaello lived, close to the border with Tibet. After a long and uncomfortable flight, two train connections and one endless and terrifying bus ride, she arrived in Dharamshala, a city surrounded by cedar forests on the edge of the Himalayas, which was home to the Dalai Lama and the Tibetan government-in-exile.

Raffaello met her and took her rucksack. He gave her the warmest hug, which took her by surprise.

'Welcome to Dharamshala, Gabby.'

Raffaello looked strange with a shaven head and wrapped in a saffron kāṣāya, rather than his erstwhile Baumler suits, pure silk ties and Stefano Ricci shirts. He wore a heavy coat, due to the coldness of the early year. The change in him went beyond his physical appearance, there was a serenity in his eyes that wasn't there before, a sincerity in his smile and a calmness in his voice.

'How are you Gabby, you look tired.'

'I am, Raffa.'

She could understand why he was here, to a certain extent – the peacefulness, the lack of pressure, no crime or pollution. But there was no excitement either, none of the conflict that was part of the human physiology and she was sure she'd get restless after a while and long for the lights. Then she thought, surely that's why she was here – to get away from all that drama and discord and to find meaning in what little time she had left?

'Do you miss London, Raffa?'

He laughed, long and loud.

She didn't laugh with him.

'Are you kidding me?'

She wasn't.

'I've tried all that meditation stuff, Raffa, but could never get the hang of emptying my mind.'

'Who can, Gabby?'

It wasn't the response she was expecting. She'd believed he'd give her a sermon about materialism, the distorted values and delusions of those living empty and unhappy lives, like herself. How fake and fragile economies, broken social structures and false notions of what happiness was, defined the Western rat race. But he didn't. Instead, he asked her a question.

'Why are you really here?'

She had to think before answering.

'I've been on an emotional roller coaster, Raffa. I want to get off, at least for a while.'

'Some time for yourself?'

'I suppose … but I honestly don't think I can be alone for too long. I'm scared of being by myself.'

She didn't tell him about the DNA prediction, it would have elicited sympathy and that wasn't what she wanted.

'We're born alone, and we die alone.'

Which wasn't true at all.

Emotional attachment stopped Gabby from being true to herself, yet she craved it. And she'd already discovered that external beauty didn't bring happiness, so no need for Raffaello to tell her that.

It was a cliché, she knew, but only internal beauty truly satisfied – the light that falls on people from the hope they feel – from the belief that there is something good, even if everything around them is bad. The rest – fame, fortune – brought a false kind of happiness but it was imitation, an imposter, not real. It belonged to other people and they loaned it to you because they liked the way you looked, or the way you fucked. But they always wanted it back in the end – one way or another. And it turned sour and left the bad taste of regret in the mouth.

Like a sin.

They took a battered old taxi to the village of Naddi, in the upper reaches of the Kangra Valley, a forty-minute drive from Dharamshala, where they were welcomed by two of Raffaello's friends – Bjørg, a sixty-year-old doctor from Norway, and Jörg, a German mechanical engineer in his forties. The three men took Gabby to a hilltop house where she dropped off her rucksack and then they led her out along a snow-covered road toward the McLeod Ganj. They trekked in silence for about an hour, passing magnificent temples with gold decorations, endless snowfields and strings of silk Tibetan flags. Gabby wondered what it was that had caused such a drastic change in Raffaello. When she knew him in London, he lived a hedonistic lifestyle, much as she had in Burgundy, and maybe that's what this was, a following in his footsteps, a making of his pilgrimage. It seemed to have worked for him – would it work for her?

There must have been a similar empty space left inside him that needed to be filled so he could get to the core of who he really was. She needed to find that secret, to rid herself of that sense of recklessness and insufficiency that had driven her to the brink of destruction. She had to find out who she could be without the material crutches she'd relied on for so much of her life. All that stuff – the apartments, the cars, the designer clothes, the jewellery, the restaurants – they all came with a big psychological price-tag of unhappiness and dissatisfaction. It was the static of want. Want – want – want – want. All that time spent wanting, listening to the want static. It seemed to Gabby, now, that what she wanted was only desirable when she didn't have it and, as soon as she got it, it lost its value and she wanted something else.

Finally, they came to an empty little café on the outskirts of a suburb, with plastic tables and chairs scattered at random around the warm interior. An Indian woman in a luminous red and yellow sari greeted them, with shining black hair and a radiant smile.

'Welcome to Little Lhasa.'

Raffaello told Gabby that the woman, whose name was Anima, had been a sex worker in Mumbai at the age of eleven. She'd moved to Little Lhasa when she was thirty, and married a Swedish man named Claes, who ran the café with her. But she still faced discrimination over her past, even in this place. Raffaello was critical of that lack of compassion.

'It's not compatible with an abundant mind.'

Gabby wondered, if bigotry existed even in a place like this, where could she go to be entirely free of it?

They had mashed banana to start with, followed by masala chai and thukpa noodle soup. Raffaello and his friends chatted to her over the humble meal. The prevailing viewpoint was that material things in themselves weren't the problem. Everyone liked comfort because the physical body craved it and, while we might be spiritual beings, we were still encased in physical shells. As such, we were incapable of understanding everything. It was like the analogy of the dog sitting in front of the television set – he could see it and knew it was there, but was incapable of understanding it. If someone was capable of explaining the television set to the dog, he wouldn't want to be a dog anymore and would probably go crazy. The same principle could be applied to humans, living in a purgatorial place where one thing lives only if another thing dies. If we found out that we're really quite primitive creatures, we'd no longer want to be human. Hence the real function of our brain, to be a filter rather than a means of enlightenment, preventing us from knowing everything and going insane. The brain performed its evolutionary function and created the illusion of waking consciousness, of filtering reality, of selecting from the wider spectrum of awareness, of preventing overload. The brain was really a tool for survival, evolved for the purpose of maximising self-life in a risky, contaminated environment, and its prime function was to contract consciousness, not to expand it.

Gabby listened to the debate and she could understand what they were saying to a certain extent – the stuff about the human ego, how it had to be killed off because it was an illusion – a temporal extension of the soul. Most of what humans did was to quench the insatiable thirst of the ego for fake emotion and, having worked in marketing, persuading people they should want stuff they didn't really need, to make money for people who already had more than enough, she nodded her head in agreement from time to time. But for the three men sitting with her this life was permanent and their infrequent trips to the materialistic West were temporary. It was the other way around for her and she couldn't see herself living in London or Paris without certain luxuries that gave her a sense of security – even if that sense was false. There had to be a middle way – something between the hair shirt and hedonism.

Next morning, Raffaello woke Gabby early. It took her a while to get her bearings and realise she was in the high-altitude village of Naddi, and not in West Kensington or Burgundy.

'I know you're tired and probably jet-lagged Gabby, but I want to make the most of your visit.'

They had a light breakfast of tsampa and sweet tea, then walked in a pithy silence for about twenty minutes. Gabby had realised that Raffaello might not have all the answers, but at least he was asking the right questions. And maybe, just maybe, she might get what she was looking for out of this trip.

'These are my children.'

Raffaello stopped in the middle of a snowy field, where a group of young boys and girls were playing with a ball, just like kids all over the world – a bunch of Tibetan children playing a local football game. As soon as they saw Raffaello, they surrounded him, jumping on his neck and swinging from his arms and looking at him with admiration and gratitude.

'Wow, they're really happy to see you.'

'Not as much as I am to see them.'

'So, what do you actually do here, Raffa?'

'I know what you think, Gabby … you think it's all about me … wealthy Westerner comes to this place to ease his conscience and build his self-esteem.'

'And do you?'

Raffaello laughed again, just as he did when they met.

'I don't have to do stuff here in order to be liked. And I don't have to explain to you why I do it.'

She felt rebuked, chastened, and fell into a sulky silence. He left her to her feelings for a while and she watched as he kicked the ball with the kids and ran around in the snow as if he was one of them. And maybe he was. He came back over to her.

'Alright … here I'm Raffaello, an imperfect man, a human being … no expensive car or Gucci watch to make me important. All I do is turn up, play football with them, read, tell them stories, listen to their hopes and dreams, and be a part of their lives. Do you get it?'

'No.'

He took her hands in his and looked deep into her eyes.

'Can I ask you to do something, Gabby?'

'Depends on what it is.'

'I want you to do nothing.'

She was puzzled.

'I want you to do absolutely nothing this afternoon. I'm going to confiscate your phone and laptop and tablet and everything else that distracts you. You can choose to go anywhere you like around here and just focus on emptying your head. Focus on your breathing, nothing else. Easy, right?'

'OK, but I can't guarantee I'll be able to empty my head.'

'Let your thoughts pass you by, as if they're strangers on a street in London and you place no judgement on them.'

'I'll try.'

'Find the universe inside you, Gabby.'

'The why?'

'The what?'

That answer told her he didn't really know.

Nevertheless, Gabby did what he asked of her. There was an outside chance that she might find the secret of true happiness in the present – she didn't want to continue living in the past and there was no future. She found herself on the plateau section of the McLeod Ganj, where there was nothing but stillness and silence in an essential sense of being. She was absorbed into the surroundings of air, water and trees and she could feel the disconnect with the universe inside her. Here she was, alone, with nothing except the feeling that life had been little more than a stream of events that brought long periods of sadness interspersed with brief flashes of happiness that soon faded. A story with no beginning and a rapidly looming end. Would what was left of her narrative continue to be blown along like a leaf in the wind? Could she do anything about it?

She closed her eyes and allowed those thoughts to pass her by, just as Raffaello suggested. Her heart began to beat uncontrollably fast and she became light-headed, as if she was about to faint. Then, imperceptibly, she stepped into an alternative reality – a multi-dimensional mandala, with walls of sand as tall as a ten-storey building. She wandered through the maze, touching the walls in wonder. It was the most beautiful place she'd ever been to. All the weight of the world had been lifted from her and she was filled with a sense of transcendence, of infinite wisdom, of wholeness and fulfilment – a state of ecstasy she'd never experienced before.

She found her way out of the mandala and came upon a shimmering pond with a huge pink lotus flower at its centre. Each petal represented a memory, some familiar and some not – her mother crying on the floor, having been beaten by a man she didn't know – a white horse galloping through a forest – a dead body, blackened by fire – Valéria, laughing and kissing a multitude of strange women – a black naja snake that tried to stretch over and bite her face. She pulled back and looked toward the last petal – a young woman wearing a mother-of-pearl clip to hold her hair back and a trickle of vomit emerging from her smile, beckoning her to come, calling her name, asking for her life back. Gabby backed away, feeling the wellness evaporating quickly and being replaced by horror. She began to run and run, through an endless grass plain toward a single tree in the distance. The black snake followed her and she called out for Raffaello to help her.

'Raffa! Raffa!'

Her voice circled round the vastness of the steppe, round and round, coming back to echo in her ears.

'Raffa! Raffa! Raffa! Raffa!'

He was holding onto her when she came out of the damaged equilibrium, trying to calm her down.

'It's alright. It's alright, I'm here. Breath in and out, slowly.'

She did as he said and her heart soon returned to its normal rhythm and the lightness left her head. She told him what she'd seen, but he couldn't explain it. She knew he wouldn't be able to because, for all his humility and self-deprecation, he didn't know.

Gabby decided not to stay in Himachal Pradesh any longer, but she still had a month left on her tourist visa. Raffaello said he'd heard of a convent of nuns in Nepal who had answers to questions that no one else had. The place was discovered many years ago when the hippies of the 1960s followed the trail from the West to Kathmandu, looking for enlightenment. If she was to succeed in her quest, she'd have to prepare properly by doing Seva, the selfless service of Sikhism.

'Do you think you can do that, Gabby?'

'I can try.'

He gave her some basic instructions, then told her, once she'd performed Seva, she'd have to recreate the essence of that bygone hippie time and travel overland at the most basic level, rather than flying first class.

The following day, Gabby said goodbye to Raffaello and promised to keep in touch, although she knew she wouldn't.

CHAPTER 25

THE CONVENT

There was no direct public transport from Dharamshala to Amritsar. Gabby had to travel by train down to Chandigarh, then back up to the Sikh capital. Raffaello told her anyone could do Seva – work that was offered to god in selfless sacrifice and, even if she didn't believe in god, it would cleanse her soul for her trip to Nepal.

The Golden Temple was impressive, standing in the middle of its reflecting pool. Sikhism advocated unity and the equality of all humankind, engaging in selfless service and striving for social justice for the benefit and prosperity of all. That seemed like a worthwhile place to be and she thought she'd give it a try. After France, she reckoned her soul needed cleansing, and maybe that was why things had gone wrong on the McLeod Ganj plateau.

Her first night in a women's dormitory was comfortable enough. She went to bed early and fell asleep almost immediately. She woke at 4:00 am and sat cross-legged on her bunk, closed her eyes and tried to meditate. She prayed to the goddess Lakshmi, reciting the three-part prayer she'd been given, ninety-nine times in her mind. Then she went back to sleep. Just before dawn, she dreamt she was walking toward the main gate of the Golden Temple, along with hundreds of other pilgrims. Someone tapped her on the shoulder. She stopped and looked back. It was Mia. She smiled at Gabby, came close and whispered in her right ear.

'Remember me.'

She woke again at 7:00 am, when the alarm clock of the woman in the bunk on her left went off. It was an old-fashioned, wind-up, spring-driven thing with two bells. The noise was loud enough to wake the whole dormitory – but not the woman who owned the clock. It took her at least three minutes to hear it and switch it off, then Gabby was able to think straight again. She sat on the bunk and remembered her dawn dream – of Mia – would she ever be able to forget her?

Later that morning, she went to the local bazaar and bought shoe-cleaning materials – black polish, brown polish, neutral polish, four pieces of cloth, three wooden handled brushes, three dusters, a sponge and a bag to carry it all in. Her mentor in the temple was a lady called Dina Kaur and she advised Gabby to buy a light linen shalwar kameez, a chunni and some sandals, which would be more practical and comfortable than the Western clothes she was wearing.

The mentor was waiting for Gabby when she got back. After saying a short prayer, they went down to the northern gateway where Dina arranged a space for Gabby to sit and do her Seva. Very soon, the pilgrims were queuing up to leave their shoes with her to be polished – her Seva had started!

She cleaned and dried the shoes with a cloth and then applied the polish, using a brush to spread it evenly, then rubbed the polish in. She buffed the shoes with spit and a dry cloth to get up a shine. The results were good as far as Gabby was concerned. She'd never done this before, but she soon got to be an expert shoe-shine girl and her speed increased with practice. She catered for all kinds of footwear – black shoes and brown shoes and white shoes – men's shoes and women's shoes and children's shoes – new shoes and old shoes – worn shoes and even some torn shoes. Dina Kaur said, for Seva to be really effective, she needed to do it for forty days – but Gabby didn't have that much time to spare.

'What about a week? I have to go to Nepal.'

'A week is better than nothing.'

On the first day, Gabby only did the shoe-cleaning Seva but, on the second day, she started doing other stuff as well. Dina organised for her to walk around holding a sign with a top-loading poster frame and a square piece of white cardboard, on which was written, in English, Punjabi and Hindi:

You May Leave Your Shoes Here
To Be Cleaned and Polished.

This gave her some exercise from the sitting and was a break away from the monotony of the northern gateway.

On the third day, she moved out of the free dormitory to a small bedsit-type room, which she rented from an aunt of Dina Kaur's. When the woman heard Gabby was doing Seva at the Golden Temple, she wouldn't accept any rent.

'Giving free accommodation to a Sevadar like you will be counted as my Seva in the Kingdom of God.'

But Gabby insisted she take some money, because she didn't want anything to interfere with the selflessness of the Seva or have anything or anyone else contribute. She was hoping this would get her to where she'd always wanted to go and she wasn't taking any chances. The aunt's name was Geena Kaur and Gabby gave her rent for the full week, even though she'd only be there four days. Geena promised she'd throw in food as well as lodgings for the money and that was everything taken care of.

Gabby liked her room. It was spacious, with two large windows that allowed plenty of sunshine in. Not that it mattered much, as she was away from early morning to late evening. The room had some basic furniture – a bed and a table and two chairs and a small wardrobe. It was above a grocery store in the middle of a bazaar, not far from the Golden Temple. There were no rats in the room, but she did see a lizard on the wall on the first night. It disappeared the next day. Geena Kaur owned two other properties in Amritsar, but they were far from the Golden Temple. This one was ideal for Gabby. A small staircase led to an open-air rooftop where residents went to sleep in the hot summer – but it was too cold for that in late February.

The rest of the week rolled by and Gabby took the Seva very seriously, working from 9:00 am to 5:00 pm, Her Sevadar colleagues were impressed, especially when they realised she was a non-Sikh, and from England too. When she wasn't doing Seva, she sometimes sat cross-legged on the floor of the temple to meditate. She didn't seem to have a problem meditating in a Sikh Temple, unlike other places where she'd tried it. She was probably closer to Buddhism than anything else and believed in the "oneness" of all things and this universal "being" was at the core of who she was and who she'd become. But the simplicity of the Seva cleared her mind – it helped her to shed the clutter of materialism and concentrated her thoughts on what was important.

Buddhists advocate removal from the material world and a solitary, singular existence – here, she was surrounded by a sea of humanity and she started to see it as it really was – for the first time. She saw herself in every woman's eyes, in every man's smile, in every child's wonderment. She was Mohammed and Jesus and Joan of Arc – she was Blake with his visions and Juliana with divine love, Alighieri with his hell and Elohim with his heaven and Nostradamus and Donne and Bayazid of Bistun and a hundred million others.

Five days into her Seva, Gabby called Raffaello on the old landline phone in the village of Naddi.

'What are you up to, Gabby?'

'Polishing shoes.'

He laughed, that long, loud laugh of his.

'How wonderful!'

March was approaching when Gabby finished her Seva. She felt refreshed when it was over, ready to move on to Nepal. The disillusionment left her and she believed the rest of her life could be worth living, despite all the greed and manipulation.

She said goodbye and thanks to Dina and Geena Kaur and set off for Delhi, taking Raffaello's advice and travelling only basic class. She found a cheap hostel in Delhi – a small shared room in which the window was a hole in the wall where some bricks had been removed.

She had to go to the Nepalese Embassy to get a visa to visit Kathmandu, which wasn't any trouble. Afterwards she took a walking tour around Delhi and had something to eat at a cheap roadside stall. By the time she got back to the hostel, the doors were locked and she had to sleep outside on the street. Luckily, she was wearing her Sikh clothes, so nobody took her for a tourist and she was left alone.

Next day, she went to Delhi Station to book a seat on the night train to Jaipur. It was the biggest train station in India and a nightmare trying to get a ticket. It was Gabby's first experience of an Indian sleeper and it was chaos trying to find the right carriage and establish her entitlement to the booked seat. The rows of open compartments meant she had to sleep with one eye open to make sure her rucksack didn't go for a walk during the night.

She got to Jaipur at 5:00 am and couldn't find anywhere to stay, so she set up a makeshift camp in Jai Niwas Garden, near the Pink City, only to be moved along by stick-wielding police. She wandered around the Pink City for a while and ate some dal baati churma with a bottle of water at the Amber Palace. The old fort was huge, overlooking an artificial lake, with long walls all around, broken by watchtowers that stretched into the distance over the hilltops. Down below, the green valley spread out toward the misty plains.

She caught the bus to Agra at 4:00 pm and managed to get some sleep on the way. From there she boarded another sleeper to Varanasi, where she met a rickshaw driver who spoke good English and offered to take her to see where the dead bodies were burnt beside the Ganges. Gabby wasn't sure at first, then thought it might be a worthwhile experience, seeing as her own death might be fairly imminent.

They journeyed through streets that got narrower and narrower, ending up in a maze of dark passageways and finally arriving at the riverbank where the bodies were burnt in large pans. Once they'd been burnt, they were tipped into the river where people were cleansing themselves just a few yards away. Gabby expected this to be a spiritual place, where she might find some meaning in death, but it wasn't – at least not to her. It was like a crematorium in England, with one funeral following another in conveyor belt fashion.

Gabby crossed into Nepal from India at Raxaul. She had some chai from a man selling it out of a big kettle and pouring it into little clay pots. Once the water had been boiled, it was OK – or so she hoped. People just threw the pots away when they'd finished and there were loads of them smashed all over the place. It was not to do with hygiene, but with the caste system – so people wouldn't have to drink from a pot that had been used by someone of a lower caste.

The Himalayas were in sight now and they were an awe-inspiring spectacle. The air was cold and rare. The people were different, they seemed imperturbable, almost nonchalant, which was refreshing. It was too cold for her Sikh clothes, so Gabby changed back into a pair of boots by Phillip Lim, dark jeans and a Canada Goose jacket. Someone wanted to buy her jeans, but she wouldn't sell them – instead, she gave them the Sikh clothes for nothing.

It was only eighty-five miles from Raxaul to Kathmandu, so she decided to hitchhike in the old hippie tradition – and she wanted to experience the road after so much travel on trains and buses. There were few cars about but the second truck she signalled stopped. The driver seemed used to picking up hitchhikers and was really friendly, even though he spoke little English. Gabby had a phrasebook and managed to make herself understood. After a truck rest stop and some interesting food that the driver insisted on paying for, he dropped her at a toll booth. The people also seemed used to hitchhikers and had no problem with her asking drivers for a lift from there. Another truck picked her up at the toll booth and took her the rest of the way into Kathmandu.

The City of Temples was the end of Gabby's journey and she arrived after a night-trip in the truck, to see the sun rise over the Himalayas. Her first task was to find a cheap guesthouse – and she did, one with a squat toilet and a cold shower. Once she dropped her rucksack, she laid her head down and slept for the rest of the day, then went and had a traditional meal of dal, bhat and tarkari, along with a local beer.

That night, she went to a temple that had an intricately carved and beautifully painted fifteen-foot high Buddha. There was a smell of incense and the sound of chanting coming from nowhere obvious. After a while, she looked around and discovered that she was the only one there – the smell of incense stayed, even after the chanting had drifted away. There was an atmosphere of pure serenity and Gabby didn't want to leave. She sat cross-legged on the floor and allowed herself to feel the same lightness of being that she'd felt on the McLeod Ganj plateau, but this time it was more familiar– as if she'd arrived where she'd started, and knew the place for the first time.

Gradually, the temple became insubstantial – shrouded in smoke or mist, undulating and drifting – the walls closed in and then retreated again. Back and forth, back and forth. Gabby saw herself when she was very young – with her father. She was moving away from him – in slow motion. He was silently calling to her, but she kept moving, toward a solitary tree in a translucent landscape. Her father was calling her to come back. Calling. Calling. But she couldn't hear his voice, just the loud rustling of the leaves as she came closer and closer to them. Everything seemed alive – glowing with life – even the grass under her feet. And she was part of it. Everything. She longed to be absorbed into it, the oneness – it was her and she was it. Her father kept calling to her as she moved further away from him, approaching the glowing tree.

The translucent landscape and the glowing tree and the rustling leaves, everything was so alive and animated and exciting and Gabby ran toward it, away from reality. If it was reality she was running from. She got to the tree and looked up into the labyrinth of leaves and waving branches, which were inviting her into their arms. The tree was smiling at her, telling her she was part of it and she could do anything. But she couldn't fly. She wanted to fly – but she couldn't, no matter how hard she tried. She could see her father coming closer, bringing his reality with him. Gabby knew he'd soon be beside her and she'd have to go back. Her father tried to move faster but his legs were lead, as in a dream. The landscape grew more opaque and her father was scared he'd lose sight of Gabby altogether – that his daughter would be absorbed into the essence of everything – become part of the oneness. There was a noise – a gong or something. Gabby looked around as a monk came into the temple.

On her second day in Kathmandu, she decided to go outside the city to find the old convent that Raffaello had told her about. She hiked west into the mid-hills. The environment was remote and solitary, with dense forest and barely accessible paths. It was fresh and vibrant and the trees around her were alive with birds. After an hour and a half of climbing fairly steep terrain, she came to a level place with an incredible view of the valley and the mountains. It seemed like the centre of the universe – a place you only get to once in your life and you feel like god. She sat down to rest and get her breath back and the lightness came again, just as in the temple the day before. The trees came alive and she could see the sap running through their veins.

The view grew hazy and the singing of birds got louder. Down on the slopes, she could hear someone calling to her – calling for her. Shouting for her to come down, that she wasn't ready. But she thought she was. Ready. The voices got louder, searching, but so did the birdsong. She lay on the ground, arms outstretched, and felt herself lifting up – defying gravity. Higher. Higher. Until she was level with the tops of the trees. The bird sounds were reaching a crescendo and she closed her eyes so she could drift into the dharma. When she opened them again, she was back on the ground, just as in that Purple Bar in Holborn, and it was getting late.

She had two more days in Kathmandu – it was Thursday and she was flying back to Paris on Saturday. She asked about the old convent and was told there were caves in the remote region to the north of the city, so she trekked up there and found it was a religious and wildlife conservation region and largely untouched. The morning was hazy and she came to a dirt road lined with elder and oak trees that led to crumbling cement steps and she could hear the sound of drums and cymbals and horns and chanting voices in the distance.

She followed the steps and the sounds to a hermitage for women and she wasn't sure if this was the convent or not.

It was called Nagi Gompa and more than a hundred nuns lived there, from young girls to old women. The nuns were there to learn the esoteric Vajrayana known as chöd, which means severing. Through practice, they are able to sever their personal demons – neurotic self-cherishing and painful negative emotions. Chöd worked in three ways: to transform harmful mental states such as fear and hatred into courage and selfless love; to understand the perfection of wisdom taught by the Buddha in the sutras; and to realise their own true nature.

Gabby had decided to keep out of the way in a small clearing and just observe what was happening from a respectful distance, when she was approached by a woman in billowing saffron robes.

'There are a hundred and seventy species of birds in the trees above your head.'

'Really? That's amazing.'

'Is it not.'

Her voice seemed to drift from her rather than being spoken. Gabby heard what she said, but not as sentences, not as strings of words. She didn't hear them – she knew them as complete things. Complete images. The complete meaning came in the same instant, not in the clumsy focus of separate sound-symbols – but as complete pictures. Concepts. Understanding of what was meant to be conveyed. The morning mist encircled her, and it was like she was herself, but not herself – a different Gabby – a Gabby who existed once but not anymore. It was this place that brought them back – the forgotten memories, the forbidden memories, if they were memories – this spiritual place of lightness.

When the mist cleared, the nuns were all gone into the little huts that were spread around the hermitage, except for the woman in the billowing saffron robes, who stood next to Gabby, looking into her soul.

'You have come here for answers.'

Again, the drifting picture concepts.

'Yes.'

'Ask.'

Gabby found that she didn't even have to articulate the questions, just think them, have them in her head. The answers came as enlightenments that glowed rather than were heard – they shimmered inside her psyche. The woman told her there was no present. As soon as the future arrived, it immediately became the past. It never actually existed as a present. A moment? A second? A split-second? She could break it down to the smallest period of time she could imagine – if it existed in time, then it didn't exist at all.

Gabby began to understand – there was no north or south, wrong or right, black or white – only a fundamental strangeness. Dreamlike. Uncertain. And it crossed over and interacted with the everyday world. All she had to do was imagine a question – and the answer came.

Hedonism?

The bread you eat is only yours when nobody else wants it. Learn to take only what is needed – not what is wanted. Learn to identify need. It takes discipline – mind control – to control desire. Distinguish it from want. Create it. Shape it. Like a child discovering the sky for the first time.

Truth?

Truth is not absolute – it is multiple and contradictory – either known or not known.

Life?

Life is not sacred – it is quick and ignominious and brutal and misunderstood. Yet it has to be lived.

Time?

You are the creator of your own time and you wear it like a ball and chain – measure it and carry it around with you. But it is an illusion. An illusion. Stumbling around in a dark age, mutilating yourself and others, mentally and physically and emotionally.

Change?

Everything must change in a changing universe – and consciousness is only concerned with the changing detail, it ignores the universal constant. A dimensionless quantum. A singularity. Where everything exists as possibility. If you alter the I-ness, you create a new creature. The you that emerges will no longer be you. It will be a stranger. It will be other. That is the human condition, with its silhouettes for which there is no responsibility and its senses for which there is no adequate control.

Life?

The mystery of life should not be a problem to be solved – just a reality to be experienced. If there is such a thing as experience. The shedding of old feelings – emotions – longings – wants. And the knowing that there will be no more disturbances.

Death?

There is not all that much difference between the living and the dead – except that the dead are dead and the living are still alive – in the human context at least – in the body and blood context. Such a small thing. Such an insignificance.

And much more. In the end, Gabby was out there – half out there – gradually coming back into a body that was independent of, yet linked to, herself. And she struggled to find herself, what was left of herself, when she was half in and half out.

Why?

The woman in the flowing saffron robes was gone, and the hermitage was derelict and decaying – no drums, no chanting, no nuns.

All gone.

Gabby left to hike back down to Kathmandu.

CHAPTER 26

A NEW LIFE?

Paris was always a place where Gabby could find a platform for new beginnings. It was where she came when she left Brazil for the first time. She came back there with Valéria and back again with Mia. Here she was again, with her mind and heart empty of all worry and the heavy load of expectation gone from her shoulders.

She joined a zouk class on the Rue des Rosiers, where she met Zooey, a tall blonde woman in her late twenties, with pale skin and an athletic figure. The class inhabited a wide room with a high ceiling and a large, mirrored disco sphere. The dancehall was dimly lit as Zooey took the lead and manoeuvred Gabby around to the rhythm of the music.

When the dance was finished, Zooey pulled her close and pressed her full pink lips against Gabby's. The kiss continued long and passionately and Gabby lost the sense of where she was, oblivious to the dozen or so couples who surrounded them. Martha, the dance instructor, interrupted the everlasting embrace and Gabby opened her eyes and glanced round at the smiling faces that circled her. It was Paris – nobody cared who kissed who in this city. At least if the guys in the class now knew she was gay it might stop them pestering her.

Martha broke up the gathering and insisted that the ladies should line up on one side and the messieurs on the other. Zooey didn't agree.

'No. I'll join the men. I want to lead.'

Gabby was already with the dames and she looked across with admiration at the tall blonde wearing a black and white fitted skirt by Marni and a sleeveless Self-Portrait top. Gabby wore a short black dress by Louis Vuitton and they both stood out from the rest of the women, who were more drably dressed in tracksuits and baggy tops.

The apartment was completely dark when they got back. Zooey turned on the lights while Gabby took off her coat, hung it on the back of the door as usual, and kicked off her shoes.

Zooey poured two glasses of Sémillon.

'I enjoyed that. Did you, Gabby?'

'Yes.'

'Thank you for introducing me to zouk.'

'You're a better dancer than I am, Zooey.'

'Not better … different.'

After the wine, they made their way to the bedroom, where their kisses became more intense and their hands more persistent. After just a few minutes, the room was strewn with their discarded clothes and they were on the bed, exploring each other's bodies freely and without restraint. Zooey took control, just as she did in the dance, while Gabby allowed herself to be consumed by the taste and smell and sound of her, until all those essences of the other person became part of her own body, her own consciousness. After a while, Gabby put up a token fight for dominance, guiding Zooey so her back was completely available to her lips, kissing every inch, all the way down to her legs. Gabby's hair caressed her body as she went, causing Zooey to emit little sing-song sounds of pleasure.

Somewhere at the back of Gabby's mind was the sound of Shostakovich – a waltz – exciting and sinister all at once. Shadows moved across the room where only one dim lamp glowed in the distance – many miles from the large bed. Gabby's head felt light from the wine she'd drunk, floating on the scent of the woman beside her – the texture of her hair, the seductive sound of her voice, the sparkle of lamplight on her teeth and the stimulating strangeness of the situation. Her skin was smooth and felt like silk – warm and slightly moist in the low light-glow. Her tongue found its way around Gabby's body and her hands were electric when they touched.

Gabby moved to the rhythm of Zooey – the tempo rubato within her. She was in tune with the body of the woman, moving in syncopation to her changing positions. Her voice purred like a leopard and her words made no sense – nor were they meant to. They were meant for herself only. And Gabby made her own sounds in the crepuscule of the satyric room. Zooey looked statuesque in the room-glow, her legs astride Gabby and her body undulating, making her breasts sway, her fingers combed through Gabby's hair and little drops of perspiration appeared on her high cheekbones. She leaned back and her hair touched Gabby's legs in this ritual of dorges and ghantas – the synthesis of sight and sound.

Zooey was pure poetry, an aesthetic experience that had claimed Gabby's attention, something that had been admired and contemplated at a distance, but which had now become part of her limbic system. She was La Primavera di Botticelli, with her symmetric shape, glowing with mild perspiration in the Parisian night. She reversed the sexual situation, exploring Gabby's body and propelling her senses to their limits until she moaned with exquisite satisfaction. Gabby exposed herself to Zooey's complete possession of her, hijacking the pleasure centre in her mind, until her sense of awareness dissipated. She guided Gabby through a beatific vision where she, like Beatrice Portinari to Dante Alighieri, ushered her through Paradiso and, in the eight spheres of heaven, faith, hope and love, made Gabby's passion for life stronger.

They came together in a rebirth of soft insubstantiality. Hearts beating. Lungs snatching at the living air. Then calmness came creeping in and sanity slowly slipped back.

They lay together in the pagan lamp-glow.

Gabby couldn't remember how long they'd been on the bed – couldn't remember if she'd slept or been awake all the time – didn't know what day it was or what month or year. She just remembered something about death. Dawn was breaking in the east and she could see faint fingers of light creeping up the window panes and knew there was somewhere she had to go.

The window flew open and a shower of light pink cherry blossom coated the room, sticking to their perspiring bodies – and the spell was broken.

Zooey was a design architect, working for a boutique Danish firm on the Champs-Élysées and Gabby had taken a part-time voluntary job helping disabled children at a special centre on the Boulevard de Clichy. The pay wasn't what she was used to, but the work gave her a tremendous sense of achievement and self-worth, which had been missing from her life up to now. In any case, after selling the apartment in London and her car and most of her other belongings, she was fairly independent as far as money was concerned and could do whatever she wanted. Gabby'd had many focal points in her life, mostly to do with trying to be the person other people expected her to be. But those requirements no longer applied, they'd been substituted with a blank canvas on which each life event was a splash of colour. The overall view didn't make much sense up close and, further back, it presented a bizarre, unfinished rendering of reality.

Still, it was an impressionist vision of reflection and contemplation, combined with grotesque darkness – an observation of Gabby's own human experience. She believed, wrongly, that it was similar to Claude Monet's *Les Nymphéas*, which she'd seen once at the Musée de l'Orangerie. Those paintings had captivated her and immersed her in the infinite and timeless beauty of clouds and water. Looking at the rich layers of paint, she was brushed by radiant sunshine. That day, in the gallery, she'd looked up at the translucid dome of the ceiling, closed her eyes and absorbed the warmth that enveloped her whole body. She lost touch with the floor under her feet and felt as if she was floating in the womb of the world.

Gabby was simply experiencing life, not from within a cage of her own making, but from a psychedelic garden, with her own personal water lilies, where she could transcend all earthly dimensions. She was letting go of her ego, as suggested by Raffaello during her visit to Himachal Pradesh. And, while she couldn't discard all the things she possessed, as he had done, and didn't feel obliged to, she'd managed to find a "middle way" between materialism and existentialism.

Now, Gaby was living with Zooey in Paris. It wasn't like her claustrophobic marriage to Valéria, or her obsessive, manipulative liaison with Mia, this was a freer, more open, healthier relationship. There were no conditions of total fidelity, but they were both happy just to see how it went. There was, however, one problem – Gabby hadn't told Zooey about the DNA prophesy and the fourth of July was approaching fast. She had to make a decision – either tell Zooey and risk an acrimonious breakup, or don't tell her and hope the fourth of July would come and go without incident.

She wasn't feeling unwell in any way and there were no external symptoms of a heart problem – no fatigue or shortness of breath or oedema or irregular heartbeat or nausea or chest pain. It was quite possible the DNA test in Doha almost two years ago was flawed and Gabby should have taken Valéria's advice and had more tests. But, as she felt at the time, if she did and it was confirmed, that would make it definite – set in stone. As it was, there was still hope and Gabby preferred it that way.

In the end, she decided to tell Zooey – it was only fair she should know, in case the worst came to the worst.

'My god, Gabby, why didn't you tell me this before now?'

'I don't know … I'm sorry.'

'Have you had a second opinion?'

'No.'

'Why not?'

'I don't want to know for sure. I just want to be like everyone else, not knowing for sure when I'm going to die.'

Like Valéria, Zooey thought that was preposterous because, even if she had a heart problem, modern medicine could fix it and it was positively medieval not to have been checked out long ago. But only six weeks were left and Gabby had gone this long, to know at this late stage that nothing could be done would be devastating.

Better to hold out and hope for the best.

After a night of dialogue and recrimination and pacification, along with several bottles of wine, Gabby was feeling fragile again – back to her old stressed-out self. This was exactly what she didn't want and she resented Zooey for making her go back there. A growing sense of emptiness began to take over – a chilling, but familiar feeling that diminished everything she'd achieved since Nepal. It now felt that Zooey had been sent to oppress her, not to liberate her. The approaching summer days grew cold instead of warm and she displayed an increasing inability to cope with even the simplest of tasks. It was coming back to her, that feeling before she'd taken the overdose in the garage in West Kensington. Zooey saw her changing, day by day, as July came closer.

'Why don't you go back to that place in London, Gabby?'

'What place?'

'Where you were treated before.'

'The Priory?'

'Yes.'

Zooey travelled with her to London, to make sure she kept her appointment at the Priory. She waited in the reception room while Gabby walked slowly and reluctantly down the long corridor, touching the door handle at the end, but not turning it immediately. She didn't want to be there, she wanted to be back in Paris and regretted saying anything to Zooey about the DNA test.

'Gabriela Pereira?'

'Yes, sorry I'm late.'

Gabby expected to see Dr Rajwana again, but it wasn't her. It was a younger woman, elegant and petite, with a delicate, freckled face. She had long straight hair, part ginger, part auburn, tied back in a ponytail.

'Hello, I'm Doctor Idoni.'

'Have we met before?'

'Have we?'

'I attended this clinic two years ago.'

'That was before I took my PhD.'

Gabby sat in a high leather chair. Idoni – that name rang a bell somewhere at the back of her mind. She was filled with a sense of déjà vu and it distressed her for some reason. She wanted to get up and leave, but the young woman had come across and sat very close to her, which unnerved her even more.

'How can I help you, Gabriela?'

'Gabby …'

'OK, Gabby it is.'

'Did you used to give zouk lessons here?'

'Yes, when I was a consultant psychologist, working for the NHS. How did you know?'

Gabby wanted to run, but she was frozen to her seat. People talked about the fight or flight response to menacing situations, but there was another alternative – fight or flight or freeze.

'Why are you haunting me?'

'Haunting you?'

'Is it because I killed you?'

'Did you, Gabby?'

Gabby didn't know what to do. She tried to stand up, but the psychologist placed a hand on her shoulder and forced her back down onto the chair.

'I want to help you, Gabby.'

'You can't help me.'

'You're not alone, you know. Focus on your internal voice, the side of your personality that's been repressed.'

'You are that internal voice, Mia!'

'Mia? Who is Mia?'

Gabby tried to focus. The room had become hazy and the figure in the chair beside her obscure.

When it cleared, she saw the white coat over the familiar coloured sari of Dr Sunita Rajwana. She was speaking in her reassuring voice of authority, about how the process of deconstructing a dependency was what drove people to inflict all sorts of psychological unkindness upon themselves. Gabby interrupted her.

'I'm sorry … I can't do this.'

Before the doctor could respond, she rose from her chair and rapidly left the room. Down the corridor, she could hear the sound of enigmatic music, coming from somewhere close by. It was both familiar and unfamiliar – music she knew, but being played in a different way – a different modality. Instead of following the sound, Gabby ran away from it, desperately searching for the reception room and Zooey.

CHAPTER 27

THE QUANTUM

Gabby poured some brandy into her glass and then looked at it as if she was trying to understand what it was. She was a little merry, waiting for Zooey to get back. She wouldn't admit it to herself, but she was. She knew what was wrong with her – she'd been like this for the past two days, ever since they got here. Uneasy. Nervous. Jumpy. Worried about something intangible – didn't know what it was. She did know but she wouldn't admit it to anyone. Not even to herself.

Tomorrow was the fourth of July!

It seemed like there were insects everywhere, outside the hotel and along Massachusetts Avenue. In the trees and on the ground and in the air and all around the whole city. Beetles and crickets and termites and flies and ants and moths and roaches and things that had never been seen before. It was late. There were plenty of people still on the streets, but she couldn't hear them. Didn't want to hear them. Gabby lay on the big bed in the Embassy Row Hotel on Massachusetts Avenue. It felt strange to be alone here – even though the ghost of Mia Idoni lay with her. She could feel it beside her. Smell the scent of it. Hear its voice saying, 'Gabby, give me back to me.'

Zooey was attending a late-niter at the convention centre. Gabby had been here and there, trying to kill time on her own, but unable to concentrate on anything. She'd seen all she wanted to see in Washington DC over the last two days and now she just wanted it to be over – the trip. Maybe it was a good idea and maybe it wasn't. Zooey thought it was. Gabby had been in the bar earlier, but it was full of politicians, talking about logjams and filibusters and gridlocks and being stuck in the Senate working the graveyard and second-degree amendments to appropriations bills. There was a time Gabby might have been interested, but not now. Now all that kind of stuff just got on her nerves because she'd moved on from the glamour and glory days. It was all last week's news to her and she hated the posturing and presumption of it, the mechanics of it, the never-ending grind of it all. So here she was – alone.

Zooey was late and she didn't trust anyone outside the hotel room. Now the cognac had hold of her. She was there beside Mia, even though she was thinking about Zooey. Maybe that's why she felt the way she did. Uneasy. Maybe it was her. The hotel room reminded her of the many other hotel rooms she'd frequented. The memories of back then – half-memories. Vague and elusive. Whatever – it was all something to do with what was approaching – inside her subconscious. Something to do with life – or was it death?

Was she a killer?

She tried to remember when and if she'd felt like this before. If it was some latent thing. But there'd been nothing like this before – there was Zooey and the others, but that was different. Nothing. So it must be new. And if it was new – then it was her. Not what went before. She didn't really believe she'd done anything wrong, used her physical strength in any way excessively. It was what had to be done and, if that was true, then there was no argument – it was all a matter of responsibility. Wasn't it? Of course it was. Mia had a responsibility not to have attacked Gabby the way she did. She had to take some of the blame.

She drank some more brandy, trying calm her nerves. It wasn't a matter of guilt – it was nothing like that. No! There was nothing. Was there? No – was there?

She tried to think about Zooey, even though she found it increasingly difficult. The others, even. But only one image came back and back. And a longing with it to see Mia again. If she ever could, even though her ghost was lying beside Gabby on the bed. It was difficult to be completely alone these days, without Zooey coming to find her – making sure she was OK, fussing over her, reassuring her. Too much! So – it would be difficult. Surely impossible. Gabby wondered why she even wanted to see the girl again. It wasn't as if – she just knew she did, that's all.

Knew why too.

There was something unfinished about it – the whole thing. It couldn't be left the way it was. It had to be settled – whatever it was that needed to be settled. And something definitely needed to be settled, she was sure of that. Since her visit to the Priory in May she'd thought a couple of times about going back there – about following the music down the long corridor. But that was too dangerous, for more than one reason. What if it wasn't Mia? What if it was? What would she say? And what about Zooey? They had a life together now – well, maybe they had, they'd find out for sure tomorrow. But it wouldn't be fair to Zooey, after all she'd done.

Gabby stood up and looked out the window. The lights of Massachusetts Avenue twinkled and stars shone bright and warm overhead and the smell of summer lingered in the hideous air. She huddled against the curtain, wrapping it around herself so she wouldn't be seen – wouldn't be discovered by the eyes passing below on the street. Music came from a faraway street band, celebrating Independence Day early. Crowds came out from the cinemas. Hot dogs and hamburgers to be had from vendors along the street – or a pizza if you preferred, or a quick kebab, and all the other fast food establishments represented in a row like tarts teasing.

Otherwise vindaloo for you. And chop suey for me.

Gabby put the brandy away and decided to stop feeling sorry for herself. Time to get ready because Zooey would want to go out somewhere when she got back – would have made some arrangement, as she had been doing for the past two days – not wanting Gabby to have time to worry. And she hadn't had time, it had been a whirlwind – until now – until tonight. Now she felt uneasy – nervous, as if something was watching her.

The temperature changed after a time that wasn't really a time. No length to it like time had – was supposed to have. It seemed to be getting colder, even though it was July – maybe the air conditioning in the hotel? She didn't know. Or maybe her body heat was dropping. Losing it. Escaping. Shivering. Shuddering. Freezing. Numbness creeping inch by inch along – from her toes. Like a spider. All feeling floating away. Leaving. Byebyebye. Nerve ends creeping into hibernation. She felt her eyelids wanting to close but she wouldn't let them. They were heavy, but held open by some force. Familiar – like when she worked in marketing and some project needed kickstarting. Like that but not like that. It felt as if they should be closing but they wouldn't. Couldn't.

All her body parts were numb now. No sense left anywhere. She should have been scared but instead she felt a kind of elation. If that's what it was. Like on crack cocaine back in Brazil with Jorge and his friends. Something like that. Not exactly like that – but happy. Kind of happy. Laid back. Anaesthetised. She thought of Zooey, but not for long. She thought of Mia – and the guilt came back. It couldn't be stopped – or blocked out by the strange anaesthesia. Couldn't be blocked out by anything anymore. Except maybe death. If there was such a thing. Maybe that's what was keeping her eyes open?

The sense of euphoria slipped away after a time. If it was time. After something that seemed like time. Warmth again – returning to her extremities and the room creeping back up to body temperature. She thought she heard a voice. It wasn't hers and there was no one else in the room – even the ghost was gone. Maybe it wasn't a voice at all, just a musical note coming from the street, far off – a street band celebrating early. What was important now was tomorrow – the fourth of July. She had to prepare for tomorrow, had to be ready – hope for the best, but expect the worst.

Washington DC always celebrated Fourth of July with a bang. Gabby and Zooey lined up with the rest of the crowds along Constitution Avenue to watch the National Independence Day Parade, with fife-and-drum bands, military displays and floats. They played Spot the VIP and cheered and whistled with the other enthusiastic observers. After the disaster at the Priory in London, Zooey didn't pressurise Gabby any further. She went along with Gabby's wishes, which were to just wait and see what happened when the day arrived. Then Zooey's firm asked her to attend an architectural convention in the American capital at the beginning of July and she thought, what better place to be with Gabby to celebrate her survival of the DNA prediction. And Zooey believed she would survive, because Gabby still showed no symptoms of illness and looked fit and healthy.

It was already noon and nothing had happened. Even though she felt well physically, Gabby was still apprehensive, trying her best to enjoy the occasion and put the prospect of having a fatal heart attack at any second out of her mind. Zooey had arranged a series of events to keep them occupied, so Gabby would have no time to brood or get distressed. Today, they'd already been to the National Park to watch a baseball game and take in the holiday atmosphere, eating real American hot dogs with mustard, sauerkraut and chilli and mixing with the Washington Nats fans.

After the parade, Zooey took Gabby to the National Archives to see costumed actors dressed up as the Founding Fathers, then on for a lunch of crab cake with remoulade sauce and French fries at the Scarlet Oak in the Capitol Riverfront. This was followed by a visit to the Bluejacket Brewery where they drank a pitcher of Yardbird authentic cask ale, which rekindled Gabby's love of the stuff. As evening approached, Zooey made a reservation at Sequoia for a dinner of grilled Creekstone steak with roast potatoes, spinach and green peppercorns in red wine sauce and they ate outside, overlooking the Potomac.

Gabby's appetite improved a little as time wore on and the best part of the day had passed.

'It's not going to happen, Gabby.'

'Don't say that Zooey … not yet.'

'That DNA test was wrong.'

'I hope you're right.'

They stayed on the waterfront, taking in the bars and live music, then went to see a show at the Kennedy Centre. Gabby was feeling more and more optimistic and she began, for the first time that day, to enjoy herself.

They found a spot on the West Lawn for a Capitol Fourth concert which began with a performance of Tchaikovsky's *1812 Overture* that featured a line-up of musicians Gabby didn't know, even though Zooey assured her they were all big stars on the American scene. The finale was a firework display over the National Mall that began at 9:00pm – three hours to go.

There were celebrations throughout the city that evening – parties and balls and cocktail buffets and concerts and galas. Gabby and Zooey visited several of them before finally settling at a corporate bash at the Hay-Adams, hosted by the organisers of Zooey's convention. The party was attended by a collage of business people and minor politicians and C-list celebrities and media and anyone who wanted a free drink in Washington DC. Zooey grabbed a bottle of mezcal and two glasses and they drank it down to the worm at the bottom.

'You have to eat it, Gabby.'

'What?'

'The worm.'

'Why?'

'It gives you a buzz. They say it's psychedelic.'

Gabby was up for anything. The day was over – just minutes away from midnight. She emptied the worm out of the bottle and swallowed it.

Zooey took Gabby on to the ballroom floor and the other guests stared as they danced to the Johann Strauss waltz 'Roses from the South'. They looked so beautiful together – made for each other. So much symmetry. Texture. Design. Correlation. Gabby with her offbeat sophistication and Zooey with her statuesque splendour. The perfect couple – even if they were both on the same side of the coin. They danced round and round. Round and round. Until the faces at the edge of the ballroom blurred. Faded to a kind of foam. Indistinguishable.

Indecipherable. Round and round. Spinning. Faster. Faster. Out of control. Spinning out of control.

Gabby wasn't dancing with Zooey anymore – she was dancing with the girl who taught her zouk. The one from the farm with the knife. Dancing faster. Dancing wildly. Faster and faster. The lights in the ballroom dimmed – then went out altogether. Blackness. Spinning blackness. Revolving. Time passing. Silence. No music. No faces. Long time. Short time. Passing time. And the sense of someone watching. Just a sense – no sight – of being looked at – by someone. Swirling in the blackness. She held on to Zooey, even if it wasn't Zooey any longer. She saw the eyes in the spinning darkness. Wild eyes – and a girl's voice. From before. Earlier. Up close. Warm breath and obscure features. Eyes reflecting the blackness all around. Lips moist. Pouting. Sounds coming from the mouth. Not human. Hostile.

'Mia?'

'I am I.'

There is no light. No glint of light from the knife. Gabby feels the blade enter under her heart. She feels its coldness. She feels the sharp pain in her chest. The floor feels like starched fur and the sky is blood-red. And a far-off door appears and lets in just a little illumination. Everything is wraithlike. Shifting. Insubstantial. There but not there. Faces hover above – in the semi-light. A circle of faces. Concentration bringing them into being and lapse of attention allowing them to fade back to foam.

'Has somebody called the paramedics?'

'I'm a doctor, let me through.'

'Give her room! Give her room!'

Voices all around. Whispering. Unseen. Skin moving. Being moved by unseen fingers. Numbness creeping inch by inch along. All feeling floating away.

'Doctor …'

'It's her heart …'

'Oh my god!'

'She's slipping away …'

'No! Do something …'
'Somebody do something!'
'I'm afraid it's no good …'
Gabby backs away. Further away. And falls over the edge. Falling. Falling. Into the flames. Just as the world explodes and everything

     is

       born

         brand new

           again.

www.ingramcontent.com/pod-product-compliance
Lightning Source LLC
Chambersburg PA
CBHW022357110726

47902CB00002BA/331